Bilal's Bread

Bilal's Bread

Sulayman X

alyson books
los angeles

Celebrating Twenty-Five Years

MANUFACTURED IN THE UNITED STATES OF AMERICA.

THIS TRADE PAPERBACK ORIGINAL IS PUBLISHED BY ALYSON BOOKS,
P.O. BOX 4371, LOS ANGELES, CALIFORNIA 90078-4371.
DISTRIBUTION IN THE UNITED KINGDOM BY TURNAROUND PUBLISHER SERVICES LTD.,
UNIT 3, OLYMPIA TRADING ESTATE, COBURG ROAD, WOOD GREEN,
LONDON N22 6TZ ENGLAND.

FIRST EDITION: JUNE 2005

05 06 07 08 09 **a** 10 9 8 7 6 5 4 3 2 1

ISBN 1-55583-861-8
ISBN-13 978-1-55583-861-4

LIBRARY OF CONGRESS CATALOGING-IN-PUBLICATION DATA
  X, SULAYMAN.
    BILAL'S BREAD / SULAYMAN X.—1ST ED.
    ISBN 1-55583-861-8 (PBK.); ISBN-13 978-1-55583-861-4
    1. GAY YOUTH—FICTION. 2. HOMOPHOBIA—FICTION. 3. IMMIGRANTS—FICTION.
  4. TEENAGE BOYS—FICTION. 5. ARAB AMERICANS—FICTION. 6. KANSAS CITY
  (MO.)—FICTION. 7. RACISM—FICTION. 8. IRAQ—EMIGRATION AND IMMIGRATION—
  FICTION. I. TITLE.
  PS3624.A13 B55 2005
  813'.6—DC22   2005041120

CREDITS
COVER PHOTOGRAPHY BY CHAD BAKER/PHOTODISC RED/GETTY IMAGES.
COVER DESIGN BY MATT SAMS.

CHAPTER ONE

"I need you to help me shave," Salim said as he stepped into the boys' bedroom and shut the door.

Bilal looked up from his trig book and adjusted his glasses nervously. By the look on Salim's face, Bilal knew his brother had more than simply shaving on his mind. It was just after eight, and Bilal's other brother, Hakim, had gone out drinking with his friends—it would be hours before he returned home.

"Come on," Salim said.

Bilal was lying on the room's only bed, which he shared with Salim. Hakim slept on the floor. Bilal frowned and put his homework aside. In the bathroom, Salim disrobed straight away and started water running in the tub. Bilal stared at Salim's naked, powerful body and felt uneasy.

"Why don't you take your clothes off?" Salim suggested. "I'll do you first."

Biting his lip, Bilal removed his clothes and let them fall in a heap. He took his glasses off and lay them on the sink. Salim made him sit on the edge of the tub and used a wet washcloth to wipe Bilal's privates before he covered them with shaving cream.

Shaving the genitals was a practice recommended by the Prophet Muhammad, so Salim took it very seriously. Yet it was not an easy thing to do, and for as long as Bilal could remember, Salim had been asking him to help. As soon as hair had begun to grow on Bilal's own privates, the ritual had turned into a mutual affair.

Islamic or not, Bilal hated it. What sense did it make? One had to shave the genitals, which no one could see, yet grow a beard—the Prophet had once said that a Muslim man without a beard would not be allowed to enter Paradise. Wasn't there a contradiction in there somewhere? Bilal glanced at Salim's "Islamic beard" and despised the fact that it made Salim look so much older than his twenty-six years.

With a plastic shaver in hand, Salim knelt on the floor in front of Bilal. He took Bilal's penis in one hand and held it while he shaved Bilal's pubic hair, the underside of his scrotum, and the insides of his legs. Salim was careful and performed the task very slowly. Bilal felt himself becoming aroused. It didn't help that his brother was purposely rubbing his penis to encourage Bilal's arousal.

"Can't you even wait till we're done with the shaving?" Salim asked, giving him a sly smile.

"Can't help it," Bilal said, embarrassed by his unruly sixteen-year-old body.

Salim made Bilal stand and lifted each of Bilal's arms in turn so he could shave Bilal's underarm hair. Then he made Bilal turn around and bend over so he could shave the hair around Bilal's anus as well. Bilal accepted all of this in humiliated silence.

When Salim was finished, Bilal took a quick bath to rinse himself off.

Salim sat on the edge of the tub—it was his turn now. Using the plastic shaver, Bilal got to work, holding Salim's thick penis with one hand to keep it out of the way and shaving with the other, just as his brother had done. As he worked, Salim's penis grew hard and he felt his brother looking at him. He kept his eyes down, looking at Salim's strong, brown belly and thick legs. Unlike Bilal, Salim had muscles everywhere.

Salim remained seated while Bilal shaved his underarms. As Bilal scraped away the thick hair, Salim reached out to grasp Bilal's penis and rub it again. Soon Salim wrapped an arm around Bilal's waist and pulled him close so that Salim could take the flesh into his mouth and suck it.

Bilal bit his lip again. His sister, Fatima, was always telling him that no girl would want to kiss him if he didn't stop biting his lip. Bilal didn't want his brother to do this, but he didn't know how to stop him, and he already dreaded the price he knew he was going to have to pay for this unasked-for pleasure. His body, which was completely uninterested in how he felt about the matter, responded with all the appropriate gasping and trembling, and soon the deed was finished.

After Bilal finished shaving his brother, Salim rinsed himself off and reached into the medicine cabinet for a bottle of lotion, which he rubbed on Bilal's privates and backside. He let one hand massage Bilal's anus for a long time, then he poked a finger into Bilal's rectum.

"If anyone ever found out about us having sex all the time," Salim murmured, "you and Fatima would be sent off to an orphanage. The government people would force you to leave. Do you want that to happen?"

"Of course not," Bilal said dully.

"We have our own ways, don't we?" Salim asked. He maneuvered Bilal so they stood face-to-face, put his hands on Bilal's bare hips, and pulled him closer so that their bellies were touching. Salim's hardness stabbed at Bilal like a scimitar. "We're not Americans. We're Kurds. We help each other. The Americans don't understand our ways, but you understand, don't you?"

Bilal nodded. He stared at the fur on his brother's chest as Salim began to slide his penis against Bilal's body.

"Look at Hakim," Salim said. "Off drinking, chasing these American whores. Is that what you want me to do, Bilal? You want me to spend our money on whores, like Hakim does? He spits in the face of Allah."

"They're not whores," Bilal said. "They're just girls." He thought of Stacey, a blond girl from Overland Park whom Hakim brought home one time. Stacey's eyes had sparkled when Bilal asked, "Are all the girls in Kansas City as nice as you?"

"All these American women are whores," Salim said dismissively. "Do you want me to get some girl pregnant? Have to marry her and leave you and Ma? Who's going to pay the bills if I leave? How are you going to survive?"

Bilal said nothing.

"I need to know that I can trust you," Salim said very softly. "I need to know that you're not going to be out there talking about our business with your friends—you would shame this family if you did."

"You know I would never tell anyone," Bilal said. He was surprised to realize he felt a bit offended.

"I know, but you don't seem to be enjoying this anymore. Not like you used to. It makes me wonder about you."

"You know I won't tell," Bilal said. Their encounters made him uneasy—he knew there was something wrong about them. He knew there had to be a reason for the shame he felt, but he was just as fearful of the consequences if anyone found out.

"You don't seem happy anymore," Salim said. He held Bilal tighter and pressed his penis against him more insistently.

"I'm happy," Bilal replied weakly.

"You're always parading yourself around, making me horny. You know that, don't you? Sometimes I just can't help myself."

Bilal lowered his eyes and felt a flush of embarrassment spread across his face.

Salim put lotion on his own penis and poked it between Bilal's legs, letting it slide beneath Bilal's scrotum as he continued to hold Bilal by the hips.

"That feels good," Salim said.

Bilal allowed himself to be pulled into an embrace. He put his arms around his brother's broad shoulders and began to feel aroused himself. After a minute or two, Salim made Bilal turn around and put more lotion on Bilal's backside.

Despite himself, Bilal bit his lip again. He felt so foolish and helplessly angry.

"I need you to help me," Salim said.

He made Bilal lift his leg and prop his right foot on the edge of the tub. Salim stood behind him and poked at his backside with his erect penis. Bilal winced when the hard flesh slowly entered his body. No matter how many times Salim had done it, it was always painful and never seemed to get any better.

Salim took about a minute to get himself fully inside before he started thrusting his hips back and forth, holding on tightly to Bilal's hips. Bilal said nothing. He squeezed his eyes shut and tried to ignore the pain in his rectum and cramping legs.

There was always terrible pain at first, with a bit of extreme discomfort, but eventually the pain lessened, though the discomfort rarely did. If it was done gently—the way Salim used to do it—it was sometimes pleasurable, but Salim was no longer gentle. Now he seemed possessed, frantic, almost desperate, as if he were trying to force Bilal's body to give him something he could find nowhere else.

Salim finally drove himself deep inside Bilal's body and stopped, gasping with the force of his orgasm. Bilal took several deep breaths and silently thanked Allah that it was over. After a minute, Salim began to move his hips again, but this time very slowly. He gently rubbed Bilal's back.

"You're always so good to me," Salim said. "You're a good boy, Bilal. You're always trying to help me. I know that. You always make me feel better. I wish you wouldn't make me so horny all the time."

Eventually, Salim pulled away and there was a long silence. Bilal sat on the floor and kneaded the cramps in his legs. Salim sat next to him and leaned against the tub.

"I need to know that I can trust you," Salim said softly. "You've always been such a good boy, but lately I'm not sure about you anymore."

"I'm not going to tell," Bilal said.

"Do you love me?" Salim asked.

Bilal nodded.

"I want to hear you say it."

"You know I love you," he said. He could not lift his eyes to meet his brother's.

"Why don't you say it like you mean it? Like it used to be. Don't you remember?"

Bilal did. There was a time when he had enjoyed doing these things with his brother. Their sex was secretive and naughty, but Salim's attention had meant the world to him. It had pleased him to know that Salim enjoyed being with him. He had been in love with his brother, had never turned away from a kiss, had never been shy about taking off his clothes and letting his brother do as he pleased. It had made him feel like an adult, someone important.

"You know I love you," Bilal said again.

"I've got no one," Salim said, moving to sit cross-legged in front of Bilal. "I can't go get a wife—who would take care of Ma and you and Fatima? I'm lonely, Bilal. Is it so wrong to be lonely? And you know I'd never tell on you. I'd never tell anyone what you've done—all those times you've given me blow jobs, all those things—I'd never embarrass you like that. It's nobody business what you do. I mean, do you want me to go around telling my friends what you do? You want me to embarrass you like that? You want everybody to be talking about you behind your back, talking about what you did? Is that what you want, Bilal?"

"Of course not," Bilal said weakly.

"Sometimes I think you've been telling your friends about us, haven't you?"

Bilal shook his head.

"You sure about that?"

"I've never told anybody," Bilal said. "Why do you keep asking me? You know I'm not going to tell anyone."

Salim gazed at him for a long time, and Bilal finally met his gaze—they both knew Bilal could never look another person in the eye if he were lying. Salim stared at him, waiting for Bilal to give himself away. But Bilal had told no one of their business, and he did not look away.

Eventually, Salim relented. "We have our secrets, Bilal. Don't you ever tell anyone our secrets. If you shamed this family like that, you know what I'd have to do, don't you?"

Bilal nodded. When he was younger, Salim used to tell Bilal that he would gut him like a pig if he ever told anyone their "business." These days the threats usually involved such things as making Bilal leave the family and go live on the streets to spare the family's reputation and honor. Salim had also hinted he might have to make use of their sister, Fatima, if Bilal decided he was no longer going to "help." Fatima was seventeen now, and Bilal was horrified at the thought that Salim might make her pregnant, which, Salim had pointed out, would mean she would have to be "sent away." Bilal was close to Fatima, and the thought of Salim raping her made him sick to his stomach. He would do anything to prevent that.

"I think about Fatima a lot," Salim said quietly, giving Bilal a coldly detached look.

"She's too young," Bilal said straight away. "And if she got pregnant…"

Salim shrugged, as if that prospect was no concern of his.

Bilal kept his father's razor hidden beneath the tub, and after Salim went to bed that night, he retrieved the razor, took off his pajamas, and sat naked on the bathroom floor.

The razor was all they had left of their father. After his death, Bilal's family had fled Iraq with little more than the shirts on their backs and a handful of black-and-white photographs. Bilal looked at the razor for a long time, thinking about his father and Salim, and himself. He wondered, not for the first time, what his life would have been like if his father had not been killed by the Iraqi secret police—"those Iraqi pigs," as Salim called them.

Dark thoughts crowded Bilal's mind.

What would Fatima do if Salim forced himself on her? What would happen if she became pregnant? Where would she go if she was sent away?

Bilal and Fatima were very much alike—they even looked the same: they were both slightly built and bookish. They both spoke English fluently. By now, they were more American than Kurd. Fatima was the only member of his family who really understood him. It didn't matter what Salim did to him just as long as he stayed away from Fatima.

Bilal gazed at the razor in his hand for a long time. Then he used it to make several small, deep cuts on his right thigh—the wounds on his left thigh from the last time had only just healed. He made these cuts slowly, cringing from the pain of each one and letting himself take deep breaths afterward to calm himself.

By the time he had made four cuts, he was feeling better.

Why the cutting helped, he didn't know. Whenever he was upset or angry—whenever that cloud of dark thoughts descended on his mind—he used his father's razor to cut himself, and he always felt better afterward. He was in charge of his body again, now that Salim was finished with his business. The pain reminded him that he was alive, that he was someone, that he existed. Sometimes he felt so numb that he just wasn't sure. Was he really alive? Was he really sixteen years old and living in America? Was he really a refugee from Iraq? Was he really a member of the same religion that produced Osama bin Laden and the Taliban?

He watched the blood bubble to the surface of his skin, then he lay his head against the tub and closed his eyes.

Why was everyone else so happy, so normal? Why couldn't he be happy the way they were?

He opened his eyes and inspected his body, which disgusted him. He was thin, panty-waisted—more like a girl than a boy. He had none of his brothers' muscles, none of their size and strength. He hated his body. It spoke of weakness—*effeminate* was the English word used to describe it.

He searched for a new place to make cuts, a place he hadn't tried before. He decided on his belly, just below the navel. He made three cuts, one above the other. He clenched his teeth and moved the razor slowly to prolong the pain and make it more satisfying. He sat for several minutes afterward to relish the sense of calmness before his anxiety reclaimed his thoughts.

He had matches stashed beneath the tub as well—several small boxes of them. He retrieved one of these boxes, lit a match, stared at the flame, and then put the matchstick against his belly to snuff it out. He gasped from the sudden, sharp pain, but kept the matchstick where it was. When he could stand it no more, he pulled the smoldering match away. He looked at the angry red mark on his belly and was surprised by how much it hurt.

He lit another match, made another mark.

Just after midnight, Hakim came home.

Bilal heard his brother stumbling around in the darkness, got out of bed, and switched on the small light by the bed that he shared with Salim. He retrieved his black plastic glasses from the bedside table and put them on.

Hakim smiled at him. He was drunk.

"Bilal, my man," he said in English. He looked like he might fall over at any moment.

"You've been drinking," Bilal said, not unkindly. He thought Hakim was sort of funny when he was drunk—friendly, affectionate, good-humored. Yet Hakim drank so much and so quickly that he often had trouble finding his way home, and when he did make it back to their house, he usually passed out on the sofa in the living room.

"Let me help," Bilal said. He bent down to help Hakim remove the ridiculous cowboy boots that Hakim loved more than anything else he owned.

"Yer a good kid," Hakim said, slurring his words. "Shoulda seen that Mary what's-her-name—the hoochies on that thing. Shit! I woulda screwed a watermelon, she made me so horny.

But that Italian guy didn't want to stop at the supermarket."

"That's nice," Bilal said, struggling with the boots and finally getting them off.

The smell of whiskey on Hakim was strong, and it wasn't a smell Bilal liked.

Hakim was a year younger than Salim. They were both big and strong with muscle, but there the similarities ended. Salim was a devout Muslim; Hakim had "fallen away." Salim hated America; Hakim loved it. Salim would never taint himself by dating "American whores"; Hakim couldn't get enough of them. Salim wore modest clothing; Hakim wore tight muscle T-shirts and tight jeans to make the most of his very obvious charms.

He struggled now to remove such a T-shirt. Bilal helped him. The pants came off next.

"Gotta piss," Hakim said, laughing to himself and stumbling off to the bathroom in his underwear.

Bilal got the mat ready on the floor where Hakim slept. He turned back the blankets and adjusted the pillow. When Hakim returned to the room, he lay down on the mat and heaved a long, exhausted sigh. "Why you not sleep?" he asked in his sloppy English.

Bilal shrugged.

"You not look happy," Hakim said. "You never look happy. You not happy?"

Bilal grinned. "I'm happy. Why don't you go to sleep?" He tried to get Hakim under the covers—it was the middle of November, and it was getting cold.

Hakim took hold of Bilal's arm, smiled up at him, and sang. "Have I told you lately that I love you? Have I told you that there ain't no one above you?"

Bilal smiled.

"Really, Bi. Yer a good kid." Hakim switched to Kurdish—the effort to speak English was becoming too taxing. "Don't think too badly of me—I like to have a drink. So what! I like to have fun. You should have some fun too. Don't take the Mad Mullah too seriously. You know? He's such a pain in the ass, I don't know how you can stand him. You know, you're a good-looking kid— you should take your glasses off once in a while, let everyone see how good-looking you are. These American girls will eat you up. They'll think you're the sensitive type. And you probably are, aren't you? I'm not so bad, am I?"

Bilal shrugged. "Why don't you go to sleep?" he said.

"Really, Bi, I'm not so bad. I like to drink. Okay, that's true. It makes me happy. Is that so bad? Just because I'm not a fundamentalist prick doesn't mean I'm a bad person, does it? Shit! I'm not hijacking 747s, am I? Peace, love, understanding—is there anything wrong with that? Should I be pissed off all the time and go on about the Jewish world conspiracy or something? Would that make me a better guy?"

Whenever Hakim was drunk, he tended to get a bit emotional. He usually wanted to make sure that Bilal didn't think he was a bad person. Bilal didn't. Hakim never seemed to remember that, so they wound up having the same conversation again and again.

"Where's my pants?" Hakim asked suddenly, sitting up now and looking around. Bilal fetched them. Hakim pulled out a pack of cigarettes from the back pocket.

"Not in here," Bilal said, making a face.

"Oh, come on, Bi, I need one," Hakim replied, lighting one up.

Bilal went to the bathroom to fetch the old saucer that Hakim used as an ashtray—it was kept stashed under the sink so that Salim wouldn't throw it out. Everyone in Bilal's family kept something hidden from Salim.

Hakim smoked his cigarette, obviously enjoying it—it was a habit he'd picked up a few months ago. Bilal hoped he would stop before he became hooked.

"Hey," Hakim said. He gazed blearily at Bilal and opened and closed his eyes several times, as if he was having trouble getting them to work properly. "A few weeks ago, I came home one night, and you guys were in the bathroom and…"

He fell silent and took his eyes away from Bilal.

"And what?" Bilal asked quietly. What else could his brother have seen except Bilal and Salim having sex?

Hakim made a face, said nothing. He lay down and began to smile to himself. "You shoulda seen that Mary what's-her-name—these American girls!"

With that, he fell asleep.

Bilal watched Hakim and wondered what he had seen.

He loved Hakim with all his heart. Hakim had ended up with the good looks in the family, and he had an easygoing charm that had served him well as a young Muslim man living in the Midwest—especially after 9/11. Bilal wished he could be more like Hakim—more honest, more fun-loving, more sure of himself, and not afraid to thumb his nose at Salim.

Just seeing his brother was comforting somehow. He was always afraid something would happen to Hakim, or his sister Fatima, or his mother—afraid they would be taken away, like his papa had been taken away. He fretted about that possibility endlessly. If he got up in the morning and Hakim hadn't returned from a night out, he would be sick to his stomach until his brother finally showed up.

Salim was another matter. Bilal never worried about losing him. In fact, he often fantasized about what it would be like if Salim went away—got married, started his own family, or picked one fight too many with the tough kids in their neighborhood and got himself whacked. In truth, Bilal spent a lot of time daydreaming about what it would be like if Salim was killed. What would the funeral be like? Who would be there? How would he act?

Bilal felt guilty about such thoughts, but sometimes he hated Salim so intensely, the hatred felt like a physical thing creeping around inside his body. One time, when Salim was holding forth about the decadence of Kansas City's suburbs, Bilal had glanced from his place at the kitchen table to his mother's butcher knives and wondered what it would be like to plunge one of the blades into Salim's chest

He lay down beside Hakim and put his arm across his brother's stomach. He breathed in the scent of alcohol, sweat, cigarettes, and maleness. Sleep finally came to him as he watched Hakim's chest rise and fall.

CHAPTER TWO

The next morning Fatima had an announcement to make.

"I'm not wearing a veil around this neighborhood anymore. I'm tired of people flipping me the finger because they think I'm a terrorist—like I have a secret plan to blow up their stupid housing projects stuck in my bra. And it's not like I'd ever marry a man who'd want me to wear a veil."

Bilal glanced at her with utter astonishment. They were standing together at the kitchen table, kneading the bread that their mother sold in the small grocery stores in the neighborhood. This was their Friday morning ritual—most of their orders had to be filled over the weekend. And since Friday was the Muslim holy day, the Abu family stayed home. While Bilal and Fatima helped with kneading, Hakim oversaw the ovens, if he wasn't too badly hungover. Salim supervised everyone else while he ate his breakfast or sat at the table and drank coffee.

Mrs. Abu, who had been rinsing mixing bowls in the sink, turned to give Fatima a deep frown, as if to suggest that Fatima ought to know better than to make such statements in front of

Salim. Mrs. Abu was a large woman and wore colorful dresses—
Kurdish women loved color.

"What did you say?" Salim asked quietly. Fatima would need
his permission to stop wearing the veil.

Fatima put her flour-dusted hands on her hips. "For those of
you who are deaf, I said that I'm not wearing a veil around this
neighborhood anymore."

Salim regarded her silently for a long moment. She stared
back at him, full of herself, full of confidence, full of a very
American sense of independence and freedom.

Speaking in Kurdish so that their mother would be sure to
understand, Fatima added, "Every day this week, the Italians or
the blacks have flipped the finger at Bilal and me, or spat at us,
or given us dirty looks on our way to school. We walked by the
projects on Wednesday, and one of those black guys put a finger
to his head, pretending it was a gun. Then he pointed his imagi-
nary gun at us and winked. I'm getting just a little bit tired of it.
And just in case you forgot, a Muslim woman has the right to
choose whether she wants to veil. At least the ones living in the
twenty-first century do."

There was another long silence.

Bilal looked from Fatima to Salim and felt his stomach
tighten into a knot. He adjusted his glasses nervously. Why did
Fatima have to antagonize Salim? Why did she always have to get
something started? Fridays were bad enough as it was—with all
of them home, the sparks flew in abundance. Why did she have
to make it worse?

Salim, in addition to his shaving habits, followed a variety of
Islamic practices: He never allowed dogs near the house, and
there was no question of keeping one as a pet. He never drank
water while walking. He never wore any item that contained silk.
He lowered his gaze whenever he met a member of the opposite

sex. He never began any activity without reciting the *Bismillah*—
"In the name of Allah, the most gracious, the most merciful." He
never said he would do something in the future without adding
In'shallah—if Allah wills. He never allowed his younger brothers
to miss the obligatory Friday Prayers at the mosque. He never ate
pork or any other meat that hadn't been butchered according to
the proper *halal* practice. He never touched alcohol or cigarettes.
He devoted himself to reading the Quran.

And he would certainly not allow Fatima to walk around the
neighborhood without a veil.

Bilal hated it when his family argued. Salim invariably flew
into one of his rages. For weeks after 9/11, that's about all Salim
did—rant, rave, curse, and bang his hand on the table to empha-
size his points. Bilal couldn't stand it.

Salim finally began to speak. "We are a Muslim family, not
terrorists," he said evenly. "We have our own ways of doing things,
and for you that includes wearing the veil. We can't stop being
Muslims because some stupid fanatics crashed airplanes into the
World Trade Center. Do I need to remind you that you're a
Muslim girl, and Muslim girls wear veils, or have you decided
you want to be like one of these American whores? About the
only thing Islam expects of you is that dress decently and not
shame your family. Is that such a big deal?"

Fatima grimaced. "Why don't you try wearing a veil if you
think it's no big deal?"

"I wear my prayer hat every day," Salim said, his voice coarsen-
ing to a snarl. "I see the way they look at me. Let them look! I'm
not afraid of them. I'm not ashamed of my religion, and neither
should you be."

"Right," Fatima said. "And you're also twice as big as I am, and
you have a penis, which I don't, just in case you might have
forgotten."

"You watch your mouth!" Salim said angrily.

"You make me!" she shot back just as angrily.

Mrs. Abu gasped. Hakim chuckled. Bilal took a deep breath.

"Well, you'll do as I say," Salim said.

"Who cares what you say?" Fatima snorted.

Salim slammed his hand on the table, making them all jump.

"Don't you talk to me like that!" he shouted. "You better care what I say! Just because we live in this shithole of a country doesn't mean you can act like these godless Americans."

With his beard and fiery eyes, he looked like Moses thundering commands down from Mount Sinai.

"Fatima, please," Mrs. Abu said quietly. She glanced at her daughter, then quickly lowered her eyes and turned back to the sink.

"Oh, that's right, Ma, just appease him," Fatima said, sneering at her mother's back. "That's what you always do, isn't it? Let him have his way. Kurdish loyalty, oldest male in the household— all that sexist, misogynist crap. Well, I'm sick of being made fun of, and I'm sick of men telling me what I can and cannot do. In case anyone forgot, we're not living in Iraq anymore, or did I miss something?"

Salim jumped up from his chair and came around the corner of the table and grabbed a handful of Fatima's long, curly hair. He yanked her head back and bared his teeth. The spark of resistance faded from her eyes and a glint of fear took its place.

"Let me go!" she screamed as she tried to get at his face with her fingernails.

"You show me the proper respect first!" Salim shouted.

"You go to hell!" she said.

"Don't you talk to me like that!"

"Would you stop it?" Hakim asked, rolling his eyes in weary annoyance.

Bilal watched in silence.

"Let me go," Fatima demanded. She tried to twist out of Salim's grasp. "I'll talk any damned way I want to!"

Salim yanked her head backward and Fatima began to lose her balance.

"You shut your mouth!" he shouted. "You're not walking around this neighborhood with your head uncovered like a whore, and that's all there is to it. If all you're learning at school is how to smart-mouth, you can just stay home and not go at all, and if you think I won't yank you out of that school, you just try me, Fatima. Talk back to me one more time, and you just watch and see what I'm going to do about it! I've had enough of you and your disobedience! I've had enough of your smart mouth!"

With that, he released Fatima and glared at her, defying her to say another word.

"I'm so sick of you!" she hissed.

He slapped her across the face.

"You son of a bitch!" she exclaimed.

He slapped her again.

Hakim got to his feet, ready to intervene.

Fatima tore off her apron and threw it on the floor. She stared at Salim, her nostrils flaring. Salim stared back at her with a familiar, cold indifference in his eyes. If Fatima had forgotten her place, she was now being reminded of it. Finally, she lowered her gaze and turned away, knowing she was defeated. Salim was the boss, Salim gave the orders, Salim's word was final.

She stomped off to her bedroom and slammed the door.

Bilal was terrified to think where this unpleasant situation would lead. He was also angry—his tongue itched to lash out and say something in response. He glanced at Mrs. Abu, who continued to rinse dishes. There would be no help from her.

"Do you have to hit her?" Hakim demanded.

"You shut the fuck up!" Salim snapped, turning to glare at Hakim.

"That kind of talk isn't exactly Islamic, you know," Hakim said.

"Don't you fucking tell me about Islam, you whoremongering *kafir* pig!" Salim shouted.

Kafir—unbeliever—was one of Salim's favorite words.

"It's not going to hurt anything," Hakim said. "You know, sometimes you have to break the rules."

"No!" Salim exclaimed hotly. "No! That's the way godless *kafirs* talk! You want us all to be *kafirs* and heretics? You want us to forget about Allah and be good Americans? You want Fatima to take her veil off and traipse around the neighborhood looking like a whore? We're not going to follow the ways of the godless *kafirs* just because it's more convenient, or because Fatima doesn't like being teased. She can just get used to it. We obey Allah and no one else. That's what Papa died for."

Bilal felt his small flicker of defiance fade. Couldn't they have even just one day in which their father's death wasn't thrown in their faces? Couldn't they have even one conversation that didn't involve godless *kafirs* and obedience to Allah?

Hakim shook his head. "Has anyone told you lately that you're a self-righteous prick?"

"Better that than an alcohol-drinking whoremonger," Salim shot back. "You want Bilal and Fatima to be like you? Is that it? A pork-eating, alcohol-drinking nonbeliever, a fucking *kafir* pig? Papa would turn in his grave—you spit on everything he stood for, everything he died for. If you love these fucking Americans so much, why don't you go live with them?"

"Why don't you fuck yourself? It's obvious you need to get laid."

"You're not the one in charge of this family!" Salim shouted.

Hakim rolled his eyes again. "From what I've seen, we'd have better luck if a doorknob was put in charge of this family."

Salim winced as if he'd been slapped. The family's difficult circumstances were his weak spot.

"Fatima's right," Bilal said. He put aside the bread dough, turned his eyes to Salim, and screwed up his courage. He was so enraged by Salim's ignorance and stupidity that he could no longer stand it. He adjusted his glasses nervously. "Women have the right to choose whether they want to wear a veil or not. Women in the early Muslim community never wore veils—only the wives of the Prophet did. There's a long history about the veil, and where it came from, and why, and not much of it has to do with Islam. Fatima's only seventeen, and she's already smarter than you'll ever be. What right do you—"

"Don't you fucking tell me about education, you four-eyed piece of shit!" Salim bellowed.

Bilal recognized the dangerous look on Salim's face, and suddenly his chest tightened up and he couldn't catch his breath. Gasping, he put his hand to his chest.

"Just lighten up," Hakim said as he rose from his chair by the ovens and moved to stand in front of Bilal. "You know, people have their own opinions, whether you like it or not. You can't control everything."

"After everything I sacrifice for these fucking bastards to get an education, and they're going to rub my nose in it?" Salim said.

"That's not what he meant," Hakim replied evenly.

Bilal fought to catch his breath. His mother came to stand beside him and rubbed his back with her large hand to calm him down. Her presence was reassuring, and his wave of panic began to subside.

"Look, your little brother here speaks Kurdish, English, Arabic, and now a bit of German too," Hakim said. "He's a smart little kid. Both of them are. They can both read the Quran in Arabic—and not just read it but also understand what it says. They've been going to an Islamic school all these years—where do you think Fatima gets all these ideas? From her teachers! She's not just making this stuff up to try to upset you, you know. You can say what you want about these Americans, but they're serious about Islam, and they know their stuff."

Salim sneered at Hakim, but didn't respond.

Hakim pressed on. "We didn't get a chance to finish school— you want to go to school now? You want to go sit in the fucking ESL class day after day? You spent three months going there, and you were pulling your hair out of your head—you want to go back now?"

Salim returned to his seat at the table. His blazing self-righteousness was giving way to self-pity. What he couldn't get by screaming or physical force, he would get by playing the martyr.

"I know they're smarter than me," he said quietly. "I didn't have a chance to finish school. Is that my fault? Does that make me stupid? Do they have to rub my nose in it?"

He picked at the remains of his breakfast, as if the matter no longer interested him.

When the Abu family arrived in America, Bilal and Fatima were only eight and nine. They truly came of age in the States. Salim and Hakim, on the other hand, were eighteen and seventeen when they immigrated and had gone to work immediately. Cultural differences between the older and younger children had created a divide in the family. Not only did East clash with West, but the old ways also clashed with the new.

"I'm trying to raise them the way Papa raised us," Salim said. "What do you think Papa would say if Fatima went around talking about not wearing a veil? A Muslim woman wears a veil. It's there to protect her, to keep men from bothering her. Nobody in this neighborhood is going to bother her because she's a Muslim girl, and they know we'll come after them if they do. But if she takes that veil off and goes walking around with all these guys hanging out on the street—with all these blacks and Asians, all these guys doing drugs—you know, there's worse things than being spit at. Is that what you want for your little sister, to get raped or murdered or who knows what?"

There was silence now. Their neighborhood was tough, and their neighbors' irrational fear of Muslims did have its advantages.

"Maybe you should try telling her that instead of accusing her of wanting to be a whore," Hakim suggested.

Salim had no rejoinder to his brother's wisdom, and the argument, for a time, was over.

"Don't forget—ten loaves for Rococco's," his mother said while Bilal packed loaves of bread into the crate on the back of his bike.

"I won't forget," he said.

"And don't be late for Friday Prayers," she added. "Your brother would be furious."

"I'm going now, Ma," he said. "It's not like you've got to remind of every little thing. I'm not stupid, you know."

She waved an impatient hand at him and went back inside the apartment.

Bilal buttoned up his jacket against the November chill and set off, in a foul mood now because of the argument that morning. It was a relief to get on his bike and leave it all behind.

Their neighborhood was a chaotic patchwork of different ethnic groups. What had once been Kansas City's Little Italy was now home to Vietnamese, Kurds, Russians, Africans,

Cambodians, and an array of Latin Americans. Each group had its own small restaurants and shops. It was to some of these that Bilal now made his way, dropping off orders and collecting money. He had been making his rounds since he was eleven, and every shopkeeper knew his face and name, even if language was sometimes a barrier.

The people out and about on the streets generally smiled at Bilal—he was a familiar, even comforting sight, with his old bicycle and his Islamic prayer hat. Though he was sixteen, with his earnest face and slight features, he was easily mistaken for a boy much younger. His black plastic glasses gave him a geekish look, but the Abus were too poor to afford wire frames.

His mother's bread was often called "Bilal's bread" because Bilal was the one who always delivered it. Customers even went into the shops asking for Bilal's bread.

Bilal always wore old hand-me-down clothes and old shoes—his family's poverty was plainly obvious. He was embarrassed to have to make the deliveries, embarrassed by the way people sometimes looked at him, embarrassed that his family was so poor. Since the 9/11 attacks, he always worried about how people would react when they saw his brown skin and prayer hat and realized he was a Muslim. He didn't blame them for being angry, but he was often astonished by their ignorance—most Americans knew nothing of Islam and lumped all Muslims together, as if bin Laden and his ilk represented the feelings and attitudes of Muslims everywhere, which they certainly did not. As if the Pope represented the attitudes and beliefs of all Christians everywhere!

There was a bite to the air now, and Bilal's fingers quickly became numb as he made his rounds.

When he finished with the main strip of shops in the former Little Italy, he headed toward the projects. There was a small convenience store there called Darby's that always took six loaves. Bilal was grateful his family didn't live in the projects, which were run-down and where many other refugee families had been resettled. Groups of young men wearing sunglasses milled around fancy cars and stared at everyone that passed. Most of the guys belonged to gangs and caused no end of trouble. Darby's was in the heart of the projects, and Bilal had no choice but to go.

Two blocks into the projects, he was accosted by a group of black guys. When they saw his white prayer hat, they blocked the road, forced Bilal to stop, and gathered around his bicycle.

"Look at this!" one of them exclaimed, grabbing Bilal's prayer hat and pulling it off his head. "Got ourselves a little Muslim terrorist!"

"Give it back," Bilal said, trying not to sound frightened. Sometimes he thought these guys were like dogs who could smell fear. He imagined they would go after you if they caught the scent, but otherwise they would leave you alone.

"I reckon this be Bilal the Bread Boy, if I'm not mistaken," another said. "The little four-eyed bread boy be off selling biscuits for his mommy."

They all laughed at this. Bilal grabbed for his hat, but it was passed from hand to hand.

"You blowed up anything lately, terrorist?" asked a tall, large man with dreadlocks and mirrored sunglasses.

"I'm not a terrorist," Bilal said. He stood with the bike between his legs.

"All of y'all are fucking terrorists," the dreadlocked man said.

"Give me my hat," Bilal said, ignoring him.

"Oh, the baby want the hat—what you think of that?" The dreadlocked man took up the phrase and rapped it. The others laughed.

"I'll give you your stupid hat," Dreadlocks said, grabbing it

from his companion and grinning at Bilal. He dropped it on the
pavement and ground his shoe into it. Then he kicked it toward
Bilal. "There's your stupid hat," Dreadlocks said, sneering at him.
"And if you blow up another building, maybe I'll just stomp on
your stupid head next time. What you think of that, you little
Muslim faggot?"

Amidst more laughter, Bilal bent to pick up his hat and thrust
it into his jacket pocket. He tried to leave, but the gang wouldn't
get out of his way. They started pushing him and his bike, cuff-
ing him on the back of the head, and laughing. Dreadlocks
snatched Bilal's glasses, snapped off one of the armbands, and
tossed the pieces into the street. Bilal lost his balance and toppled
to the street with his bike. Two dozen loaves of his mother's
bread spilled onto the pavement.

An elderly black woman came striding down the sidewalk
and confronted the gang. "What do y'all think you're doing?" she
demanded in a loud voice. She glared at each young man in turn,
disapproval written across her ancient face. "You get on out of
here! You go on home to your mamas. You ought to be ashamed!
What's wrong with you? You leave this boy alone! Mercy, Lord,
what a bunch of fools you is!"

Dreadlocks and his pals laughed off the old woman's scold-
ing, but slowly retreated to the black Mercedes on the other
side of the street. Dreadlocks leered at Bilal and waved his hand
dismissively at the old black woman.

"You all right, honey?" the woman asked, giving Bilal her
hand as he tried to stand.

Bilal nodded and glanced fearfully across the street. As he
brushed gravel off his trousers, he kept his eyes on Dreadlocks.

"Don't pay no attention to 'em," she said. "Ain't got nothin'
better to do than harassing folks and making asses of themselves and pardon my language."

Bilal looked around for his glasses, picked them up, and retrieved the broken armband. He put both pieces in his pocket. Then he picked up the bread, grateful that it hadn't been ruined—his mother would have had a fit. He repacked it in the crate, thanked the woman, and jumped on his bike, embarrassed and frightened.

When he was safely away, he began to tremble. He was terrified of those guys and all the others like them. He was afraid of fighting, afraid of violence. It made him sick to his stomach. It reminded him of how his father had been tormented before he was put to death.

When he got to Darby's, he parked his bike by the door, smoothed out his jacket, and tried to steady his nerves by taking several deep breaths. His heart was pounding uncomfortably in his chest.

He went inside the store. Contrary to her usual habit, Mrs. Darby, the owner, did not offer him one of her hearty smiles or "How ya doin', Bilal?" Instead, she looked upset, as if she were bracing herself for a confrontation.

"Hi Mrs. Darby," he said in greeting as he approached the cashier's desk hesitantly, wondering what was wrong.

"Bilal, I'm sorry, I don't need no bread today," she said abruptly.

Bilal frowned.

"In fact," she said, "I don't think we'll be needing your bread anymore."

He gave her a long, confused look, then lowered his eyes. His face burned with embarrassment.

"You know," she said, as if explaining, "since that World Trade Center thing, and the war in Iraq, well, I'm sorry, but I just can't do business with you people no more. You people killing Americans—that just don't sit right with me. Don't sit right with me at all. You just go on now. Tell your mother I'm sorry."

Bilal raised his eyes to look at her again. Two of the Italian shops had stopped taking his mother's bread, and he wasn't looking forward to telling her that another shop was now going to do the same.

"I understand," he said quietly. He turned away quickly, his eyes stinging with unwanted tears.

Bilal stood in the prayer line between Salim and Hakim as he went through the motions of the Friday Prayers. He responded to the prayer call in Arabic, bowed, prostrated himself with all the other men and boys in the mosque. He tried to forget about Dreadlocks and his cronies, Mrs. Darby, and the argument that morning—everything.

He had tried to wash off his prayer hat in the bathroom, but it was too soiled to be worn. He had been surprised by the paleness of his face when he looked at himself in the mirror. Without his glasses, he looked naked, strange.

Now that he was at the mosque, standing between his older brothers, he felt safe.

During the *kutbah,* or sermon, Imam Malik—a large black man who always wore an African-colored prayer hat—talked about the real meaning of jihad, which was not, he said, hijacking planes and enlisting children as suicide bombers to make a political point.

"The real jihad is the struggle with oneself," he said, "with one's lower nature. Striving to overcome selfishness—that's jihad. Striving to be kind to widows and orphans—that's jihad. Striving to resist the allure of the flesh—that's jihad."

The Imam's sermons did not sit well with some of the people in the mosque, especially those from Arab countries and young men like Salim, who were on fire with hatred for the West and the rest of the world. They wanted Imam Malik to preach about how evil Americans were, how righteous the Taliban were, how noble bin Laden was. But Imam Malik would have none of it. If some of the more restive members of his flock abandoned him, he was not going to lose sleep over it.

During the sermon, Bilal saw his friend Nu Haidar sitting with his older brother, Ahmed. Whenever he saw Ahmed—who was nineteen and going to college—Bilal felt something stir in his belly. Ahmed was handsome and finely built, with strong shoulders and a slender waist. Everything about him was attractive to Bilal in a disturbing sort of way. Bilal feared he might be gay.

The thought of that shamed him—hadn't the Prophet once said, "Homosexuals should be killed wherever you find them"? Hadn't the people of Sodom been destroyed for being homosexuals? Wasn't the Islamic position on the matter extremely clear?

Talk about jihad! No matter how Bilal struggled against his feelings, he found no relief.

He took his eyes away from Ahmed, embarrassed by his unruly feelings. When he looked in the other direction, he saw his best friend, Muhammad Jackson, who was one of the Imam's sons. Muhammad and Bilal had been pals since they were ten. Muhammad had lately become the subject of erotic fantasies that came to Bilal's mind unbidden.

Whenever Bilal spent the night at Muhammad's house, they showered together—Muhammad had three brothers and two sisters, and bathroom time was usually scarce. The last time Bilal had stayed over—two weeks ago—the sight of Muhammad's beautiful black skin and bare butt had given Bilal an erection that Muhammad had noticed. They had said nothing about it.

Muhammad had taken longer than usual that night to finish his bedtime bathroom routine. At one point, he stood in front of the sink, staring at his face in the mirror and picking at something in his eye, completely naked, for a rather long time. It seemed like he had wanted Bilal to get a good eyeful—and Bilal certainly had. Bilal couldn't stop himself from staring at the line of vertebrae that disappeared into the small of Muhammad's back, which gave way to the plump, soft buttocks...the dark line between them...the long legs, strong with muscle...the graceful shoulders...the flatness of the boy's belly...the patch of black hair below it...the thick bit of flesh that sprung from it...

Gazing at Muhammad made Bilal dizzy with longing. Nu Haidar was always going on about getting his hands on Britney Spears's tits, and Bilal couldn't have cared less. But to get his hands on Muhammad Jackson...suddenly, he understood what Nu meant.

Glancing at Muhammad across the crowded prayer hall, Bilal thought about what he had felt the last time they were alone together. He was ashamed. Why did he have to be a faggot? Why couldn't he be normal? Young Kurdish Muslim men were expected to take wives, and have children, and carry on the family name. They were not expected to spend Friday prayers wondering what it would be like to lie in bed naked with Muhammad Jackson.

Salim saw that Bilal had drifted off into his own thoughts and poked a finger in his ribs. With a jolt, Bilal awoke from his reverie.

The Friday Prayers ended and the men filed out of the mosque to go stand outside and socialize. Bilal remained where he was, kneeling but leaning back on his calves with his hands in his lap and his eyes closed. Salim always said extra prayers to make a show of his piety. Hakim went off to talk to his friends.

Bilal put his face in his hands and felt completely miserable. Why did he have these shameful desires when he didn't want them? When would they ever stop and leave him in peace? Why wouldn't Allah make these feelings stop?

That wasn't the only issue that Bilal wanted to take up with Allah. Why was Salim so troublesome? Why couldn't they get through just one day without all the screaming and drama.

And Bilal missed his father. Eight years had gone by, and for most of those years, he had quietly accepted his father's death as martyrdom—as the will of Allah. But these days all he could do was think of his father and miss him and wonder what life would have been like if his father had lived and Salim had never taken charge of the family. Sometimes after the Friday Prayers, Bilal watched his friends with their families. Most of his friends had affectionate, happy relationships with their fathers. It made Bilal utterly wretched. He would give anything to have his father back. His friends complained about their fathers—"They're stuck in the '60s." "They're total dorks." Bilal wanted to lash out at them for being so stupid. What would they do if they didn't have a father? How would they feel then?

Salim finished his extra prayers and knelt down next to Bilal. "Why are you crying?" he asked in a whisper.

Bilal was ashamed to realize he'd been crying. He couldn't look at Salim.

"What's wrong with you?" Salim said more insistently.

"Nothing," Bilal said, wiping his eyes.

Salim looked at him strangely. "Where's your glasses? Why aren't you wearing your prayer hat?"

Bilal shrugged. He still couldn't look at Salim.

There were difficult feelings between the two brothers, but there was love too. Bilal loved Salim's certainty, his strength, his seriousness, and his devotion to the family. He loved those rare

times when his brother sang old Kurdish songs—the ones their
father had taught the boys many years ago. He loved everything
about Salim except his beard, which made him look old and
ugly, and his temper, which could so easily get out of hand.

"You can tell me," Salim said quietly. He was tender now and
draped an arm protectively around Bilal's back.

Bilal shook his head. He couldn't find the words for everything he felt.

"You know you're going to tell me," Salim said. "You can't
hide anything from me."

Bilal looked up at him. Thus far in his life, that had certainly
been true. He had never been able to hide anything from Salim.

"Come on, tell me," Salim said. "We're not going anywhere
until you tell me why you're crying."

"It's not your business," Bilal mumbled, wiping his eyes.

"It *is* my business. You're my baby brother, and I want to
know why you're crying. Now tell me."

"No. You can't make me. It's my own problem."

"Bilal…"

"No."

"Bilal…"

Bilal lowered his eyes. He was going to have to say something.
In a voice hoarse with sadness, he told Salim about what had
happened in the projects and what Mrs. Darby had said. He said
he was upset about those things, which was only partly true.

Salim immediately became angry. "Who were they?" he
demanded. "Those black guys?"

"I'm not telling you," Bilal said. "It doesn't matter now."

"Yes, it does matter," Salim snapped. "Come on, get up."

Bilal followed his brother as they left the prayer hall to
retrieve their shoes in the courtyard. He wiped the tears on his
cheek to get them dry before anyone else saw him.

Salim found a group of his friends and went over to them. Bilal hung back, watching Salim stir up the group's anger and wondering why he hadn't kept his mouth shut. But what else was he going to say? What other reason could he give for crying in the mosque? How was he ever going to be able to tell Salim the truth about himself?

Salim's voice rose. "They took his prayer hat off and stomped on it and broke his glasses," he said so everyone in the courtyard could hear. "I'm going down there."

This provoked a heated debate, and Bilal was dragged over and made to repeat exactly what had happened. More and more of the "brothers," as the men were known, joined the congregation and kindled the collective anger that one of their kids had been messed with.

Muhammad Jackson and Nu Haidar pushed through the throng to stand next to Bilal. Bilal told them what had happened and what the men were talking about. He felt nervous when Muhammad put his arm around him.

Nu looked bewildered. "Frigging kooks," he said softly. Nu's vocabulary was full of colorful substitutions for swear words, which he could not bring himself to say—his mother had washed his mouth out with soap on more than one occasion, and he lived in fear of the day when it would happen again.

"They don't know any better," Bilal said. He felt more at ease now with his friends close by.

"You're defending those turd-lickers?" Nu asked.

"I'm just saying they're stupid and don't know any better."

"Well, someone ought to teach them," Muhammad said.

"Yeah," Nu said. "Frigging fags ought to pick on someone their own size."

Bilal cast a resentful glance at Nu. "Fags" didn't come under the category of a swear word, so Nu used it freely.

A group of about ten of Salim's friends decided they were going to walk down to the projects and confront Dreadlocks and his cronies. Bilal felt sick to his stomach.

"Please don't do this," he said, screwing up his courage. Then he spoke in Kurdish: "Salim, you'll just make it worse. Those guys down there have guns and drugs and all the rest of it, and you're just going to make trouble. Fatima and I have to walk to school every day, you know."

"*In'shallah,* we're going to teach them to have some respect," Salim replied.

"Don't be stupid," Bilal said.

"Stupid?" Salim said incredulously. "We have to protect ourselves. If we don't protect ourselves—if we don't go there and show them that we're not going to stand for it—it's only going to get worse."

Hakim and some of his friends joined the throng and Hakim asked what was going on. Bilal explained as best he could. Hakim was immediately pissed off about the matter, and just as eager to go marching into the projects as Salim was.

Bilal felt overcome with despair and leaned into Muhammad's embrace despite his anxiety.

There were soon about sixteen men—most of them in their twenties like Salim and Hakim and none afraid of a fight.

Nu nervously excused himself, saying his father was waiting for him. Muhammad insisted on going, for which Bilal was grateful. The men and boys got into assorted cars and made a convoy. A few minutes later they got to the projects and found Dreadlocks and his group of friends standing by the black Mercedes.

"You stay with the car," Hakim said to Bilal and Muhammad as the other men in their car got out.

Salim walked right up to Dreadlocks and pushed his chest with both hands.

Bilal stood by the car with Muhammad, watching and feeling uneasy.

"You want to fight with somebody?" Salim shouted angrily, pushing the man's chest again and forcing him backward. "Is that it? You want to fight? Or do you just sit around waiting for little Muslim kids to drive down your street on their bicycles so you can have a good time?"

Salim's English wasn't the best, and what came out was more like: "You want fighting? That it? You want fighting? Or you like to sit and waiting for little kids drive on this street on the bike so you have a good time?" But it was enough to make himself understood.

"You're crazy, man!" Dreadlocks said. He removed his sunglasses so Salim could see the fierceness in his eyes.

The group of black men arrayed themselves on either side of Dreadlocks, and the Muslim brothers flanked Salim. The blacks were outnumbered and they knew it. But Dreadlocks had his pride to consider, and Salim was obviously ready to draw blood.

"You touch my little brother again, and I'll kill you," Salim said. He pushed the man again.

"Stupid terrorist!" the black man exclaimed. "Y'all just violent terrorists—why don't you go blow up a building or something?"

"You shut your mouth!" Salim shouted.

"You make me," the man replied with a sneer.

Salim grabbed Dreadlocks by the lapels of his leather jacket and shoved him. Quickly recovering his ground, Dreadlocks shoved Salim back. A fight threatened to break out, but Salim's friends were quick to grab hold of him and drag him away, and Dreadlocks's friends did the same with him. The fracas ended before any real damage could be done.

Salim strained against the arms that held him back and bellowed, "You leave my brother alone!"

Dreadlocks's friends urged him to walk away gracefully as they cast wary glances at the Muslim brothers, who remained ready for a brawl if the need arose.

"This ain't finished," Dreadlocks said. He spat on the ground. "I'm gonna get that faggoty little bread boy—you just watch and see. Tell that little faggot to watch his back."

Salim charged at Dreadlocks, but the brothers held him back.

Dreadlocks and his crew backed away, then turned and entered the dark brick apartment building.

Bilal was despondent. This was all he needed—a pissed-off group of black guys waiting to settle the score when Salim was not around.

"What's wrong?" Muhammad asked.

Bilal didn't answer. When Salim approached, he said in Kurdish, "Thank you. That was enormously helpful."

"You shut up," Salim shot back. "They're not going to bother you anymore because they know they can't get away with it, so you shut your mouth about it."

Bilal grimaced and shook his head. He said nothing as they drove back to the mosque.

CHAPTER THREE

"Why don't you spend the night?"

Bilal and Muhammad stood outside the mosque as the men dispersed. The rest of Bilal's family had gone home already, leaving Bilal to stew in his anxiety and desire.

"We could do our trig homework," Muhammad added, as if the pot needed to be sweetened.

"I'd rather have a spike pounded into my forehead," Bilal said.

"Trust me, the trig is easier," Muhammad replied.

"You sure it's all right with your mom and dad?"

Muhammad nodded.

Bilal considered what had happened the last time he had spent the night—his embarrassing erection—and was not at all sure that Muhammad's proposition was a good idea. In fact, he was uncomfortable around Muhammad now. Bilal feared he would say or do something to give himself away. Would he get an erection at the wrong time—or worse yet, wake up in the morning to find that he'd been hugging his friend in his sleep?

"What is it?" Muhammad asked.

Bilal shrugged.

"Something's different about you now," Muhammad said. "It's like you don't want to talk to me anymore. You mad at me about something?"

Bilal shook his head.

"Well, what?"

Bilal shrugged again. "I'm not mad about anything."

"Is it your brother?"

Muhammad let that question hang in the air between them. Over the years, they had grown to know each other so well that they could communicate with a look, a shrug, a twitch of the lip, or just a few words. When Muhammad inquired about Bilal's brother, he was really asking: Did Salim beat you again?

Bilal shrugged again to let Muhammad know he was on the right track, but that he wasn't much inclined at the moment to discuss it. It was the second time that day that Bilal had been deliberately deceptive, and he didn't much like the feeling.

"So, what do you say?" Muhammad said, bringing the conversation back to a more appealing subject. "Come on, man. If I have to play Monopoly with the twins again, I'm going to kill myself."

"You sure it's all right?" Bilal asked.

"Oh, please, Bilal, you ought to know better than that."

Bilal did know better.

There were six children in the Jackson family, and they lived upstairs in the house attached to the mosque, which had once been a Catholic church and rectory. It was to the former rectory that Bilal and Muhammad headed for the post-Friday Prayers lunch, which was always a large but relaxed affair. All of the Jackson kids brought friends over, and the Imam always invited one or two families to join his brood.

At sixteen, Muhammad was the second-oldest of the Jackson children. Zubair, the oldest at twenty, was away at college. The two girls, Aisha and Jamilla, were fourteen and seventeen respectively. Both of them were good friends with Fatima. The last of the lot—the twin boys Hamid and Hamad—had just turned twelve. Muhammad's father, Imam Jackson, was also known as Doctor Jackson—in addition to being an Islamic scholar and an Imam, he was also a resident psychiatrist at the Missouri Medical Center's psychiatric care unit.

The Imam had been appointed to the mosque soon after Bilal had started to go to school there. In those days, Bilal's English wasn't good, and instead of making fun of him, Muhammad, the new boy, had befriended him. They became best friends, and in the intervening years they had done and shared everything together.

Muhammad was fascinated by the '60s—JFK, flower power, and especially Malcolm X. Muhammad had made Bilal sit through the Spike Lee movie about Malcolm X's life so many times that Bilal had memorized most of the dialogue.

For his part, Bilal was interested in words—he wrote stories, poems, lyrics to songs. He had notebooks full of the stuff. It was an interest he kept quiet about, lest the other boys make fun of him. He rarely shared his work with Muhammad, even though Muhammad did nothing but encourage him and express admiration for Bilal's talents.

Lunch was noisy. Muhammad's sisters had a clutch of girls around them who giggled and cast furtive glances at Muhammad and Bilal to try to get the attention of one or the other. The twins occupied the living room coffee table with their friends from the neighborhood. Imam Jackson sat at the dining room table with an old Palestinian man and his three sons. Muhammad and Bilal loaded their plates and disappeared to the bedroom that Muhammad shared with the twins.

"You write anything lately, Stephen?" Muhammad asked as they settled on the floor with their food.

"Don't call me that," Bilal said.

"He's a rich man—all you gotta do is write another *Carrie* or *Salem's Lot* and you'll be set for life."

Both Muhammad and Bilal devoured Stephen King books, but sitting down and writing another *Carrie* was not Bilal's cup of tea.

"I did write something," Bilal said softly.

Muhammad sat cross-legged on the floor next to him and ignored his lunch while he tried to repair Bilal's glasses with Super Glue. "What?" he asked.

"It's a song, I think. I'm not sure yet."

"Well, what is it?"

"Don't laugh."

"Man, you know I never laugh at you. I think you're cool."

"Really, don't laugh at me. It's a song. It's called 'Killed by Love.' But maybe it's a poem. I don't know. You have to speak it—when you speak it, it has this sort of ring to it."

"Let's hear it."

"Promise you won't laugh?"

"Bilal!"

"Okay…it goes like this…"

Bilal composed himself and pretended that he needed time to recall the words. He didn't. All the words were right there in his mind—he could recite them backward too. There was a melody as well, but he was too embarrassed to sing. So he spoke the words:

She wore a big, black dress and shiny shoes,
and when she talked about love, she could really parlez-vous

and I was just a fool with nothing better to do
and she caught me in her witch's spell
and the web she weaved, she weaved so well
and I remember thinking it was gonna be hell
but I was tongue-tied and petrified,
driving through Dallas when she hitched a ride,
and by the time we'd got to Tennessee
I'd been killed by love in the first degree.

He paused, wondering if the words sounded as ridiculous to Muhammad as they did to him.

Muhammad laughed, but not in a mocking way. "Is there more?" he asked.

"Why are you laughing? You said you weren't going to laugh!"

"Bilal, it's great. 'Killed by Love'—that's inspired, man! Sounds like it ought to be an Eminem song."

"There's more," Bilal said. He sat up straight and continued.

Well, she talked so sweet, like a chocolate bar,
and she was smoking cigarettes in the back of my car,
said, "Son I've got to find me some heroin—
it's the only cure for this mess I'm in
and I don't care much for reality
'cause reality ain't never been a friend to me
and, oh, these things my eyes have seen,
so many things you just wouldn't believe,"
but it couldn't last and I knew that
there was only room for one in that sleeping bag,
so I dropped her off at a Nashville shack,
put the pedal to the metal and never looked back,
but still sometimes at night I dream
about the big black dress and those eyes so green

and I wonder what it was those eyes had seen
and I wonder what it was that she couldn't tell me.

Bilal fell silent, thinking he must surely be making a fool of himself.

"And you were killed by love in the first degree?" Muhammad asked, smiling.

Bilal shrugged.

"That's wicked," Muhammad said. "Really, Bilal. That's really good."

"You think?"

Muhammad nodded. "So, what was it that she couldn't tell you?"

Bilal bit his lip. "I don't know. You know, everybody has secrets, don't they, things they can't tell other people?"

Muhammad frowned. "Not everybody has secrets, Bilal. I don't have any secrets, not from you."

"I know," Bilal said, shrugging. "It's just…you know."

"What about that one you did the last time—something about the little boy black and blue. I can't remember how it goes."

Bilal obliged:

Little boy black and blue,
someone's been hurting you—
was it your mother, was it your father?
There in your eyes I see
hints of the misery—
was it your brother, was it your sister?
Don't want to pry,
it's none of my business,
but why do you cry
for no reason?

Little boy black and blue,
someone's been hurting you,
and if you want, I'll protect you.

"Speaking of secrets," Muhammad said grimly.

"What's that supposed to mean?"

"I remember that one because you're telling the whole world what your brother's doing to you."

"It's not about my brother," Bilal said defensively.

"Yeah, right. I believe you."

"Well, it's not."

"Okay, pardon me for caring."

"He's not half as bad as you make him out to be," Bilal said.

"I worry about you sometimes, that's all. You've been acting really weird lately."

Bilal sighed and looked at his half-eaten lunch. How was he supposed to act when he couldn't stand being who he was?

"You been thinking about that contest?" Muhammad asked.

Bilal gave Muhammad a terrified look. The contest was a "Poetry Hoedown" sponsored by the Kansas City School District—Muhammad kept urging Bilal to give it a shot. One winner from each school would be chosen to compete in the grand finals.

"I could never get up there in front of all those people," Bilal said. "Just the thought of it makes me want to puke."

"It'll be a hoot," Muhammad said. "It'll be fun. They'll probably love your stuff. What have you got to lose?"

Bilal sighed and frowned. "I'd never be able to get up there and do that," he said.

"Not if you keep talking that way," Muhammad replied. "Look, the first round is early next month. At least give it a shot. If you win, you'll represent our school at the finals. I mean, how cool is that? You'll have loads of time to prepare. So, what do you say?"

Bilal's head was spinning. He was thrilled by Muhammad's enthusiasm and overwhelmed by the force of his fears.

"Do the monster thing," Muhammad suggested. "That's the one I like the best. That's the one you ought to do for the hoedown. They'll love it."

Bilal grinned. The "monster thing" was a poem he wrote called "The Ogre Ode."

"You have to say the 'hey' part with me, all right?" he said. Muhammad nodded.

Eat his flesh and gnaw his bones
and leave him roasting on the stove—
smash and trash and dash and crash
and eat the meat from shin to bone—
with bellies fat and greasy lips
we'll eat his arms and bite his hips,
tear and swear and scare and dare
and chew the tasty greasy bits.

"Hey!" they shouted in unison.

He's just a lowly villager;
there's hardly any consequence.
We'll take his land and eat his hands;
we'll fry his kids and eat his wench.
He'll learn his place, he surely will,
and if he doesn't then we'll kill him—
eat his flesh and gnaw his bones,
we'll eat the meat from shin to bone

"Hey!"

Grab his eyes and make a stew,
any pair of eyes will do—
boil and toil and roil and boil—
tongues are also tasty too;
cut his fingers one by one,
fry them in the morning sun,
spy them try them hack them crack them—
O how festive, O what fun!

"Hey!"

He's just a lowly villager,
country fed and muscle strong,
and in our roiling, boiling pot
he'll find the place where he belongs—
don't forget the family jewels:
they're succulent, nutritious too!—
hack them off and fry them up,
garnish them with herbs and blood.

"Hey!"

The sweetest meat is on the breast
so take a cleaver to his chest—
hack, attack, and whack and smack—
when we're finished, we will rest,
and if he begs and if he pleads
and if he cries and if he screams,
then pay no heed, no heed indeed,
just separate the bone from meat.

"Hey!"

Eat his flesh and gnaw his bones
and leave him roasting on the stove—
smash and trash and dash and crash
and eat the meat from shin to bone.

"Hey!"

The boys collapsed into a fit of giggling—this poem always did that to them.

"That's just too wicked!" Muhammad exclaimed. "That's the one you ought to enter for the contest. They'll love it!"

"You think?" Bilal asked, a small bit of hope flaring in his heart. Would people actually like his stuff? Wasn't it just too weird for public consumption?

"Oh, come on, Bilal, you did that one for us at dinner once— everyone laughed themselves to tears. Don't you remember? My dad about split his sides. I mean, it's funny, man. It's bizarre."

"Yes, but it's about eating people," Bilal pointed out.

"Exactly!" Muhammad exclaimed. "But it also has this 'exploitation of poor people' thing about it, doesn't it? That's what it's about, right? 'Eating up' the poor people?"

Bilal shrugged. It really wasn't about that—he'd written it after reading *The Hobbit* and thinking about Bilbo trying to rescue the dwarves from the three trolls who were planning to eat them. Still, if Muhammad wanted to think it was about social issues, that wouldn't hurt.

"So you really think I ought to try?" he asked, fishing for a little more praise.

Muhammad slapped his hand to his forehead. "Duh!"

"What if I make a fool out of myself?"

"You won't," Muhammad assured him. "And anyway, who's

your competition going to be? I bet no one from our school will even try out, and you'll be miles ahead of anyone who would. Come on, man, you've got to have a little bit of confidence in yourself! You'll be great."

Bilal was blossoming in the warm glow of his friend's encouragement, but he still wasn't so sure about making himself vulnerable in front of an audience.

Afternoon gave way to evening, and Muhammad suggested they take their shower before the others finished their Monopoly game. "They'll all be knocking on the door at the same time," he said

They took their pajamas and towels to the bathroom and locked themselves inside.

Muhammad disrobed straight away, and Bilal stole longing glances at the boy's lean chest and arms, his smooth black skin and long legs. He tried not to look too much lest he become aroused.

Bilal peeled off his brothers' hand-me-downs and looked at himself briefly in the mirror. The face that gazed back at him looked like Fatima's—when they were younger, they looked so much alike that most folks thought they were twins (people often mistook Bilal for a girl). Everything about him was spare, delicate, feminine—almost fragile-looking. His skin was light brown, hair jet black, and his eyes were a pale brown-green combination. He was a few inches shorter than Muhammad.

As they had done countless times over the past six years, they got into the shower together. Muhammad adjusted the water temperature and got himself wet. Bilal took in Muhammad's strong back, the curve of his buttocks, and the long legs that tapered down to handsome feet. Just once, to take the boy in his arms, to touch that flesh…

They soaped up and talked and carried on like nothing new was passing between them. Bilal's eyes kept straying to Muhammad's penis, his belly, and the muscles on his chest.

"Let me wash your hair," Muhammad said in a strange, hesitant voice. They had never washed each other's hair before—that wasn't something boys did. Bilal offered a small smile and a shrug in reply and turned around. Muhammad shampooed Bilal's hair and massaged his scalp. Every now and again his belly brushed against Bilal's back.

When he finished shampooing Bilal's hair, Muhammad soaped Bilal's shoulders and back. Muhammad's hands moved down to the small of Bilal's back, then to his buttocks and hips. Muhammad reached around to rub Bilal's belly, up to his chest. All the while Muhammad pressed his body close so that Bilal could feel his growing erection.

Embarrassed and exhilarated, Bilal said, "That feels good."

"What are friends for?" Muhammad asked quietly. He continued to run his hands over Bilal's body. "Have you ever, you know, done stuff with someone?"

Bilal slowly shook his head.

"You want to?" Muhammad asked.

Bilal turned around, nodded, and felt a broad smile spread across his face. Their erections brushed against each other.

"Did you ever, you know, kiss someone?" Muhammad asked very quietly.

Bilal had kissed Salim many times in the past, though not in recent memory—at least not willingly. But he didn't want to tell Muhammad that, so he shook his head.

"You want to?" Muhammad asked. For all his boldness, he was suddenly unsure of himself.

Bilal turned his head up and put his lips close to Muhammad's. Muhammad kissed him. His first go at it was just a quick peck, but Bilal made him do it again. The second time Muhammad didn't pull away. He drew Bilal closer to him and let his hands slide down Bilal's back to his buttocks.

When they pulled away, Muhammad said, "I think I'm gay. Sometimes I think maybe you…maybe you understand."

Bilal did. His eyes grew wide and bright.

"If I'm embarrassing you…"

Bilal shook his head.

They kissed again for a long time and embraced each other. Muhammad let his penis slide between Bilal's soapy legs and he began to move his hips back and forth. It took him no more than a minute to come, and when he did, he refused to look Bilal in the eye. Still breathing heavily, he soaped up Bilal's penis and encouraged him to do the same to him. Bilal eagerly complied.

Having sex with Muhammad was unlike anything Bilal had ever experienced. With Salim, Bilal sometimes had known pleasure, but more often he had felt brutalized. Now he felt himself ablaze with passion—alive and incredibly happy.

After he came, he was so astonished by his ecstatic feelings he couldn't bring himself to pull away.

"I've been trying to tell you for a long time," Muhammad said.

"Tell me what?" Bilal asked.

"You know," Muhammad said, shyly pressing his lips into the crook of Bilal's neck.

"What?" Bilal pressed.

"You know," Muhammad murmured. He would say nothing more.

"Isn't it a sin?" Bilal asked after breakfast the next day while they worked on their homework. "I mean, two guys… you know."

"It doesn't feel like a sin to me," Muhammad said. "It's not like we're robbing a bank or something. We're not doing anything wrong."

"But the people of Sodom were destroyed for being...what they were," Bilal said.

Muhammad chuckled.

"What?" Bilal asked, offended by his friend's laughter.

"I think there was more to it than that," Muhammad said.

"Like what?" Bilal demanded.

Muhammad gave him a long, searching look. "My dad knows about me—we sat down and looked at the verses in the Quran that talk about homosexuality, and he explained a lot of things to me. There was a lot going on in Sodom. They were thieves, highway robbers. They broke the desert hospitality laws, did lewd things in public, went around raping men and young boys. When the two angels showed up on Lut's doorstep warning him about the impending destruction of the city, the men of Sodom gathered outside Lut's house, demanding that he turn over the angels so that they could rape them. I mean, what does this have to do with us? We're not going around raping people, are we? We're not thieves. We're not hurting anyone. I mean, it's a bit too simplistic to say that the people of Sodom were destroyed because they were homosexual. It was obviously more complicated than that."

Bilal started to bite his lip, but stopped himself. He began to turn Muhammad's words over in his mind.

"My dad told me that people in those days probably wouldn't even understand what we mean when we use the word 'homosexuality' today. The word itself might have meant something really different to them. When they condemned 'homosexuals,' they might have been talking about men who rape young boys—so the condemnation might have become a

religious law to protect young boys, not to condemn gay people. Do you know what I mean? Things change."

Muhammad spoke quickly, passionately.

"My dad's a real radical, you know," Muhammad said. "He's
real progressive about some things. He's not shy about casting
doubt on the decisions reached by scholars eight hundred years
ago. He says we know a lot more now than they did then, and
we have the right to form our own conclusions and decide for
ourselves how we're going to live out our Islam. Each generation has that right, and my dad doesn't have much patience for
Muslims who blindly obey everything and never question.

"Anyway, he told me to just be a good person and not to get
involved with someone unless I loved him—you know, not to
be out there going to bars and engaging in drinking and casual
sex and all of that, but to save myself for someone I love, to
respect the limits that Allah has placed on sexuality, not to just
be giving in to lust all the time. I mean, come on, Bilal, what
else are we supposed to do? You are who you are. Why should
you feel bad about something you can't change?"

Bilal imagined what Salim would say to all of that. "But what
about all those things the Prophet said?" he replied. " 'Kill the
one who's doing it; kill the one it's being done to.' "

"You don't believe all that, do you?" Muhammad asked.

Bilal gave him a consternated look.

"So many of those sayings were fabricated," Muhammad said.
"It's hard to take any of them seriously, especially questionable
ones about killing people. Come on, Bilal, we're Muslims. We
follow the Quran. We don't base the decision about whether to
kill someone on a saying that may or may not be authentic.
We're supposed to use our reason and intelligence, not blindly
follow whatever sayings people attribute to the Prophet."

"But what if he *did* say those things?" Bilal pressed. "We

can't just ignore them because we don't like them."

"No," Muhammad said, "we can't. But they have to be consistent with the spirit of the Quran. The Quran comes first. And then the Hadith sayings. And among the Hadith sayings, there are those that are strong, some that are weak, some that are doubtful, and so on. So you have to look at each one of those sayings and try to determine where it came from—was it a strong source, or a doubtful one? And even then, Bilal, these were the opinions of Muhammad. They're not part of the Quran. They're his opinions. He could have been wrong, you know. His words could have been misinterpreted over the years to mean something quite different."

"So you don't believe he said those things about killing gay people?" Bilal asked.

Muhammad shook his head.

Bilal was quiet for a moment. "So your dad knows about you?"

Muhammad nodded. "He was a bit upset at first, but he said it was better for me to be honest than to lie or pretend to be someone I wasn't."

"My brother would kill me if I told him," Bilal said.

"We're not hurting anyone," Muhammad said earnestly. "And if we love each other, if we respect each other, if we try to help each other—what's wrong with that? What's wrong with wanting to love someone?"

"But it's unnatural," Bilal said.

Muhammad rolled his eyes. "It didn't feel unnatural to me. And I don't feel the slightest bit guilty about it."

Bilal didn't either, really, yet he felt like he ought to.

"We didn't hurt anyone," Muhammad said again quietly. He opened his trig book—tucked into the back were two photographs. One was a snapshot of Muhammad at a swimming pool. His dark skin gleamed against a bright yellow swimming suit. The picture had been taken over the summer during a trip to the YMCA—Mrs. Jackson often took the boys and Bilal there on Saturday afternoons. The other snapshot, taken the same day, captured Bilal as he was climbing the ladder out of the water.

Muhammad handed the picture of himself to Bilal. "Just in case you miss me," he said with a grin.

Bilal blushed and smiled.

"And I'm keeping this," Muhammad said, taking the picture of Bilal and putting it back in the book. "In case I miss you."

"Will you?" Bilal asked.

"Of course," Muhammad said. It was a straightforward, honest statement of fact.

Bilal watched him for a long moment. Was he falling in love with this boy? That would be so easy to do. But what on earth did Muhammad see in him?

"You don't really love me," Bilal said. It was more a question than a statement.

"You don't really know me very well, do you?" Muhammad countered.

"But I'm the ugliest guy in the whole school. You could have anyone you wanted."

Muhammad chuckled and shook his head.

"Why are you laughing?"

"Oh, Bilal, listen to you. You're so full of shit sometimes, it surprises me. You think I take showers with all my friends? No. Only you. You think I ever let them see my tally wacker? No. Only you. You think I invite them to spend the night? No. Only you. Always, it's just been you, Bilal. And you're not the ugliest kid in the school, not by a long shot, and you know it. You've got this cute Arab thing going on—haven't you ever heard all the girls giggling when you walk by? Why do you think they're giggling? Because you're cute. And one of the reasons you're so cute is that you're so completely unaware of it. You wear those Elvis Costello glasses and never comb your hair, and it's like the harder you try not to be cute, the cuter you are. And every time I look at your brown butt in the shower, I get the nastiest thoughts going through my mind."

Muhammad's brazenly lowered his eyes to take in Bilal's body. Bilal felt self-conscious at first, but then his erection returned and he felt—what? Bold, embodied, alive.

"But it isn't just that, Bilal. You're my friend. Nobody knows me the way you do. Nobody ever could. Sometimes I think about you and me being together always, all our lives—that's what I want. I've never wanted anybody else. Always, it's been you. I would never have sex with anyone else 'cause I think that would be wrong, that would be sinful. But if you and I were together, and you loved me as much as I loved you, and we took care of each other—how could that be sinful?"

Muhammad put his hand on Bilal's face and smiled.

Bilal smiled in return. His heart raced. The words were wonderful to his ears. But was he only fooling himself? Would he ever be able to let himself fall in love with another boy? What would Salim say about it?

"Doesn't the Quran say that we will all have 'companions' according to our own needs?" Muhammad asked. "If other people don't understand, that's their problem, not mine."

Bilal gazed into Muhammad's eyes—eyes that he had looked into countless times in the past, eyes that now revealed new things about Muhammad. Bilal was humbled by his friend's words, excited by the thought of having a "companion" according to his own needs.

"I don't want to rush things," Muhammad said, a twinkle in his eye. "I'm just talking, you know."

"You're looking happy," Fatima said. She dropped her history textbook on the kitchen table and gave Bilal a cartoon frown.

It was Sunday evening, and they were finishing the last of their homework. Since there was no television in the Abu household—Salim would not permit it—they did not, as their friends did, sit around watching CNN for the latest news on the "war on terror," though Fatima often wished they could.

The kitchen, with its constant smells of bread and Arab spices, was the heart of the household. It was large, with a round table situated in the middle under an overwrought chandelier from the 1950s. The table itself was not much to speak of, and the chairs were mismatched, as was just about everything in the two-bedroom apartment. The blue linoleum underfoot did not match the green wallpaper, but it was home.

"Is it a sin to be happy?" Bilal asked.

"In this family it is," Fatima said, smiling. "So you had a nice time with Muhammad, eh?"

"What's that supposed to mean?" Bilal asked. He felt the blood drain from his face.

"Oh, everybody knows you two are in love with each other," she said breezily.

"We are not!"

"Whatever," Fatima said. "Aren't you just a teeny-weeny bit too old for sleepovers and all that stuff? Jamilla said you guys still shower together. I mean, hello? Inquiring minds want to know."

Bilal warily appraised his sister. She had a way of figuring everything out—often way before Bilal even had a clue.

"What, you think we're in love?" he ventured.

"You can tell me," she said sweetly. "You know I won't tell anyone."

"We're just friends," Bilal said after a beat. He tried to look offended.

"Okay, fine," she said. She took a seat on the other side of the table and held him in a steady gaze. "Then are you ever going to start dating girls? Are you ever going to show *interest* in girls? Hello? You do know what a girl is, don't you? Most boys your age are so full of hormones they can't think straight, but you…well, you're different, Bilal. Aren't you?"

Sensing that an offensive was wiser than being on the defense, Bilal said, "Aren't you still pining away for Omar Hanif?"

"That creep?" Fatima replied, raising her voice.

"Everybody knows you've got the hots for him."

"Oh, please!" she exclaimed. She did, of course, but since Omar never paid her the slightest attention, she had decided he was a creep.

"Tears on your pillow and all of that," Bilal said, rubbing it in.

"As if!" Fatima replied.

"Anyway, why are you doing all this studying?" Bilal said, pressing his advantage too far. "You know, all you're going to do is get married and make babies. It's not like you need to know calculus for that."

"Don't even joke about that," Fatima said. There was a hint of warning in her voice.

"It's true," Bilal said earnestly. "You should be learning how to cook—something useful."

"Then who's going to tutor you in math, huh?" she asked, mad now. "Trig was a breeze, but you whine about it so much I'll be surprised if you don't flunk it. I'm surprised you even passed algebra."

"When you're barefoot and pregnant, I'm sure those cosines will come in handy," Bilal said, enjoying himself.

"Just don't even," Fatima said, giving him an angry glare. "I know you're kidding, but it's not a laughing matter, Bilal. I have just as much right to an education as anyone else, and just because I'm a girl doesn't mean you're smarter than I am, which you are obviously not. I mean, jeez, if you can't do trig, forget calculus."

"One might think you were an American," Bilal said.

"One might think you were in love with your best friend," Fatima replied, getting back to the matter at hand.

Bilal lost his nerve and blanched again.

Fatima regarded him carefully. "Don't let Salim find out," she said quietly. All her playfulness was gone. "That's what I'm trying to tell you."

"There's nothing to find out!" Bilal said too shrilly.

"Whatever," Fatima said. "I'm just warning you. He'd blow all his gaskets."

Bilal frowned and bit his lip. Fatima reached across the table and gently touched his chin to make him stop. She knew the truth of things. There was no hope of fooling her.

"We're not hurting anyone," he said quietly.

"I didn't say you were," she replied. "I'm just saying, maybe you ought to try to be less obvious about it—around Mr. Super-duper Holy Man. Don't forget we're talking about a Neanderthal here, not some enlightened being of the twenty-first century."

"It's not his business what I do!"

"Keep saying that."

Bilal took in the seriousness of his situation. "Does everybody know?" he asked, shifting in his seat nervously.

"Of course not," Fatima said. "And that's the way we're going to keep it. Don't forget who Muhammad's father is, Bilal. You could make a mess of things for that man if the community found out his son was…well, you know."

Bilal had never considered this. He would hate to bring unhappiness to Muhammad or his family.

"You don't want to get the man fired," Fatima added.

On the nightstand next to the bed, within easy reach, Salim kept a bottle of lotion. When Bilal felt Salim moving around in the bed that night and reaching over in the direction of the nightstand, he knew what it meant.

Salim moved closer to him, pulled back the covers, and reached for Bilal's pajama bottoms. He pulled them down just far enough to expose Bilal's buttocks. Bilal cringed, but he didn't dare complain. He didn't turn to look at his brother and he made no effort to be cooperative.

Hakim was already sleeping—Bilal heard the gentle, heavy rhythm of his breathing in the darkness down near the foot of the bed, where Hakim kept his mat.

Salim moved closer still and poked at Bilal with his erection, which he had greased with the lotion. Then he settled himself just behind Bilal and forced his penis inside Bilal's body.

Bilal tensed up from the sudden, unwanted pain. Despair and helpless anger rose in his stomach. He groaned and twisted his hips so that Salim's intrusion would be less painful.

For several minutes, Salim lay on his side, holding onto Bilal's hips and thrusting himself quietly in and out. Bilal could tell Salim was in one of his moods—he would "make love" for half an hour or more, moving slowly and steadily, pausing every now and again, in no hurry to finish. Whether Bilal was in a similar mood was never an issue, so there was little he could do but lie still and endure it.

When Salim touched him these days, Bilal thought he might jump right out of his skin—he did not want to be touched by his brother anymore. Increasingly, that unwelcome contact produced feelings of revulsion and anger in him. Bilal feared he would not be able to hide them for much longer.

His experience with Muhammad had been completely different: pleasurable, arousing, satisfying. They had not "sodomized" each other. There had been no pain in their lovemaking, no feelings of confusion or fear, just a heady mix of passion and happiness and delight.

"It hurts," Bilal whispered. He glanced over his shoulder and reached back to push against Salim's hip to try to get him to stop—or at least to fuck more gently.

"It feels good," Salim whispered in reply, ignoring Bilal's rare protest. Instead of being more gentle, he forced Bilal to lie on his stomach. He pushed back the covers all the way and straddled him, pushing his penis deep inside Bilal's body.

Bilal was in agony. Salim gripped Bilal by the shoulders to steady himself while he rocked his hips back and forth.

Bilal began to cry. He didn't want to, but he couldn't help it. Salim reached around and clamped a hand over Bilal's mouth, just as he had done when Bilal was little and couldn't control his sobbing. Bilal felt a surge of panic—with Salim on top of him and Salim's hand clamped over his mouth, he felt utterly trapped. To prevent Bilal from moving around, Salim grasped Bilal's hair with his free hand and kept the other clamped over his mouth. He began to thrust frantically now, determined to finish as quickly as possible.

Bilal struggled uselessly. He tried to bite the hand over his mouth, but Salim jerked Bilal's head by his hair to make him stop.

Finally, Salim came. He gasped in Bilal's ear and lay the full weight of his body on top of Bilal. When he caught his breath, he rolled off of Bilal and lay very still. Soon his breathing was keeping time with Hakim's.

CHAPTER FOUR

On Monday, Nu found Bilal and Muhammad on their lunch break. He frowned as he joined them in the cafeteria at their table.

"You know, the way you guys carry on sometimes, people might think you're queer for each other."

Bilal was suddenly paralyzed with fear, but Muhammad only chuckled. "I thought everybody knew that I was queer for you, Nu," he said.

"Yeah, right," Nu replied, rolling his eyes. "If you were talking about my faggy brother, I'd believe you."

"Ahmed?" Bilal asked, his eyes growing wide.

Nu nodded. "He's got queer porno magazines in his bottom dresser drawer—like nobody's going to notice. I found them yesterday. I can't wait till my mom flips one of those open and sees those guys sucking on each other. Jeez, the turds'll hit the fan for sure."

"He's *gay?*" Bilal asked.

Nu nodded. "Faggy as a three-dollar bill. I mean, can you believe that—guys giving each other blow jobs? What a bunch of queerbait losers."

"It feels good," Muhammad said, grinning. "You should try it. Tastes a bit salty, though."

"Oh, please," Nu said, making a sour face. "You'd have to be mental. Now, wait till you see Miss December."

Licking his lips, Nu took a large folder from his book bag, which was stuffed with his Arabic class notes. He lay the folder casually on the table and slid it across to Muhammad, who opened it carefully so that no one but he and Bilal could see what was inside.

The latest issue of *Playboy* was tucked into one of the pockets inside the folder.

Muhammad gave Bilal a sly grin as he took out the magazine and flipped through the pages. Bilal tried to look duly impressed, but he kept glancing around to make sure they weren't going to get caught—they could be expelled for looking at pornography.

Bilal glanced at the bare female flesh on display and felt...nothing. If anything, he was embarrassed for the young women who were flaunting their charms in such a fashion. Their curves and swells, their breasts and backsides, their pouty lips—none of it was even mildly arousing to him, though he desperately wanted it to be.

Muhammad thumbed past every page, but said nothing. After a couple of minutes, he offered the folder to Bilal, who politely declined. "You don't want to see Miss December?" Muhammad asked, an incredulous look on his face. Bilal couldn't tell whether he was being serious or sarcastic, taking a dig at Nu. Muhammad was always making subtle jokes that Nu wasn't bright enough to pick up on.

"I just don't want to get caught," Bilal said. He hoped he managed to convey reluctance and hide his relief. He adjusted his glasses nervously.

"Mr. Goody Two Shoes," Muhammad said.

"I can think of several things I'd like to do to some of those chicks," Nu said enthusiastically. He adjusted his Harry Potter glasses and leered at Muhammad and Bilal.

"We could throw them off a cliff," Muhammad said, glancing at Bilal and smirking. The Prophet had once said homosexuals should be thrown off a cliff.

"Oh, please," Nu replied. "The only place I'd throw them is on their backs. Then I'd show them Paradise—all twenty inches of it."

Muhammad laughed. "Probably need a magnifying glass, is more like it."

"That's not what the chicks say," Nu replied, looking smug.

"You mean those day-old chicks they got on the farm, the ones just crawling out of their eggshells?"

"Get real," Nu said. "We're talking babes. We're talking ba-da-booms like you wouldn't believe. We're talking squeals of delight here."

Muhammad rolled his eyes.

Nu grinned goofily. "Anyway, I've got to go. See you later."

He excused himself, leaving Muhammad and Bilal sitting side by side in the sudden silence.

Toward the end of lunch, Bilal thought again about searching the Internet for information on homosexuality—and frowned. For weeks, he had been trying to gather the courage to go to the computer lab and conduct such a search. He was almost compulsive when it came to looking up words like "homosexuality" and "gay" in dictionaries and encyclopedias. He desperately wanted to learn more about what was happening to him.

The school library offered little help—the subject was rarely mentioned. One brief entry in an encyclopedia on Islamic ethics stated that homosexuality was the sin of the People of

Sodom, for which they had been destroyed by Allah. Another book stated that homosexuality was a sexual perversion similar to pedophilia, bestiality, and necrophilia. Bilal also looked up those words, and was horrified to find himself classed among people who wanted to have sex with children or goats or even dead bodies.

After what had happened with Muhammad—as he began to realize that he was probably in love with the boy, and the boy was probably in love with him—he had to know more. He was sure there would be a lot of information on the Internet, but if he was caught using the school's computers to look at such information, there would be hell to pay.

After he told Muhammad he would catch up with him later, Bilal went to the computer lab and sat at one of the terminals in the back where no one could see what he was doing. If nothing else, he could check his e-mail and see what other silliness Nu might have sent him. He logged on, launched the Internet browser, and checked his e-mail. Then he took the plunge; he called up an Internet search engine, typed in "gay Muslim," and hit the return key. He furtively glanced up from his screen to make sure nobody was watching.

On the first site he visited, he read:

In order to maintain the purity of the Muslim society, most Muslim scholars have ruled that the punishment for this act should be the same as for fornication (i.e., one hundred whiplashes for the man who has never married, and death by stoning for the married man). Some have even ruled that it should be death for both partners, because the Prophet said: 'Kill the doer and the one to whom it was done.' (Related by Al-Bayhaqi)

Bilal let out a dejected sigh and moved on.

The next site said homosexuality was "dirty" and led to AIDS and venereal diseases, because the rectum was not designed to be penetrated by the male sexual organ:

Homosexuals are only interested in satisfying unnatural lusts and pose a danger to the smooth ordering of society and therefore cannot be tolerated in any Muslim family or community, lest they spread their perversion to others.

Another site pointed out that the Prophet had once cursed homosexuals by repeating three times, "Allah has cursed anyone who does what Lut's people did." Then the Prophet commanded: "If you find any persons engaged in homosexuality, kill both the active and the passive partner." To this passage the commentator Ibn Abbas had added, "Find the tallest building in the town and throw the homosexual down from its roof, then stone him to death."

The Prophet also said that those who will be consigned to the flames of Gehenna include both the active and passive partners in homosexuality, men who have sex with animals, men who marry both a mother and daughter at the same time, and those who masturbate regularly. Ibn Abbas speculated that an unrepentant homosexual would be turned into a pig in his grave.

The general opinion of Muslim scholars, past and present, was that homosexuality was unnatural. Each man and woman was created heterosexual by Allah. Only later did a person choose to deviate from the normal sexuality he or she had been born with. The more recent scholars said this deviation was the result of environmental factors, such as childhood sexual abuse, or an absent father, or early exposure to pornography. In any case, homosexual feelings were described as a temptation from

Shaitan that had to be endured until it pleased Allah to allow the temptation to stop.

Bilal discovered several "gay Muslim" sites. He quickly scanned the articles written by Muslims who were gay and who had posted their life stories. A few of these articles refuted or reinterpreted the Islamic teachings on homosexuality. Most of the stories were about having boyfriends and going out to bars and discotheques and living the gay lifestyle.

One site led Bilal to a discussion of the Hadith literature—the sayings and deeds of the Prophet Muhammad—and how these texts related to such sayings of the Prophet as "homosexuals should be killed wherever you find them"—an injunction that hard-line Muslims took seriously. The article asserted that Muslim scholars and educated Muslims in general knew that a great deal of the Hadith literature had been fabricated, and that some of the sayings and deeds attributed to Muhammad were downright disgraceful. The site reminded Bilal of what Muhammad had said the other day.

The author of the article cited the well-known story that Muhammad used to go around to his thirteen wives every night, satisfying each of them sexually. The writer noted that this might have been an honorable or praiseworthy notion to ignorant Arabs in the desert, who invented such stories to glorify Muhammad and make him "greater" than he was. But to the modern mind, attributing such things to Muhammad, rather than glorifying him, made him seem lusty and vulgar, while all the other evidence of his life suggested he was not.

Bilal glanced up from the screen and looked around to make sure no one was watching. His heart was racing. These ideas, these thoughts—they made his head spin.

Bilal next came across a site put together by an older Muslim man who talked about how he had been gay all his life. This man had lied to himself, pretended, denied, gotten married and divorced, stayed in the closet, prayed, begged Allah to "cure" him—nothing had worked. In the end, as he neared his fortieth birthday, he had to conclude that he was what he was, and could never be anything else. He wondered why Allah would create him in this fashion, only to condemn him for being what he was—what sense did that make? He also wondered why the Muslim world demanded that he lie about himself. Wasn't honesty to be preferred in all things?

Bilal glanced at his watch, moved on to another site, saw a link for "hot boys," and clicked on it. He arrived at a site full of gay porn. He clicked on several of the pictures to enlarge them, then followed another link to another site. He stared at the pictures in astonishment. For the rest of the day, after he logged off the computer, he couldn't get those pictures out of his mind.

CHAPTER FIVE

Just before dawn the next day, Bilal rose with Salim.

The first of the day's five sets of prayers had to be said after light entered the sky, but before the sun itself could be seen. Bilal and Salim performed their ablutions at the bathroom sink, got their prayer rugs, and lay them side by side on the floor next to where Hakim was sleeping.

It had been a long time since Hakim had joined them—he'd stop praying years ago. He slept on, oblivious to their ritual, as he did every morning.

Salim led the prayers, and Bilal followed. Afterward Salim said his "litany" of those whom Allah ought to bless and those whom He ought to curse. The latter list was always much longer than the former.

At breakfast, which Mrs. Abu had waiting for them, Bilal said, "There's a poetry competition at my school. I was wondering if I could have permission to enter."

Salim glanced at him and frowned. "Poetry?"

Bilal nodded.

"That sounds lovely," Mrs. Abu said. She didn't notice the disgusted look Bilal was getting from Salim. "I'm sure you'll do wonderfully."

"Oh, please," Salim said. "His stupid poems—who's going to like them? He'll just embarrass himself."

Bilal said nothing and picked at his breakfast. His brother had a way of making him feel as if everything about him was stupid—his interests, his habits, the way he looked, the way his hair was combed, the sort of books he read.

"Don't talk like that," Mrs. Abu said, giving Salim a disapproving scowl.

"It's a waste of time," Salim said dismissively. "And the Prophet hated poetry. Why is an Islamic school having a poetry competition? Don't they have anything better to do?"

Bilal quietly seethed with frustration. Salim was wrong again, but he didn't dare point it out. There were those who claimed the Prophet hated poetry and music and stories and anything else in life that was cultured and enjoyable—but those were baseless claims, the sort of foolishness that the Taliban resorted to when they outlawed music and stage dramas. It was ignorance, never questioned, never challenged, and passed on from one generation to the next—just like all the other ignorance that passed itself off as "Islam" but had nothing to do with true religion.

"Please?" Bilal said quietly.

"Why don't they have a Quran memorizing contest?" Salim asked with a wave of his hands.

Bilal wanted to say that no one had time to memorize the Quran anymore—and no one wanted to—but he didn't dare. Of course, memorizing the Quran was considered part of a proper Islamic education, but it was done at the expense of other subjects. In consequence many Islamic countries had fallen far behind the rest of the world in science and technology. What good was memorizing the Quran when it came to putting down roads and building power plants and running hospitals?

"*Please?*" Bilal said again, allowing a bit of despair into his voice.

"Why do you have to be interested in these sissy subjects like poetry? Why don't you learn how to do something useful, be a lawyer or a doctor? How are you going to pay the bills if you write poetry for a living? You'll starve to death," Salim said.

"I'm *not* going to write poetry for a living!" Bilal said angrily.

Fatima, who was sitting across the table from him, shot Bilal a wary look.

"I was hoping you might come," Bilal said firmly, determined not to back down. "I'm going to be nervous, getting up on the stage by myself."

Salim rolled his eyes, but something in Bilal's voice made him relent. "If it's so important to you, then go ahead."

It took Bilal a moment to accept that he'd heard Salim correctly. "Thank you," he replied when he'd gathered his wits. "Like I said, I was hoping you'd come and listen." And he was hoping. Just once, he'd like his brother to see him do something daring, something to make the family proud.

"Oh, please," Salim said. Salim never attended any of their school functions, never showed any interest in their schoolwork or activities.

There was a long, uncomfortable silence.

"Go wake your brother up," Mrs. Abu said to Bilal. "It's getting late."

Bilal began to bite his lip, but stopped when he saw Fatima flash an encouraging smile. He got up from the table and went to wake Hakim.

After Salim and Hakim left—they both worked at a lumber-yard and had to catch the 6:30 bus to go across the river and into the North Side—Fatima got out their old, beat-up boom box and put on a Billie Holiday tape. Salim wouldn't permit music to be played, so Fatima kept the small, portable stereo hidden in her closet.

Billie launched into "Good Morning, Heartache," and Fatima sang along as she helped Bilal clear the table.

Bilal smiled at her. They both loved Billie Holiday and Ella Fitzgerald and Patsy Cline. John Denver and Elvis Presley were also favorites. Their tastes were dictated partly by economics: There was little money to spare in the Abu household, so the tapes they bought when they could beg a few dollars from their mother were always secondhand, or recordings by singers that people no longer wanted to hear. Muhammad was also a Billie Holiday fan and had turned them on to many of the great blues singers his parents enjoyed.

"So you're going to do the Poetry Hoedown," Fatima said. She tried to stifle a fit of giggles.

"Why are you laughing?" Bilal asked.

Fatima collected herself and beamed at her little brother. "I think you'll be brilliant. You do know that Jamilla is in love with you?"

Bilal put his hands on his face and shook his head. Jamilla was Muhammad's sister, and Fatima and his mother often teased him about her. She was a nice girl, but Bilal was not interested.

"She'll be your biggest fan," Fatima said. She sensed she had struck a nerve.

"Thanks," Bilal said coyly, hoping to steer Fatima away from the subject.

"My hero," Fatima said, feigning a swoon. "My four-eyed poetry man. I just want to kiss him. Kiss, kiss, kiss, kiss, kiss."

"I can't help it if you're lusting after Nu Haidar all the time," Bilal said.

"Oh, please," Fatima replied. "I don't want to have to compete with his inflatable doll."

They spoke in English, so their mother, who was chopping vegetables for the evening meal, couldn't possibly follow the conversation. They were enjoying their little bit of naughtiness.

"Well, really, I'm impressed," Fatima said, serious now. "I like your stuff. I think you're going to be surprised when you discover that other people do too. I just never thought you'd have the guts to get up and do that, but what do I know?"

"I can still back out," Bilal said.

"Uh-huh," Fatima said forcefully. "You're not backing out. It'll be good for you. And who knows—you might win."

"So I take it that at least you'll be there, if I do it," Bilal said hopefully with a backhanded gesture toward Salim's place at the table.

"Forget about him," Fatima said. "He wouldn't understand what you were saying anyway. Then again, you could memorize the whole Quran and make him sit there for two hundred years while you recite it. He'd love that."

He probably would, Bilal thought, nodding.

During his last class that day, Bilal was shocked when Salim appeared at the classroom door and motioned for Bilal to collect his things.

Salim worked all day and usually didn't get home till about six or so. Mystified, Bilal put his books in his bag, nodded a goodbye to Muhammad and Nu, and collected his jacket and lunch box. He'd been on a high all day, hanging out with Muhammad, thinking about the Poetry Hoedown, wondering if he really did have a chance of winning, and fantasizing about representing the Harun Mosque and School at the citywide finals. He might even get his name in the paper.

"What is it?" he asked in the hall. Salim didn't answer. Instead, he turned and walked toward Mr. Washington's office.

Mr. Washington was a large black man who had a serious way about him that could be intimidating. He had just begun his duties in September, and was much stricter than the previous principal. In addition to being the principal, he was also the trig teacher—two solid reasons why Bilal disliked him intensely.

Washington stood when he saw Salim and Bilal appear at the door. "Come in," he said, "Mr. Abu, Bilal. Please close the door. Sit down."

After they settled into the two folding chairs in front of Washington's desk, the principal regarded them for a long moment.

"Mr. Abu," he said finally, looking at Salim, "I'm sorry to have asked you to come down to the school. I know you have to work. I do indeed apologize. I don't mean to cause inconvenience. But I wouldn't have asked you to come if it wasn't important."

Bilal frowned. What had he done?

"Is something wrong?" Salim asked in English.

Washington glanced briefly at Bilal and nodded. "Yes, Mr. Abu, I think there is. You must understand that I'm not unaware of your situation, concerning your father and all."

Salim stiffened in his chair. "What about my father?" he asked, not following the train of thought.

Washington shook his head. "It's not about your father, Mr. Abu. It's because Bilal doesn't have a father—I'm bringing this problem to your attention because of that, since you're the man of the family, so to speak."

Salim frowned. Though he generally understood conversations in English, subtleties were easily lost on him.

"I'll get to the point," Washington said, putting his hands together and laying them on the desk. "The computer administrator has informed me that Bilal has been using the school computers to search the Internet for material of a sexually explicit nature. But first, in fairness, we need to ask Bilal whether this is true, and then decide what should be done about it. Now, the thing is, Bilal signed in at the computer lab yesterday. Or, at least, someone using Bilal's I.D. signed in. Now, Bilal, I need to ask: Were you the one who signed in, or was it someone else?"

Bilal looked at the man in horror. How had they found out? Had someone seen him? Had someone turned him in? He thought of the pictures he had seen—young guys doing things he could not even bring himself to mention—and felt such a powerful surge of shame sweep through him that he wanted to sink through the floor and disappear.

He nervously adjusted his glasses. Suddenly, he felt incapable of speech.

Salim looked at him and asked him in Kurdish to translate. In a constricted voice, Bilal translated what Washington had said. As he did so, a look of disgust spread over Salim's face.

"Bilal?" Washington said again, trying to get his attention. "You didn't answer my question."

Bilal looked at him. He had never been able to lie, though he wanted to now. "I was the one," he said very quietly.

Washington continued on, implacable. "Mr. Abu," he said, addressing himself to Salim, "There's more to this, I'm afraid. Bilal was searching for information on homosexuals. Specifically 'gay Muslims,' as if there are such things. He visited several sites of this nature. In addition, he also visited pornographic Web sites that featured pictures of naked men, some of which were very sexually explicit, involving acts of sodomy and other things that are best not mentioned in polite company. I'm very rightly worried about the sort of effect looking at such pictures will have on a young boy like Bilal."

With a sinking feeling in his stomach, Bilal translated this quietly for Salim's benefit.

"All of this, of course, is very worrisome," Washington said when Bilal had finished. "Islam is very clear on the matter of homosexuality, and if Bilal needs information on this matter, he should seek it from the appropriate sources, either myself or the Imam—although I think our Imam is a bit too liberal, but that's just my opinion—or the men in the community. But such information ought not to be sought on the Internet or anywhere else; otherwise, Bilal could be led spiritually astray."

Bilal suddenly found it hard to breathe. Salim asked him to explain what Washington had said. His disgust turned to horror as the situation became clear to him.

Washington slid a piece of paper across the desk over to Bilal. "Bilal, when you signed up for the computer lab, didn't you sign this agreement with the school?"

Bilal picked up the sheet of paper as if it were a snake that might bite him. He slowly nodded his head.

"Now, in item number eight, this agreement clearly says that the school's computers will not be used to search for or to display material of a sexual nature. Isn't that what it says, Bilal?"

Bilal nodded. He couldn't look at Washington or his brother.

"Now, we made an agreement, didn't we, son? You signed your name here. You gave your word. We put this paper in the files. It's binding, Bilal. But you've broken your word. And since you've broken your word, there are consequences."

Bilal was completely overwhelmed. He didn't know what to say.

"Of course, *In'shallah,* I will punish him," Salim said.

Washington nodded. "He should be punished, of course. It's best to deal with these sorts of things firmly, right away, before the matter gets worse. Homosexuality is simply not permitted, and the school will not tolerate any students being involved in sexual perversions or immorality. Let me say it up front, Mr. Abu: It's a matter over which Bilal could be expelled. We've seen in the past that such students start talking to other students, trying to engage them in such activity—it's a very unwholesome influence. We have a duty to our students to protect them from the danger a homosexual could pose. As it is, *In'shallah,* we will call a board meeting concerning this matter and also whether Bilal will be allowed to continue his studies here. Bilal is going to have to reassure the board that he will follow the Islamic teachings regarding sexuality and that he will not pose a danger to the other students."

Washington paused for a long moment while Bilal struggled to translate for Salim.

"In the meantime, I must ask Bilal to keep his side of the agreement we have made concerning the use of our computers," Washington said. "*In'shallah,* I will notify Bilal as to when the board meeting will take place. I hope I have made myself clear on this matter."

There was silence.

Salim stood and took Bilal by the arm. "He not cause any more trouble," he said in English. "I take care."

"Well, I thank you for your time, Mr. Abu."

Salim pulled Bilal behind him as he strode out of the office, down the hall, and out of the building.

Fatima was waiting for them on the steps out in front. "What is it?" she said.

Salim looked at Bilal with disgust on his face. He pushed Bilal's chest, knocking the book bag and lunch box out of his hands.

"What are you doing?" Fatima demanded.

"You stupid shit!" Salim exclaimed loudly. He shoved Bilal again, and Bilal staggered backward. He couldn't speak.

Salim slapped him. It was a sudden thing—his hand flew out, caught Bilal full across the cheek, and sent his newly fixed glasses flying off his face. Then Salim shoved him roughly, and Bilal tripped and fell backward, landing on his buttocks.

Fatima pleaded with Salim to stop, but he ignored her.

"You stupid shit," Salim shouted again, looking down at Bilal. "How could you shame this family like that? What the hell's the matter with you?" When Bilal didn't reply, Salim kicked one of his legs, landing the point of his shoe in Bilal's thigh. "Answer me, damn it!"

"What?" Bilal exclaimed, grimacing with pain.

Salim's foot shot out again, landing on Bilal's shin and causing him to cry out. Students waiting for their parents began to take notice, and Salim stalked off, leaving Bilal and Fatima to walk home by themselves.

When they got home, Bilal went to the boys' bathroom to change and wash up and capture a few precious minutes of privacy. He was humiliated. For a long time he washed his face in the sink, as if he might wash away the shame he felt. Standing in his underwear as he prepared to take a shower, he bent close to the mirror and looked carefully at his face. There was a red mark on his left cheek where Salim had struck him. If he was lucky, it wouldn't turn into a bruise.

The door banged open and Salim barged in.

Bilal turned to look at him, and his stomach knotted up into a ball of pain.

Salim gazed at him, so angry he could not speak. He carried the switch, which he set on the edge of the sink.

Bilal lowered his gaze, and a nameless terror swept through him.

Salim slapped him, then backhanded him, making both sides of Bilal's face sting as if he'd been burned. Bilal kept his eyes lowered, hoping his brother wouldn't do anything more.

"You fucking shit," Salim hoarsely. "What were you doing in that computer lab? Why were you looking at those pictures?"

Trembling, Bilal looked at his brother. He didn't know what to say, so he said nothing.

"Why, goddamn it?" Salim demanded. He slapped Bilal again when he didn't answer right away.

"I don't know!" Bilal exclaimed, putting his face in his hands to protect it.

"You don't know?" Salim asked. "You go looking at pictures of guys fucking on the Internet, and you don't know?"

Bilal tried to get hold of himself. When his brother's temper got out of control, there was no telling what could happen.

"Why were you looking at those pictures?"

"I don't know," he said again quietly.

Salim grabbed him by the shoulders and shook him. "Don't fucking tell me you don't know! Wrong fucking answer!"

"Please," Bilal said, bringing his hands up and trying to push his brother away.

"Why?" Salim demanded, spitting the word out.

Bilal couldn't answer.

"*Why?*" Salim roared.

Bilal took a deep breath. "Because—" he said. But he could say no more.

"*Because what?*"

"Because I'm gay," Bilal said. His mind reeled with fear but there was no turning back. "I was trying to find some information on it. I didn't look at those pictures on purpose."

Salim released him and stood gaping at him. Then a hardness came over his features, and his lips turned into a sneer. He started slapping Bilal's head, first on one side, then the other, with both hands, forcing Bilal against the wall.

"You're going to be a faggot?" Salim asked, sneering at him. "Is that what you think you're going to do? You think I'm going to let that happen? You think I'm going to let you shame this family? Is that what you think?"

Bilal futilely tried to dodge Salim's hands. Salim punched him, first on the arm, then on his chest.

"Don't!" Bilal cried. The punches hurt.

"Stop me," Salim ordered, punching him again.

"Stop it!" Bilal said, cringing.

"Make me stop it," Salim said, punching him. "Come on, you little fairy. Make me. Don't just stand there and take it like a god-damned girl."

Bilal slid along the wall into the corner by the sink. Now there was nowhere to go. Salim slapped and punched him.

"Stop it!" Bilal cried again. The words were hard to get out—his mouth felt like it was full of molasses.

"Make me!" Salim said.

Bilal brought his arms up to protect his face, and tears sprang to his eyes.

Salim stopped his assault and stared at Bilal disgustedly. "Crying all the time like a goddamned girl. Why don't you fight me—act like a man? Pretend like you have at least a little bit of a spine?"

Bilal said nothing.

"This is just what I need," Salim said in a strange voice. "After all I sacrificed on your behalf, and this is what I get—you come home and tell me you're a faggot. All my effort and all my sacrifice, and this is how you thank me. Well, we're going to see about this, Bilal. We're going to see about whether or not you're going to shame this family. You can trust me on that. And if you get yourself kicked out of school, after all the money we've paid so that you could have a proper Islamic education—you better hope to God that doesn't happen. You better fucking hope to fucking God that doesn't happen because I'll fucking kill you."

Salim yanked on the elastic waistband of Bilal's underwear. "Give me these," he demanded.

Baffled, Bilal just stared at him.

"Give them to me, goddamn it!" Salim shouted.

Bilal took them off and handed them to Salim.

Salim balled up the underwear and grabbed Bilal by the jaw, forcing his mouth open. He stuffed as much of the underwear inside Bilal's mouth as he could, his face ablaze with rage and disgust. "You want to be a faggot?" Salim demanded. "Is that what you want, you little fairy? You want to shame this family? You want to be a fucking pervert? Is that it, Bilal?"

Bilal was gagging, trying to breathe through his nose as he struggled to remove Salim's hands from his face to no avail. "You liking it now?" Salim now demanded. "You want some more of this?"

Bilal tried to shake his head.

Salim finally stepped back, and Bilal pulled the underwear out of his mouth, gasping for breath.

Salim grabbed for the switch on the sink.

Bilal looked at it with terror in his belly. The switch was a thin, supple birch branch, about three feet long, that had been smoothed from frequent handling.

"You've punished me enough already," he said in a small, frightened voice.

"Excuse me?" Salim bellowed.

A tremor passed through Bilal's body. He felt a wave of rage rise in his mind. "Enough!" he said in a voice that surprised him.

"Bilal, don't make it worse for yourself," Salim said, almost in a whisper.

"You leave me alone!" Bilal said through clenched teeth.

Salim used the switch to strike him on the arm, causing a quick flash of angry pain. Bilal cringed away from it. "Stop!" he exclaimed.

Bilal tried to catch the switch, but Salim was too fast for him.

Salim grabbed Bilal by the arm and forced him to turn around. "I want you to think about this the next time you're tempted to do something you know is wrong."

The first blow landed across Bilal's shoulders. It was quiet, almost inaudible, but the pain of it rang through Bilal's body. It was like fire spreading across his back. He gasped and tried to kick Salim's shin with his heel. Salim began to strike him repeatedly in a rage. Each blow made Bilal gasp, and a shrill cry of agony escaped his lips, though he did not want it to. From his shoulders down to the back of his legs there was sharp, bright pain. Bilal got down on his hands and knees and tried to scramble away from Salim's grasp, only to find himself pinned to the floor while Salim struck at his exposed back and buttocks.

Bilal crouched on the floor, the brief flame of his defiance fading as Salim landed blow after blow. Why had he looked at those pictures? Why had he been such an idiot?

"How can you do this to me?" Salim screamed, an edge of hysteria sharpening his voice. Salim ended his rain of blows and stood over Bilal, his chest heaving and sweat gleaming on his brow.

"In Iraq, they would kill you, you four-eyed piece of shit," Salim rasped. "They'd stone you. Throw you off a cliff. Are you stupid? Is that what you want for yourself? You want to bring shame on all of us because you can't control yourself?"

Bilal turned his head and peered at Salim over his shoulder. An erection bulged inside Salim's trousers. "I'm not the one who can't control himself," Bilal hissed.

A cloud passed over Salim's eyes as he reached down to free

his erection. He knelt, grabbed Bilal by the hips, and forced his hardness into Bilal's body with one quick plunge.

Bilal screamed as a thunderclap of pain reverberated through the middle of his body.

Salim pounded Bilal brutally. For the first time in his life, Bilal screamed for help. He hoped his mother might come, yet he knew better: Salim had trained her never to enter the boys' bathroom for any reason.

Salim came with a grunt and pulled away. Bilal was overwhelmed by pain and curled up by the tub, hugging his arms to his chest. He began to sob.

"Fucking crybaby," Salim said. "Maybe you better think about the consequences the next time you decide you want to be a fucking faggot."

Bilal glimpsed the razor he kept hidden beneath the tub. He wanted to grab it and slash Salim's face, but all he could do was curl himself around the wrenching, burning pain in his middle.

"Stop crying," Salim said, kicking him. "You're such a fucking baby. It's not like I hurt you."

Bilal suddenly felt cold—a powerful wave of shivers wracked his body. Salim walked out of the bathroom and slammed the door.

The family sat at the dinner table in silence.

"Can somebody please tell me what's going on now?" Mrs. Abu asked.

Salim's anger was like a living thing. They all felt its looming presence. It pervaded the entire apartment and reduced them to whispering among themselves, terrified they would provoke it.

"What is it?" she asked again. The warm smell of the food she had worked so hard to prepare—noodles, beef, bread rolls, tea— filled the kitchen.

Salim turned to her. "Your son Bilal is a goddamned homosexual, Ma."

Mrs. Abu, Fatima, and Hakim exchanged anxious glances across the table. Bilal lowered his eyes. He felt like he was standing on the edge of a cliff, waiting for that one little push that would send him plunging into madness. The lingering pain in his rectum kept him rocking from one hip to the other.

"What do you mean?" Mrs. Abu asked.

Salim put down his fork and knife, folded his hands, and put them on his lap, all very carefully, ready to make his case. "Mr. Washington, at the school, called me in today for a meeting about Bilal," he said. "He told me Bilal has been using the school's computers to look at naked men on the Internet—pornography, Ma, naked men doing God knows what with each other—and that he was also searching around and looking for information on homosexuality."

Everyone stopped eating.

"You must be joking," Mrs. Abu said quietly, casting an odd glance at Bilal.

Salim glared at all of them angrily. "I have been trying and trying to keep this family away from these American perversions, but none of you will listen to me, and now look at what's happened. What's next? Is Fatima going to come home and tell me she wants to be a motorcycle-riding lesbian? Are the two of them going to start smoking crack and drinking alcohol instead of doing their homework? Is this what we get for sacrificing so much on their behalf so that they can get an education? Well, if you won't choose to listen to me, I'll *make* you listen to me, and you better believe that. You fucking better believe that."

He stared at them, defying anyone to disagree.

"Bilal and I are going to fix this little problem, *In'shallah*," he said at length, "because if he thinks he's going to shame this family, he's got another thing coming. If I ever catch him doing something like this again—and we're not even going to talk about what's going to happen to him if the school calls me and tells me he's been caught sucking somebody's dick in the bathroom—if I ever, ever catch him doing something like this again, I swear by Allah I will kill him. You watch and see if I don't. I will not have this family shamed. I will not have Papa's memory mocked."

There was a long, shocked silence. Bilal quietly got up to leave. He couldn't bring himself to look at anyone. He felt sick and wanted to lie down.

Salim banged his hand on the table, making everything rattle—and everyone jump. "You're not excused!" he shouted. "You sit down! You fucking do what I say!"

Bilal sat back down, lowered his head, and burst into tears.

"Stop fucking crying!" Salim shouted. "Fucking crying about every goddamned thing! I'm sick of it! Stop your fucking crying!"

Bilal choked back his tears and bit his lip.

Salim banged his hand on the table again. "And fucking stop biting your lip, you goddamned fairy!"

Bilal put his face in his hands, trying to hide his tears and get hold of himself.

"Stop talking to him like that," Hakim said, finally roused to anger. "He's just a kid."

"He's a fucking faggot," Salim said, throwing a dirty look at Hakim.

"That's not your business," Hakim said. "You don't have to scream at people to get their attention. He's only crying because of the way you treat him. Didn't the Prophet say Allah has no mercy on those who are not merciful? You're the one who's supposed to be such a big believer."

Salim glared at him. "Haven't I told you not to fucking talk to me about religion, you goddamned fucking *kafir* pig! Don't you fucking tell me about religion! When was the last time you said your prayers, you alcohol-drinking, whoremongering piece of shit?"

Hakim lost his nerve and looked away from Salim, whose eyes glinted with murderous rage.

There was a long silence. Finally, Mrs. Abu said, "But surely there's some mistake."

"Ask him, Ma," Salim said. "Ask him what he was doing. He already admitted it to the principal and me. Just ask this little faggot what the hell he thinks he's doing—he's supposed to be studying at that school, not looking at naked men fucking each other on the Internet."

Mrs. Abu looked at Hakim with sadness and incomprehension in her eyes. Fatima gazed at Bilal with pity. The words "I told you so" were written across her silent lips. Salim glared at them all, as if it was their fault that Bilal was homosexual.

Hakim took up his fork and spun a mouthful of noodles around it. "Would you lighten up?" he said, throwing a look of contempt at Salim. "Talking about killing him—what the fuck is that about? Is that what good Muslims do, go around killing children because they're gay?"

"The Prophet said homosexuals should be killed wherever you find them!"

"Well, the Prophet was full of shit, then, wasn't he?"

"You shut your mouth!" Salim shouted, slapping his hand on the table again. "Don't you talk like that."

"Well, the Prophet was wrong, and if he really did say that, then he's just as much of a fucking moron as you are. Anyone with common sense would know that," Hakim said curtly.

"That common sense will take you straight to Gehenna!" Salim said, his voice becoming a screech.

"I'll have fun on my way too, and I won't spend my life making everybody else miserable."

"Well, I'm in charge of this family so it doesn't matter what you think one way or the other!" Salim said shrilly. Fatima and Mrs. Abu looked at him wide-eyed, and Bilal watched Salim's knuckles grow white as he gripped his knife.

"Just because you're the oldest doesn't mean you're right," Hakim snapped. "It may come as a shock to you, but we're not in some filthy hovel in Iraq anymore. People do things differently here. It's called 'freedom,' in case you weren't paying attention. You don't get to stone people to death here."

"We have our own ways!" Salim shouted, standing up and sending his knife clattering across the table. "We're not fucking Americans!"

"You're not, that's for sure," Hakim said.

"I will not let Papa be mocked like this!" Salim shouted. He grabbed the tablecloth and yanked it as hard as he could, spilling everything onto the floor. The others shouted and jumped away from their seats. The bread rolls, the glasses of tea, the noodles and beef their mother had prepared, the plates, spoons, and forks—all of it crashed to the floor.

They stood in a shocked silence while Salim raged on: "We are a *Muslim* family! We have our own ways of doing things! We are not perverts and fucking homosexuals! I will not let this family become a bunch of godless *kafirs*, like these fucking Americans! Do you *hear* me? Is there *anybody* in this fucking family who doesn't understand what I'm saying?"

Everyone stared at him, fearful of what he might do next. Even Hakim looked frightened. Salim glared back at them with a fiery madness in his eyes.

Bilal burst into tears again—he was so frightened, terrified, and overwhelmed that he could nothing more than gape at the mess on the floor and cry. Salim grabbed him by the front of his shirt, whirled him around, and slammed him into the refrigerator, screaming at him in a wordless fury.

Bilal felt something shake free from inside of himself. "You're the faggot, you fucking monster!" he screamed.

Salim slammed him against the fridge again. "You shut up!" he screeched. Then he backhanded Bilal, sending him sprawling to the floor. He advanced on Bilal, his feet flying, catching Bilal in the stomach and chest.

Hakim lunged at Salim with his fists. Mrs. Abu screamed. Hakim fought with Salim, trying to get him out of the kitchen, but Salim was fixated on Bilal now, kicking him in the ribs, the groin, his legs. Fatima launched herself at Salim, scratching at his eyes with her fingernails and kicking his shins fiercely. Together Hakim and Fatima finally forced Salim from the kitchen.

Bilal curled himself up into a ball, and Mrs. Abu wailed as she clutched her head with both hands.

"Ma."

Bilal tapped at the door to her room, opened it quietly, and stepped inside. He didn't ask permission to enter her room, as was required at this late hour.

"What is it?" she asked. She was in bed. Fatima, who usually slept in a cot next to her bed, had gone to spend the night with Jamilla.

"It hurts, Ma," Bilal said quietly. He took off his pajama top and turned around so that she could see the welts on his back. He was in such pain he could not sleep.

She gasped and put a hand to her throat.

He went to the bathroom that adjoined her room, and she followed—they had done this before. She took a jar of aloe vera from her medicine cabinet and had him lean against the sink while she applied it gently to the welts.

When she finished with his back, he turned to her, embarrassed. "Ma, they go all the way down my legs."

She gave him an anguished look and her eyes filled with tears. He removed his pajama bottoms and leaned against the sink again while she continued to apply the balm to his wounds. She said nothing as she worked.

When she was finished, she took him into her large arms and let him cry. She held him for a long time, stroking his hair and telling him everything was going to be all right.

Bilal was not much inclined to believe that everything was going to be all right.

Without really knowing what he was doing, he grabbed a handful of flesh on his left arm and began squeezing it. He began to rock from the pain.

"Stop it," Mrs. Abu said, trying to pull the hand away. "I've told you before, don't do this to yourself!"

Bilal gritted his teeth and squeezed even harder, as he began to feel faint.

"Bi, stop it!" she cried.

She wrestled with him a moment and managed to pry his hand loose.

"Why do you do that?" she asked, frowning.

He just stared at her dully.

She led him back to the bedroom and made him lie down with her so she could hold him. When she tried to get up to turn the light off, he grabbed her nightgown and wouldn't let her leave, burying his face against her stomach.

The door to the bedroom banged open. It was Salim.

"What the fuck is he doing?" he growled.

"You leave him alone," Mrs. Abu said.

"He knows he's not supposed to be in the girls' room."

"He's terrified of you," Mrs. Abu said angrily.

"He's a fucking sissy."

"Just leave him alone," Mrs. Abu said, pleading with her voice for Salim to just go away and stop causing trouble. "What's wrong with you? Your father never treated you this way, did he? Why do you do this to him? Just leave him alone."

Salim stared down at the two of them. "Is he having one of those fits again?"

"Just leave him alone," Mrs. Abu said.

"Is he?"

"Yes. Just go away and stop bothering him. Don't you realize that you're almost twice as big as he is, and when you start shouting at him and hitting him—what do you expect? How can you treat your little brother this way? What's wrong with you? If your father was here, he'd kick you out of this house. You're supposed to take care of this family, not destroy it."

"He's the one who was looking at pornography on the Internet, Ma, not me!" Salim exclaimed, as if this explained everything.

"And this is how you're going to teach him not to?" she asked. "Taking that damned switch to him? Screaming at him? What the hell's the matter with you?"

"He needed to be punished," Salim said. "What, Ma, you want him to be some fucking faggot? You want him to shame this family like that? Is that what you want?"

Mrs. Abu looked at Salim sternly. "I want you to treat him with kindness, the way your father treated you. If he makes a mistake, you need to talk to him, explain to him what he did wrong, help him learn how to fix that mistake. You can't just beat him and scream at him all the time. All you're doing is making him crazy."

Salim seethed with anger. He couldn't touch Bilal now without doing violence to his mother, and even he couldn't countenance that.

She held his gaze resolutely.

"I wish we'd never come to this fucking godless country," Salim snorted. "You think I'm going to be silent when he thumbs his nose at me? You think I'm going to break my fucking back every day so he can sit at school and look at pictures of men fucking each other? You're going to sit there and defend him while he mocks our religion and spits at Allah? He's lucky I don't break his fucking neck."

With that, he turned on his heels and stalked off.

Bilal grasped his mother around the waist and pushed his face into the fabric of her nightgown. He cried soundlessly, his jaw clenched and his body rigid, his fingers gripping the fabric so tightly she was afraid he was going to tear it.

CHAPTER SIX

"Well, His Highness has gone off to work at the factory, and I think it's high time we had a talk about him, because he's getting worse and we're going to have to do something. I don't care if he's the oldest male in the household. I'm sick of the way he's treating us."

Bilal moved cereal around in his bowl and ignored Fatima, whom he resented for fleeing to Jamilla's house when he needed her.

"He's getting worse," Fatima said in Kurdish now so their mother would understand. "We have to do something."

"What do you want to do, Fatima?" Mrs. Abu snapped, turning around from the sink suddenly to look at them. "What do you suggest? Go to the police? Have him arrested? Have the government people come and poke their noses in our business?"

"Ma, I'm just saying it's getting worse. We have to do something."

"Yes, but what? You and your smart mouth—you know everything! So you tell me what, Fatima. How will we pay the bills without your brother's help? What will happen to him if he's deported and sent back to Iraq?"

Fatima rolled her eyes, but she had no reply to her mother's questions.

To talk about turning Salim in to the police was a sin against family loyalty—and Kurds could be loyal to the point of madness. They had not been able to reorganize themselves into a nation after the fall of the Ottoman Empire because their loyalty was always to local leaders and to their own tribes and families, which made collective action and organization all but impossible. Because of their stubborn tribalism they were now the largest homeless ethnic group in the world—almost thirty million of them were spread across Iraq, Iran, Turkey, and Syria, with no homeland of their own.

"Okay, Ma," Fatima said when she grew uncomfortable under her mother's gaze. "We'll just wait until someone gets taken out of here in a body bag, and then we'll think about doing something."

Mrs. Abu took the plate she had been washing and smashed it on the floor. A small shriek escaped from her lips. She turned back to the sink and began to cry.

Bilal squeezed his eyes shut, and darkness washed over him. If the people around him didn't stop arguing, he feared he would start screaming and never stop.

"Goddamn it," Fatima mumbled. "Bilal, do you have to bug out like a fucking loony all the time? Can't you help me out here?"

Bilal began to rock back and forth in his chair to soothe himself.

Mrs. Abu turned around and stared at Fatima bitterly. "Don't you talk to me like that," she said quietly. "Your father was a good man, and he would never have punished any of you the way Salim does. But your father's not here. Your brother's here. That's what I have to live with. Do you hear me, Fatima? That's what I have to live with as a Kurdish woman every day of my life, because my husband is dead. I'm in a strange country, surrounded by strange people, and I can't understand what they're saying. All I have is what's right here, Fatima—you and your brothers. I have no way to make a living, to support myself, to pay the bills. I have no family to turn to, no relatives, no in-laws. I'm not even a U.S .citizen! Everything I had I lost back in Iraq—my family, my house, my husband, my relatives—everything! Do you hear me? And all that's left is you children. So don't you sit there and run your mouth about what you think I ought to do. Don't you sit there and talk about threatening what little I have left."

Fatima was angry, but she couldn't look at her mother.

Bilal stopped rocking and tried to get hold of himself.

"And I'll tell you another thing," Mrs. Abu went on. "I'm the one who has to watch while my children are beaten, and all I can do is pretend that it isn't happening, that my babies are not being treated this way. Don't you know I'd rather die? I've begged him and pleaded with him again and again and again—what do want from me, Fatima? You want to joke about a body bag? Is it a joke to you? What sort of cruel little person are you? You want the government people to take you away, put you in an orphanage? Is that what you want? Fine, Fatima—go to the police. Go tell them every goddamned thing you want to."

Her lower lip trembled, and she put her hand to her throat.

"No, Ma," Fatima said angrily. "You're not doing this to me. Don't give me that Kurdish family loyalty crap. Don't try to make me feel guilty because of what happened in Iraq. It wasn't my fault and I didn't do it. I'm trying to find a way to help this family—to help you, Ma, so that you don't have to see your kids slapped around and punished. Maybe in the old days all you could do was bite your tongue and be loyal to the tribe and bow your head to the oldest male in the household, but we're not in

Iraq, and we don't have to do things like that anymore—not if we don't want to. And especially not if the oldest male in the household is a raving maniac!"

They glowered at each other. Somehow their confrontation had brought Bilal to his senses, and he glanced from one to the other.

"Fatima, tell me—what?" Mrs. Abu spoke very slowly. "What can we do? Don't just run your mouth. I don't know what to do. Do you understand me? I don't know! Please tell me what to do." Her ire crumbled, and she burst into tears.

As the other students drifted into their trig class, Muhammad asked Bilal, "What happened to you?" He gave Bilal a concerned look.

Bilal looked at his friend, desperate to communicate, then looked away.

"Let me guess—your brother again?"

Bilal shrugged.

"Bilal, I'm telling you, that idiot is out of his mind. When are you going to do something about it?"

"Don't start in with me," Bilal said, annoyed. "Just don't."

Muhammad pursed his lips and shook his head. "Do you think I like to see you getting hurt by that fucker?"

Bilal turned away from him and pulled his trig book from his backpack. He had a ritual that he performed at the beginning of every class. The book had to be positioned a certain way on the table. His pencils—always two of them, in case the lead broke on one of them and he needed a spare—had to be arranged to the right side. Clean sheets of paper had to be neatly folded and stacked beneath them. The eraser went at the top of the book. The calculator went on the left side.

He performed the ritual now, trying to ignore Muhammad.

"What did he do, little boy black and blue?" Muhammad asked gently.

Bilal didn't answer.

Muhammad watched as Bilal adjusted the objects in his work space until they were exactly in the right spots. He knew the ritual and understood why Bilal did it.

"Why don't you just tell me what's wrong? Why won't you let me help you?"

Bilal folded his hands on top of his book and gazed silently toward the front of the room.

Annoyed, Muhammad nudged Bilal's trig book out of place. Bilal immediately set about putting it back where it belonged.

"Talk to me," Muhammad said, nudging the book again.

Bilal squeezed his eyes shut and clenched his fists.

"Oh, fuck it," Muhammad said despairingly. "Fine. I won't mess with your book."

Bilal continued to ignore his friend. He was so upset this morning, he didn't know how he was going to get through the day.

"Bilal, I'm sorry," Muhammad said, putting a hand on Bilal's back. "If you don't want to tell me about it, that's fine. I just want to help you."

Bilal opened his eyes and remained silent, but he gently leaned into Muhammad's touch. It was the only communication he could manage.

Nu arrived, sat down, and frowned when he noticed the bruises on Bilal's face.

"What the hell happened to you?" he asked.

"I fell," Bilal said flatly.

"Yeah, right," Nu said. "And I'm the Queen of England."

Bilal put his face over his hands. He felt like his head was going to explode.

"Jeez," Nu said breezily. "Okay, so I'm not the Queen of England."

"Would you leave him alone?" Muhammad said.

"Okay, fine, he fell," Nu said angrily. "Pardon me for caring."

A student assistant to the principal pulled Bilal out of lunch early and told him to report to Mr. Washington. He approached the principal's office with a sense of dread—he absolutely hated the man now.

"Bilal, sit down please," Washington said when Bilal appeared at his door.

Bilal sat down obediently. He stared at the picture of the Dome of the Rock on the wall behind Washington.

"Bilal, you probably despise me, and that's quite all right with me. That's not really the point here. When I look at you, I see someone in trouble, and I hope to be able to do something about it. You know, a lot of folks in my position would just look the other way. You get tired of it after a while—tired of trying to help. But I haven't reached that point yet."

Bilal said nothing and refused to look at the man.

"I'd appreciate it if you would look at me, Bilal."

Bilal gritted his teeth and clutched the sides of the folding chair. He thought about the conversation that had taken place in this room the day before. His humiliation turned to bitter anger when he considered Washington's role in the violence Salim had done to him.

He heard Mr. Washington sigh. "All right, fair enough. You've got a right to hold a grudge. Now, Bilal, I would like for you to go see Imam Malik and have a talk with him. In fact, I want to insist on it. I'd like you to talk to him about what we discussed in this office yesterday.

"I understand how you must feel—this must be embarrassing

for you. But the point isn't to embarrass or humiliate you, Bilal. The point is to try to get some help for you. What we don't want is for you to simply give up and run away from this problem or abandon your religion. We want to help you hold fast to the rope of Allah and keep yourself away from this dangerous thing. So please, Bilal, please understand there's no shame in discussing a problem and trying to find a solution to it. In fact, it's just the opposite. It takes a real man to admit he has a problem and to be willing to listen to others who might be able to help him. It takes real courage. And I can assure you it will be easier to fix this problem now than to let it go untreated. It's a bit like cancer, son—a little radical surgery now will save you a whole lot of suffering later on.

Washington paused. When Bilal remained silent, he sighed again and finished his speech.

"Now, Imam Malik is a very intelligent man, as you must know. He's a psychiatrist and a Muslim scholar. If he can't help you figure out what's going on, then I don't think anybody can."

Bilal thought about Imam Malik—he saw him, in his mind, sitting in the living room of the Jackson household, reading one of the numerous books that were always stacked on the little table by his chair. How was he going to be able to talk to the Imam— Muhammad's father—about what he had done? The notion made him shudder.

"Now, Bilal," Washington said, "when the board of directors have their meeting about you, Imam Malik will be there, and it would mean a lot to the board if the Imam put in a good word for you. But that means you're going to have to keep yourself away from this homosexual business."

Bilal nodded. He wished Washington would just shut up and get on with this excruciating process.

"*In'shallah*, I'll let you know when the board meeting is going to be held, because you'll need to attend it. The board will ask you some questions, and you'll have to answer honestly. Then they'll talk amongst themselves and come to a decision about whether to let you continue your studies here. You'll have an opportunity to say something in your defense, and I suggest you start working on that, start thinking about what you're going to say."

Bilal glanced at Washington and tried to hold his gaze, then turned away.

"Have I made myself clear?" Washington asked.

Bilal nodded again.

"Of course, I don't think we need to talk about what will happen if there's a next time, Bilal. Because if there's a next time, you will simply be expelled, and that will be the end of it."

Long moments of silence passed between them.

Bilal felt his defiance flicker to life when he realized that Washington was more uncomfortable with their wordlessness than he was. He loosened his grip on the sides of his chair and regarded Washington coolly.

"You better run along now," Washington said after another moment. He glanced down at his hands, which were folded primly on the top of his desk.

In the afternoon, Mrs. Owen, the school nurse, poked her head into Bilal's history classroom and asked that Bilal be excused for a few minutes.

Bilal felt his stomach tighten into a familiar knot. He got up and followed Mrs. Owen silently to her office. He already knew what she wanted, and his anger simmered inside him.

"Would you mind explaining?" she asked, when the two of them were seated on either side of her desk. A large black woman, she wore a dark but colorful veil that she arranged fashionably around her head and shoulders. She had a friendly smile and keen eyes that could spot a lie almost immediately.

Bilal said nothing. What did these grown-ups expect from him?

Mrs. Owen had his file on her desk. She flipped through it, frowning. "Bilal, we're not even three months into the school year, and this is the fifth time I've seen you with bruises on your face. Now, I have no idea what the rest of your body looks like, but I have my suspicions. Do you want me to insist on having a look, or would you rather just tell me what's going on?"

"I fell," Bilal said. What was he supposed to do—point a finger at Salim? All the truth would get him was another beating.

"Uh-huh," she said, frowning even more deeply.

"It's true!" he exclaimed.

"Why do you keep lying to me?"

"I'm not lying!"

"Is there something going on at home, Bilal?"

Bilal didn't answer, and a long silence passed. The vacuum no longer worked to his advantage.

"Okay, young man, can you get undressed please?"

He looked up at her with despair in his eyes. "I told you, I fell! It's nobody business."

"That's where you're wrong," she replied evenly. "It's *my* business. And if I think you're being abused at home, I'm required to notify the authorities. If I don't do my job, the school could be sued, and since you're not going to cooperate, we'll just have to do it the hard way. Now, can you get undressed please?"

Bilal stood up and looked from her to the door. He wanted to run—but to where?

"Bilal, I'm not trying to upset you. I'm trying to help you," she said gently.

"I don't need your help!" he cried. He bolted out the door.

"Bilal, please!" she called after him.

Bilal ran back to his class and grabbed up his books.

"Where are you going?" Muhammad asked.

The rest of the class, shocked by his behavior, turned to look at him.

Not looking at anyone, Bilal fled.

When Salim got home, he was already angry, and the tension in the house hung like a pall over everything. Hakim had gone out drinking with his friends, leaving Bilal and Fatima at home with their mother.

A half hour after Salim walked through the door, as they sat down to eat, Salim made a pronouncement. "I want Bilal to leave this house."

Bilal, Mrs. Abu, and Fatima regarded him in stunned silence.

"You can't be serious," Mrs. Abu finally said, shaking her head as if she were waking from a dream. "Where do you want him to go?"

Bilal felt a wave of horror wash over him. Indeed, where would he go if he was forced to leave his family? How could Salim even suggest such a thing? Surely he was joking.

There was more silence as Salim heaped noodles on his plate.

"Ma!" Fatima exclaimed, breaking it. "Don't just sit there! He can't make Bilal leave. This is madness!"

Salim glared across the table at his mother, daring her to challenge him.

"Ma!" Fatima said again when her mother looked down at her plate.

Fatima turned to Salim. "You're not kicking anyone out of this family. How Islamic is that? Is that what they're teaching you at the mosque? Imam Malik certainly didn't teach you that. Are you out of your mind? If Hakim was here, he'd beat the crap out of you. You don't have the right to kick people out just because you're mad. Are you listening to me? You know, sometimes I think you're sick—I think you're mentally ill. I think you don't understand what you're doing. Are you listening?"

Salim began to eat his dinner and ignored her.

"Salim," Mrs. Abu said, "the boy made a mistake. Tell him how to make it right. Tell him what he can do to fix his mistake. You can't just make him leave—that's not how problems are solved. That's not how you teach a child to learn to do the right thing. For God's sake, it's cold out there! It's November already!"

Fatima folded her arms across her chest. "Bilal isn't going anywhere," she said firmly.

"Don't be too sure of that," Salim said, not bothering to look up from his food.

"You're not sending him anywhere. You're not making him leave," Fatima said, her temper rising.

"Shut up," Salim said, putting down his fork.

"No, I will not," Fatima said forcefully. "You don't have the right to kick him out."

Salim got up, rounded the table and grabbed the front of Fatima's dress, then dragged her to her feet. "You shut the fuck up," he said as Bilal and Mrs. Abu watched in horror. "You don't make the decisions around here. You don't get to tell me what I can and cannot do. You're not the fucking boss in this family, so shut your fucking mouth and stop telling me what to do."

He shoved her backward so that she fell over. "You say one more fucking word and I'll rip your fucking tongue out. I'm sick of you, Fatima. I'm sick of your fucking disobedience."

Fatima crouched on the floor as tears rolled down her cheeks. A dazed, disbelieving expression distorted her delicate features.

Salim sat down and resumed eating as if nothing had happened.

Bilal put his hands in his lap. He didn't want to give Salim any further reason to be upset. Without another word, Fatima picked herself off the floor, got her coat, and left the house.

Mrs. Abu pushed her plate away and sat staring at Salim. He didn't look up at her.

When Salim finished his meal, he went to the boys' bedroom and returned with Bilal's prayer rug. He grabbed Bilal's jacket off the hook by the door and dumped the items at Bilal's feet.

"Take your stuff and get the fuck out of this house," he said in a cold, hard voice.

Bilal got to his feet and looked at him uncertainly.

"Pick them up," Salim said, nodding to the rug and jacket.

Bilal did, trembling.

"I want you to get out of this house. I want you to know what it's like to try to make it on your own when you've got nothing. Maybe next time you'll think twice about mocking this family. Now, I don't care where you go or what you do, but just get the fuck out of this house before I kill you."

Bilal, clutching his prayer rug, could hardly breathe. It was already dark outside. "Please don't make me leave," he said desperately.

"You can't do this!" Mrs. Abu said.

"You shut up, Ma! You shut the fuck up! You shut your god-damned mouth!" Salim screamed.

She flinched when these words struck her. She put a hand to her throat and another to her forehead as if she couldn't believe what she was seeing.

"I said, GET OUT!" Salim shouted at Bilal. He dragged Bilal by the arm to the back door, flung it open, and shoved Bilal outside.

Bilal turned back, clutching his prayer rug to his chest, just as Salim slammed the door in his face.

"Bilal, what is it?" Imam Malik asked when he opened the front door. "What happened to your face?"

Bilal opened his mouth but no words came out. Imam Malik put an arm around Bilal's shoulders and guided him into the study. When they were both seated on the sofa, he said, "Take your time. Tell me what happened."

Bilal nodded and calmed himself. "My brother...told me to leave the house. He threw me out. Imam, I don't have anywhere to go. I'm sorry to bother you, but I don't know what to do or where else to go."

"Threw you out?" Malik asked, astonished. He put a large hand on Bilal's shoulder.

"He told me to get out," Bilal said, lowering his eyes, ashamed.

"Why?" Malik asked.

In a halting voice, Bilal told him about the Internet search he had conducted, the pictures, the meetings with Mr. Washington, and the convening of the school board to discuss the matter.

"Come upstairs," Malik said. "It's cold down here. We'll fix you up—you know you're always welcome in our house, Bilal."

Bilal followed the Imam upstairs. The house was quiet—everyone had gone to bed. The clock on the mantle said it was almost eleven.

"Why don't you sit down, son?" Malik said, motioning to a chair at the kitchen table. "I'll wake Muhammad. Are you hungry?"

Bilal shook his head. "I'm really sorry, Imam Malik. I'm so embarrassed. I'm sorry to bother you, to wake you up."

"Don't be sorry, Bilal. You need to get some sleep, and, *In'shallah,* we'll talk about this when you're feeling better, all right? If your brother thinks he can throw kids out on the street, well, I'm going to have to talk to that man. You're welcome to stay with us. You know that. It's no bother at all. Now, what happened to your face?"

Bilal shrugged. "I fell."

Malik gave him a long, searching look. "Didn't you say that the last time?"

Bilal sighed wearily and nodded.

Malik disappeared down the corridor and, after a few moments, returned with Muhammad, who gave him a quizzical look as he wiped sleep from his eyes.

"I'll wake you up for prayers in the morning," Imam Malik said.

After his father left them alone, Muhammad looked at Bilal. "What are you doing here?" he asked. "Not that I'm not happy to see you."

Bilal explained about Salim.

"The way he treats you is despicable," Muhammad said when Bilal was done.

They went to Muhammad's room, and Muhammad handed him some pajamas. Bilal began to feel better—less afraid, less upset. He shrugged off his clothes. Before Bilal could get the pajama top on, Muhammad noticed the welts on his back.

"What the hell is this?" he asked.

"It's nothing," Bilal said, embarrassed.

"*Nothing?*" Muhammad said. "Nothing? Are you out of your mind? Did your brother do this to you? He did, didn't he?"

"It's nothing," Bilal repeated. Annoyed, he tried to put on the pajama top.

"Oh, I suppose you're going to tell me you fell down again," Muhammad said.

Bilal gave him an exasperated look.

Muhammad frowned, left the room, and returned a couple of minutes later with both his parents. Bilal looked at the three of them with a feeling of dread in his stomach.

"Bilal, what's this about?" Imam Malik asked.

"You didn't have to tell your parents!" Bilal said angrily to Muhammad.

"Your brother has no right to beat you," Muhammad shot back. "Let them see. Mom, Dad, look at it!"

Bilal looked from Imam Malik to Mrs. Jackson, feeling miserable.

"We don't want to embarrass you," the Imam said gently. "Can we take a look?"

Bilal felt cornered, but he took off the pajama top and turned around. From behind, he heard the soft hiss of air sucked through clenched teeth.

Bilal had yet to see his back in the mirror, but he could imagine what it looked like—it would be the same as the last time, and the time before that, and the time before that. He'd lost track of how many times Salim had taken that switch to him.

Imam Malik pushed down Bilal's pajama bottoms a little bit.

"How far do these go down?" he asked, making Bilal turn around to look at him.

Bilal wouldn't meet his gaze. He felt mute.

"Please, son. We're not going to hurt you."

Bilal took a breath, tried to steady himself. "They go down to the back of my legs."

"Can I look?" Imam Malik asked.

Bilal nodded slowly and turned around again.

The Imam pulled down the fabric enough to see that the marks did indeed continue down the backs of Bilal's legs.

"Did your brother do this?" Malik asked. "Please turn around."

Bilal turned to face the Imam, but said nothing.

"Bilal, who did this?" Malik insisted.

"I shouldn't have looked at those pictures," Bilal replied. "It's my fault."

"You don't deserve to be punished like this," Malik said. He knelt beside Bilal so that the boy didn't have to look up at him.

A shudder of panic rippled through Bilal's body.

"We'd like to help you, Bilal," the Imam said. "This is not how a Muslim man deals with a child. Muhammad's right. Your brother has no right to beat you."

"Well, try telling him that!" Bilal cried. "You don't know what he's like."

"Tell me, then," Malik said.

"We can't say anything," Bilal said. "We could put his immigration status at risk. He could go to jail. He could have all sorts of trouble, and so could we. The government might take Fatima and me away—I don't want to go live in some foster home. What do you want me to do? If they put him in jail, how can we pay the bills?"

"What are you talking about?" Mrs. Jackson asked. "What is this about foster homes? What is this about bills?"

Bilal's mind reeled. "I can't tell you," he said miserably. "If he knew I was telling you our business, he would kill me. It's my fault anyway—I shouldn't have been looking at those pictures. I'm always doing something to make him mad. If I didn't make him mad all the time, there wouldn't be a problem. Please, can't you just leave me alone?"

"Listen to me, Bilal," Mrs. Jackson said. "Just because you make him mad, he has no call to beat you like this. He can just get over it and deal with his problems like the rest of us do. Don't you even think about blaming yourself."

"But it's my fault," Bilal said.

"That's simply not true," she replied. "He ought to consider himself lucky to have a brother like you."

Bilal knit his brow. No one had ever talked to him like this before.

"How long has this been going on?" Imam Malik asked.

Bilal shook his head.

"You don't know?" Malik said. "Or you won't tell me."

"I can't tell you," Bilal said. "Please don't ask me."

"How long?" the Imam insisted.

Bilal didn't answer.

"How long? Bilal, I want an answer."

Bilal started to bite his lip but stopped. "I don't know. A long time, I guess," he said.

"Son, let me tell you some of the facts of life. Fact number one: This is called child abuse. It's illegal in this country. Your brother could go to jail for this. It doesn't matter what you've done; he doesn't have the right to do this to you. Fact number two: You have the right not to be physically harmed in your own home, and if someone is infringing on that right, well, *In'shallah,* we're going to straighten that out. And fact number three: For a Muslim man, abusive behavior of this sort is not acceptable, and if Salim has forgotten that, then I intend to remind him."

A desperate longing for hope fought the old habit of despair in Bilal's mind.

"We can put a stop to this," Malik said gently.

Bilal put his face in his hands and struggled to contain tears he didn't want to cry. He was getting agitated again, finding it hard to breathe.

"What is it, Bilal?" Malik asked.

"He's going to kill me now," Bilal said. "You don't know what he's like. You don't know what he does to me. And if you confront him—if he knows I told you what he did…"

He shook his head, couldn't finish the sentence.

"If you're that afraid of him, then we should call the police," Malik said.

Bilal was horrified. "You can't!"

"Yes, I can," Imam Malik said. "And I will, if I have to."

"But what about his immigration status?"

"Who cares about his immigration status? That's not the point, Bilal. The point is, he doesn't have the right to do this, and we have to make him stop."

"If you turn him in, he could be arrested. He could go to jail. How are we going to pay our bills? What if he can't get a job when he's released? What if we don't have money to pay our rent? What if he's deported and sent back to Iraq?"

Malik gently took Bilal's hands in his. "Well, we'll just remind him about all those things, won't we, Bilal?" he said. "We'll just point out to him that when he breaks the law, he's putting his own immigration status at risk—he has no right to expect you to be silent while he abuses you. That's sick, Bilal. That's dysfunctional. If he chooses to break the law, he has to bear the consequences if he gets caught."

"You're just going to make trouble for me," Bilal said quietly.

"No, we're not. We're going to make sure this doesn't happen anymore. Trust me, when you confront them, most abusers sober up real quick. If your brother doesn't want to go to jail, then he has no choice but to stop breaking the law. If he's not aware that he's breaking the law, then, *In'shallah,* we'll enlighten him."

Bilal tried to let the good sense of the Imam's words sink in, but all he could think of was how furious Salim would be when he found out that Bilal had told someone their business. He looked at the Jacksons, from one to the next, and felt overwhelmed with panic. "I'm sorry," he said. "I have to go. I shouldn't have bothered you. I know it's late. I'm really sorry. Please don't say anything. You'll just get me in trouble."

He started gathering up his clothes. Muhammad moved to stop him, but his mother held him back.

"Please don't tell him I talked to you," Bilal said. "I mean, he just got upset this one time. It's no big deal. It's not a problem. He never does stuff like this."

"And where are you gonna go?" Mrs. Jackson asked, putting her hands on her hips. "It's almost midnight. This fine fellow you're talking about kicked you out of your house, or did you forget that? Where are you gonna go now—you gonna find some Dumpster to sleep in?"

"Please," Bilal said. "Don't make trouble for me. He'll kill me."

"Then we'll call the police," she said.

Bilal let out a small cry and began putting on his clothes.

"You're not going anywhere!" Muhammad said.

"Just a minute," Imam Malik said, giving Muhammad a stern look. "Bilal, if you want to go, we won't stop you."

"Dad!" Muhammad exclaimed.

"Just a minute, son. Please. Bilal, if you want to go, we won't stop you. But you're welcome to stay here with us. We're glad to have you. Please understand, we're not going to force you to do anything you don't want to do. If you don't want us to say something to your brother, we won't. Okay? Yet I have to say that if you're so afraid that your brother won't listen to reason and would continue to hurt you, knowing the risks—well, Bilal, I have to say that your brother is dangerous, and we don't have any choice but to turn him in."

Bilal considered this in silence.

"Bilal, I'm a psychiatrist. You know that. I sit down with families every day, and we work these kinds of problems out. Okay?"

Bilal frowned. He wanted to say his brother was mean and vicious. "He has a temper," he said instead.

"What we do in these situations, then, is document the abuse—I have a Polaroid camera I use for that. We take pictures. We have witnesses. We invite the family to sit down. We show the perpetrator the pictures. We talk about the consequences of being turned in to the police. We make sure all of this is made known to everyone in the family. The negotiator—that's usually me—keeps the pictures, and the perpetrator is made aware that if any future abuse occurs, the negotiator will call the police and turn over the pictures. Unless the perpetrator is mentally ill, or involved with narcotics, this approach generally works. The abuse stops."

Malik paused for a moment to let Bilal absorb his words.

"If you like, we can do this for you," he continued. "We can do it tomorrow after Friday prayers. We can all sit down, hash it out, and put a stop to this."

Bilal gave the Imam a long, searching look. He was torn between wanting to trust this man and tell him about all the other things and his fear of betraying Salim.

"Bilal, let my dad help you, okay?" Muhammad said. "Come on, put your pajamas on, stay with us. It's going to be all right."

Bilal twisted his hands together nervously and wiped his eyes.

"Come on, Bilal, please," Muhammad said quietly.

"I don't know where to go," Bilal said. "I'm sorry...I don't know where to go."

"Then stay with me," Muhammad said.

Bilal began putting his clothes on. The Jacksons watched him in silence. He fumbled with the buttons on his shirt. His hands were shaking. Suddenly, he felt very strange. His whole body began shaking, and he couldn't stop it.

Muhammad put his arms around Bilal and held him until Bilal's shuddering stopped and the sobs finally came. As Muhammad gently rocked Bilal in his arms, the Imam and his wife slipped from the room and closed the door behind them.

CHAPTER SEVEN

After Friday Prayers the following day, Bilal found himself standing next to Muhammad in the Imam's conference room, which was next to his office downstairs in the former rectory. Across the table from the Imam were Mrs. Abu, Salim, Hakim, and Fatima. Salim looked nervous. Hakim looked bewildered. Fatima looked worried and annoyed. Mrs. Abu kept putting her hand to her throat.

Sitting next to the Imam was Mrs. Owen, the school nurse—the Imam had called her that morning to ask for her help. Next to Mrs. Owen was the school principal, Mr. Washington, who now regarded both Bilal and Salim from a rather different perspective.

Bilal was glad that Salim was finally going to be confronted in a context where his bullying would be of no use. He was also completely terrified. If they were all so worried about what he had told the Imam last night, what would they think if they knew the whole story? What would they say if they knew Salim had repeatedly raped him?

So now Bilal watched and waited while his insides seized up with apprehension. Surely when the Imam, the principal, and the school nurse were all arrayed against him, Salim would think twice before touching Bilal again.

Imam Malik put a snapshot of Bilal's face on the table and

slid it over to Salim. That morning, the Imam and Mrs. Owen had taken many pictures of Bilal for documentation purposes, being very careful about his modesty.

For a long time, Malik said nothing. He merely stared at Salim, who would not touch the photograph or raise his eyes to look at anyone.

Now Malik slid another photograph across the table. This one showed the welts on Bilal's back and buttocks. Still Salim said nothing. He glanced at the photographs, then took his eyes away.

Mrs. Abu peered timidly at the photographs and began to weep quietly.

"Fatima," the Imam said, "would you translate for your brother? I want him to be sure to understand what I have to say today."

Fatima nodded.

Malik spread the rest of the Polaroids across the table.

"Salim, we took these photos to document what you did to Bilal. Now, if we wanted to, we could call the police, show them these photos, and tell them that you forced a minor to spend the night outside. You would be arrested and put into jail for child abuse. You'd be in a lot of trouble. Is that what you want, son?"

Fatima translated. Salim shook his head.

"Would you like to explain to us why you did this to your brother?" the Imam asked.

For a long moment, Salim said nothing. Then, in Kurdish he said, "Fatima, tell him that Bilal has been involving himself in sexual perversion and shaming this family. I'm trying to make him understand that it's not acceptable. The people of Sodom were destroyed for such things. I'm trying to keep him in the way of Allah."

Fatima translated for the Imam.

"You're talking about the pictures on the Internet?" Malik asked. Salim nodded.

"Is that what you think you've accomplished by making him spend the night outside and beating him? When you were beating him, was that to teach him how to respect the limits that Allah has placed on sexuality?"

Salim grimaced as Fatima translated this.

Malik went on. "Didn't the Prophet—peace be upon him!— say that the wrongdoer should be admonished gently with compassion, that we ought to reason together to resolve problems and show mercy and be tolerant of the weak among us who are not yet mature in the way of Allah?"

"He's a faggot!" Salim exclaimed in English.

Malik sat back in his chair and regarded Salim for a long time, making Salim increasingly uncomfortable. "I'm not sure that Bilal's sexuality is any of your business," he said at last. "And I'm not sure how you plan to help him with this matter, if you're more interested in shaming him than providing compassionate guidance. Bilal may or may not be a gay person. Curiosity about the matter doesn't mean much."

It took Salim a while to digest the Imam's words. "What the hell is he talking about?" he asked in Kurdish, looking at Hakim and Fatima.

"I think he's trying to tell you that you're an asshole," Hakim said.

Salim gave his brother a murderous look.

"Here's what we're going to do, Salim," Imam Malik said, trying to diffuse the volatile situation. "I'm going to hold on to these photographs, and if Bilal ever suffers these kinds of injuries again, then—*In'shallah*—I will call the police and have you arrested. If Bilal ever knocks on my door again in the middle of the night because you've kicked him out, I will call the police. If

Mrs. Owen, the school nurse, ever sees bruises on Bilal's face again, we will call the police. If Bilal goes to Mr. Washington and tells him that he's been having more problems at home, we will call the police.

"I would like to impress upon you that a Muslim man does not act this way. We all have problems. I have six children, Salim—if I had to beat them every time they annoyed me, there would be no end to it. We have to find other ways to deal with problems. Physical abuse is never acceptable, not for any reason. Allah puts children in our hands so that we will care for them, not hurt them."

There was another lengthy silence. Bilal watched Salim's face, but his look was indecipherable.

"I'd like you to think about these things," Imam Malik said. "And I'd like your assurance that Bilal will not be subject to such treatment in the future. I want you to promise me that you're going to find a more compassionate and Islamic approach to any problems that Bilal might be having. Can you do that for me?"

Grudgingly, Salim nodded his head.

"Now, Bilal is going to stay with us for the weekend, to give you some time to cool off and start thinking clearly. Is that all right with you?"

Salim nodded again.

"Now, son, if you need help dealing with teenagers—I'm not unaware that you're the man of the family and filling your father's shoes and you have both Bilal and Fatima to raise— I am always available if you wish to talk. Allah has put you in charge of this family, and I'd like to see you fulfilling your responsibilities in the right way so that everyone will benefit. This community is here to help and support you."

Salim listened to these words, but his gaze was directed at Bilal. When the Imam finished speaking, Salim said very quietly in Kurdish, "I told you not to discuss our business with others, didn't I? You're going to pay for this. You just wait and see."

Bilal felt dread settle into his bones.

Before Fatima had a chance to translate Salim's threat for Imam Malik and the others, Salim turned to her. "Don't you tell him what I said—not if you know what's good for you."

"This is just like the last time," Hakim said softly, glancing at Mrs. Abu. A fearful sort of look passed between them.

Bilal frowned at both of them. *Just like the last time? What was that supposed to mean?*

"Salim," Fatima said quietly, "don't you understand what you're doing here? This man has just told you that he's got pictures of what you did to your little brother, and he'll call the cops the next time—and you're sitting here and making threats? All Bilal has to do is tell this man that you're making threats, and that's it. He'll go upstairs, call the police—off you go. Is that what you want? Don't you realize what's going to happen to you if the police are called in? Do you know what happens to guys who go to prison for child abuse?"

"I told him not to be talking about our fucking business!" Salim snapped.

"Well, stop beating him and there won't be anything to talk about, will there?" Fatima replied evenly. "Look what you did to him! Look at these pictures! Are you out of your mind?"

Salim shook his head, a look of disgust distorting his features. "Can we leave now?" he asked.

"What are you talking about?" Imam Malik asked, gazing at all of them.

"We were just reminding Salim that he's lucky you didn't call the police already," Fatima said.

"I want his assurance that these things aren't going to happen anymore," Malik said. "I don't want this boy being hurt like this again. If I have the slightest doubt in my mind about Bilal's safety, then *In'shallah*, I will call the police and that's that."

Fatima translated for Salim.

Salim's mouth curled into a sneer. "Tell him if he's so fucking concerned, he can have a talk with Bilal about what happens to faggots. If he can do better than I can, fine, let him have at it. Just tell him I don't want to see this crap anymore—I don't want Bilal looking at pornography or sucking somebody's dick. I don't want him to make a mockery of everything Papa died for. Tell him that. Tell him we're a Muslim family, not a bunch of fucking *kafir* perverts."

Leaving out the profanity, Fatima conveyed Salim's words to the Imam.

Imam Malik nodded. "Fine. Bilal and I will discuss this matter, *In'shallah*, so that he can develop a proper Islamic response to it. Now Fatima, remind your brother that all we can do is equip young people with information and guidance: That's all. They have to make their own choices and decisions. Allah has given them this freedom, and we can't take it away from them. Each of us answers only for his own self, not for anyone else. We raise our children the best we can, but ultimately it's up to them to decide how they want to live their lives. You need to tell Salim to back off and let Bilal make his own decisions. Bilal's not a child anymore. Tell him a little bit of kindness and understanding will get him a lot further than a stick will."

With a dubious look on her face, Fatima translated.

Salim did not respond.

"Fatima," the Imam said, "I need to know that your brother is going to be safe when he goes home."

Fatima steeled herself and looked directly at Imam Malik, Mrs. Owen, and Mr. Washington, then spoke very quickly so that Salim wouldn't be able to follow. "If you knew the half of what this monster has put us through, you'd have made that call already, and you wouldn't waste your time sitting here. How can I promise you what he will or will not do? He does whatever he pleases, and no one can stop him. As far as I'm concerned, a straitjacket is about the only thing he needs."

"Even so," Imam Malik said quietly.

Fatima turned angrily to Salim. "Here's the deal. You need to tell this man that you're not going to beat Bilal anymore, or he's going to call the police. So you decide. I want to tell him to just call the police and to hell with you. If you've got any brains at all in that fat head of yours, you'll cooperate and lighten up a bit. What you're doing is illegal in this country. You could go to jail. Do you understand that? If you go to jail, you could be deported. In any case, you'll have trouble finding a job afterward because nobody wants to hire an ex-convict. Are you listening? Is there anybody home? Is this what you want? Do you understand what I'm trying to tell you? Do you have any brains at all?"

Salim was seething with rage, but there was no denying Fatima's logic. "All right," he said quietly. "Tell this man I know I have a temper. I'm sorry. *In'shallah*, it won't happen anymore."

Fatima translated.

Imam Malik nodded, collected the photographs, and put them in an envelope. "Fatima, you tell your brother I'm deadly serious. If he gives me any reason to believe that he's been abusing Bilal again, I will call the police and turn these photographs over to them. You tell him the people in this community are not going to stand for this kind of behavior—we're not going to sit back in silence while our kids are mistreated. And you also tell him that this isn't a matter of you and Bilal being removed from your home. *He's* the one who will be removed. And if that happens, this community will take care of your family, and you're not to worry about that. The Quran's got more verses in it about taking care of widows and orphans than you can shake a stick at. You tell your mother that—tell her not to worry on that account. And you tell your brother I'm going to be keeping an eye on things. I take my duty to this community very seriously indeed."

Imam Malik came to the bedroom after dinner to ask Muhammad to go help wash the dishes and give him some time with Bilal. After Muhammad was gone, Malik sat on the bed and regarded Bilal for a long time, not speaking. Bilal had the feeling that the Imam was really *seeing* him. There was no judgment, no condemnation in the Imam's eyes, only understanding and compassion.

"You look like the butter's about to slide off your biscuits," Imam Malik said gently.

Bilal laughed. The sound of his laughter surprised him—he couldn't recall the last time he'd heard it.

"It's curious," the Imam said. "Those welts go all the way down to the backs of your legs. That tells me that you must have been forced to pull your pants down. Was that what happened?"

Bilal recounted his last experience with Salim but left out the bits about Salim stuffing underwear in his mouth and raping him.

"Well, that's curious, isn't it?" the Imam said, gazing steadily at Bilal. "That sort of punishment often has a sexual connotation to it. Do you know what I mean?"

Bilal frowned and shook his head.

"I was reading about the Salem witch trials the other day," Malik said. "Before they burned these supposed witches at the stake, the priests or ministers would rip off the women's blouses, exposing their breasts. It was supposed to humiliate them—but I suspect those these priests and ministers took a bit of sexual pleasure in seeing a woman's private parts. That's what it means to be a sadist—someone who takes pleasure in the pain they cause others. Do you know what I mean?"

Bilal squeezed his palms together.

"It's curious that your brother would make you expose yourself, isn't it?"

Bilal looked distraught.

"I'm not trying to embarrass you," Malik said gently. "It's just that I'm wondering if your brother has ever touched in ways or in places that make you feel uncomfortable. Has he done things that maybe you don't like, things of a sexual nature?"

Taking a deep breath, Bilal searched the murk of his unhappiness for the spark of defiance that had flickered yesterday. He was weary of the way things were—weary of the way he felt all the time. He was ready to try to change all that. He had to make a move, take a risk. If he did not, the future would only hold more of the what the past had held. More fear, more abuse at Salim's hands.

"Have you ever had sex with your brother, Bilal?" the Imam asked quietly.

Bilal looked at the Imam squarely for the first time. The Imam's face brightened and he nodded encouragingly. Bilal was tempted—powerfully tempted. "You won't say a word?" he asked steadily.

"Not a word," Malik replied.

Bilal continued to hold the Imam in an even gaze. The man obviously knew the story, without even having to be told. All Bilal had to do was supply the details. What difference would it make? And maybe, just maybe, the Imam could help him find a way to make Salim stop.

"I'm terrified," Bilal said, lowering his eyes now. He didn't look away from Malik, but tears rolled down his cheeks.

"That's understandable," Malik replied. "I took a good look at your brother today, Bilal. He's big, isn't he? He looks like he could get into a fistfight with a grizzly bear and he'd be the winner. I don't blame you for being afraid of him."

Letting go felt good. Bilal straightened his posture and continued. "He said I'd have to go away if anyone found out what we were doing. I'd have to go live on the street or something."

Malik nodded encouragingly.

Bilal fought against the tears. He had to get the hard words out now. "He said if I didn't help him, he'd have to do something to Fatima, and if Fatima got pregnant, then she'd have to leave. I don't want him to hurt Fatima."

"Of course you don't," Malik said.

"When I was little, he used to say he would gut me like a pig—he said that's what they do to traitors. I was so afraid of him, I didn't dare say anything to anyone 'cause I just knew he would do it."

Malik put a comforting arm around Bilal's shoulders. He didn't interrupt—Bilal was doing just fine.

Bilal thought about how he longed for and missed his father, and began crying again. The Imam's touch felt safe, comforting, and strong—not dangerous, not sexual, not threatening.

He cried until he was ready to stop. Malik didn't accuse him of crying about every "goddamned thing" like a baby, did not attempt to stop him or silence him or shut him up.

The whole story came out in bits and pieces, starting from the time when Bilal was nine, right up to the other evening when Salim had beaten him and raped him.

When Bilal was finished, Malik offered a wry smile. "Well, to tell you the truth, Bilal, I want to march over to your house and break that man's neck. But I promised you I'd be silent, so I will. I just don't understand how you could have kept all this inside yourself for all these years. It must have been horrible for you."

Bilal gave him a wide-eyed looked and nodded. It had been a living hell.

"I'm going to think about this for a while, Bilal, and see if I can come up with some way to help you. There are a lot of different things we could do, and we'll have to talk about them, *In'shallah*, and see if maybe one of them seems right to you. But for right now, I think you should take a rest—let your mind take a rest. We'll figure this out, okay?"

Bilal nodded again.

The Imam gave him a firm, affectionate hug, and it felt good. Bilal thought maybe things would really get better.

"What was that song you were telling me about the other day?"

Muhammad, propped up on an elbow, regarded Bilal carefully.

" 'Killed by Love'?" Bilal suggested.

Muhammad smiled. "Yeah, 'Killed by Love.' Recent events have given that song a whole new meaning."

Bilal frowned. "What's that supposed to mean?"

Muhammad smacked his forehead and said, "Well, duh!"

"Well, what?" Bilal demanded.

It was late at night, and neither boy wanted to sleep. Just lying in bed together was enough.

"Bilal, come on. You're always telling me about these songs, and you don't get it—you put down, in words, all the things that are happening to you, but you're the only one who doesn't understand it. 'Killed by love'—what the hell does that mean? Are you being 'killed' by someone that you love? Is that person's love 'killing' you? Come on. It's obvious, isn't it?"

Bilal looked aghast. Maybe it really was obvious. He hadn't told Muhammad about the conversation he'd had with his father. He wasn't ready for Muhammad to know all that about him—not yet.

"And that other one—'Little Boy, Black and Blue.' Plain as day, isn't it?" Muhammad said.

Bilal rolled onto his back and put his hands on his face.

Muhammad got up, tip-toed over to his desk so as not to wake the twins, and searched for a piece of paper. When he found it, he brought it back to the bed and handed it to Bilal.

Bilal recognized his handwriting. It was a poem called "Carmelita" Bilal had given Muhammad last year.

Carmelita was sixteen.
She put on her makeup,
she put on her dreams,
she say she got to go—
and Lord, you don't know—
every night, her father's touches
burning like a bonfire out of control;
every night, her father's touches
leaving wounds on her soul,
but she wanna be free and take to the sky
    with a thousand butterflies.
Carmelita bought herself a gun,
say he gonna pay for the things he's done.
I try to stop her, try to tell her no,
but she say she got to go.
Every night, the memories burn
and they don't heal with time—
then one night she found him sleeping,
then found the strength to draw the line
'cause she wanna be free and take to the sky
    with a thousand butterflies.

Bilal finished reading the poem. He couldn't look at Muhammad, so he stared at the ceiling.

"Now, who's this Carmelita chick?" Muhammad asked. He

sat cross-legged on the bed and gazed earnestly at Bilal.

Bilal shrugged.

"She's you, isn't she?" Muhammad asked. " 'Every night, her father's touches burning like a bonfire out of control'—how obvious is that? So you write this poem about this Carmelita girl, and you try to stop her, you tell her no—you're just talking to yourself, aren't you?"

"I suppose your dad taught you how to psychoanalyze people," Bilal said angrily.

"My dad taught me to think about why people do what they do," Muhammad replied. "He also told me that every single day we're all sending out signals about ourselves—through the way we dress, the way we look, the words we use, the things we write, the things we like, the books we read. He said if you pay attention to these things, you can quickly figure out what people are really all about, no matter what appearance they try to project."

"Isn't that nice?" Bilal said sarcastically.

Muhammad shook his head in frustration. "When you gave me this poem last year, I just scratched my head. I didn't understand what it meant. But I read it now, and it makes a lot of sense to me. You were trying to tell me something, Bilal, and I didn't know it. That's the point. I'm not trying to psychoanalyze you. You're always writing things like 'Lord, you don't know'—it's like you're telling the reader, 'You don't know what's going on.' Well, what's going on? All these secrets, Bilal. All these things you can't say. What is it?"

Bilal closed his eyes. He was not in the mood for more of this sort of conversation.

"Bilal, it's a beautiful poem. 'Take to the sky with a thousand butterflies'—is that what you want? Isn't that what we're doing, you and me? That's the way I feel. I mean, you put it down in words, just exactly how I feel. You've got a way with words, a real talent. But what about those other things? 'Her father's touches burning like a bonfire'—what is that about?"

"Nothing," Bilal said. "It's just a stupid poem."

Muhammad gave him a hurt look.

"Come on," Bilal said, urging him to lie down. "I don't want to fight with you. I don't want to talk about these things right now. I just want to be here with you."

Muhammad lay down and took Bilal into his arms. Bilal was grateful for the warmth of his friend's body.

"Someday you've got to tell me the truth," Muhammad said quietly, kissing Bilal on the forehead.

"I will," Bilal said. "But not today."

Bilal spent most of the weekend in Muhammad's bed, wishing he would never have to leave it. They held each other all of Thursday night, all of Friday night, and all of Saturday night. They wore only their pajama bottoms, and after the twins went to sleep, they removed these too. They reveled in their intimate contact and the lust their nakedness produced. When they weren't in bed together, they could hardly keep their hands off each other.

When they made love in the shower, Muhammad was careful and tender. He didn't want to hurt Bilal by inadvertently rubbing against the welts on his back or buttocks.

On Sunday evening, when it was time for Bilal to go, Muhammad walked him all the way home. They spent more than twenty minutes saying goodbye as they stood on the stoop behind the Abu's duplex apartment.

Salim was sitting at the table paying bills as Bilal walked through the kitchen, but he said nothing. Later on, as Bilal took a bath, the door to the bathroom opened and Salim walked in. He closed the door behind him and sat down on the edge of the tub, staring at Bilal and waiting for Bilal to look up to him.

When Bilal did, he asked, "What did you tell that man?"

Bilal simply stared at Salim defiantly.

"What, goddamn it?" Salim snapped.

Bilal shrugged. "He could see the welts on my back, what you did to my face—what was I supposed to tell him? I mean, you kicked me out of the house. Where was I supposed to go? What was I supposed to do?"

Salim glared at him. "Did you tell that man our business?"

Bilal shook his head. Surprisingly, the lie came easily.

"Don't you ever do that," Salim said quietly. "It's not my fault if these Americans don't understand the way we do things. And anyway, if you weren't coming on to me all the time, there wouldn't be anything to talk about."

Bilal felt anger flare. Salim's logic used to seem irrefutable. Now it seemed preposterous. But he didn't want to provoke Salim, so he said nothing.

"I was too hard on you the other day," Salim said. "I know that. I didn't mean to be, but I don't think you understand what you're doing. If we were living in Iraq and you had been caught having sex with a man, at the very least you would have been given a hundred lashes. You think I hurt you the other day? That was nothing. A real whipping—you wouldn't survive it. You'd be dead before they finished."

"We're not living in Iraq," Bilal quietly pointed out.

"No, we're not," Salim agreed.

Bilal locked his jaw and looked away from Salim.

"We don't have anything in this country, Bilal. All we have is each other. I have to make sacrifices. So do you. The family has to come first. We have our image to think about."

"And what about the truth?" Bilal asked. "Doesn't the truth matter to you?"

"What truth?"

"The truth about what I am," Bilal said. "Do you want me to lie about it?"

Salim gave him a look of disgust. "There are things you keep your mouth shut about. If you were a thief, would you be going around telling people that you like to steal things? If you were a drunk or a drug addict, would you go around telling people? If you had murdered someone, would you tell everyone you were a murderer? Just because you do something shameful and sinful doesn't mean you have to tell everyone about it—you don't have to rub our fucking noses in it."

"But I'm not a murderer," Bilal said. "I haven't done anything wrong."

"Homosexuality is a crime!" Salim exclaimed. "You haven't done anything wrong? So it's all right for you to look at men fucking each other, but I can't look at pictures of naked women? It's all right for you to give in to your lusts, but I have to control mine? Does being a faggot mean you don't have to answer for your sins? Is that what you're telling me?"

Bilal shook his head in frustration. "And the other day when you raped me—what was that? Wasn't that giving in to your lusts? It's all right for you, but not for me?"

"I was teaching you a lesson!" Salim snapped.

"You *raped* me!" Bilal shot back.

"I have a right to do as I please," Salim said, his eyes narrowing. "You should be glad it wasn't worse. And I didn't rape you—don't be getting all melodramatic like it was some big deal."

"Don't you get it?" Bilal asked, throwing caution to the wind. "What have you and I been doing all this time? That's not homosexuality? Fucking each other? Giving each other blow jobs? Isn't that what the people of Sodom did? You're a hypocrite!"

A moment passed, then Salim said, "Don't you love me?" His voice was plaintive and full of hurt.

Bilal felt his resolve teeter off balance. "Of course I do," he said, looking at Salim.

Salim shook his head. "I thought you enjoyed what we did. I thought you liked it—why didn't you just tell me to fuck off if you didn't like it? Are you going to blame me for everything now? Are you going to have a nervous breakdown because I tried to love you and make you happy—and tried to treat you like an adult and not a little baby?"

Bilal didn't answer. Salim's words suddenly made him feel small, ridiculous, and petty.

Salim stood. "When are you going to grow up and start acting like a man and help me with this family, instead of crying about every goddamned little thing? After what they did to me in Iraq…and you can't help me when I'm feeling bad, when I need someone…what a selfish little prick you are."

He stalked out of the bathroom without waiting for Bilal to answer.

Bilal felt his head might burst from the pressure inside it. When he was certain that Salim wouldn't return, he toweled off and fetched a box of matches from beneath the tub. He burned himself six times before his head cleared and he began to feel better.

He plunged into dejection once more. That weekend with Muhammad and his family, he'd felt optimistic. Not that he was home, he was right back where he started.

CHAPTER EIGHT

On Monday morning, Bilal rose, as he always did, just before dawn. Salim was already up, moving about the room, arranging his prayer rug, preparing for the early morning prayer. Bilal did his ablutions in the bathroom sink, then put his prayer rug next to Salim's. He waited for Salim to finish his own ablutions and start the prayer.

Salim gave Bilal a dirty look when he returned from the bathroom and saw Bilal waiting for him. He grabbed up his prayer rug and went into the living room to pray by himself. Bilal felt unwanted tears sting his eyes. He refused them. He would not cry. He was sick of crying. He said the prayers by himself, and for a long time afterward he remained kneeling on the floor, leaning back on his calves, pouring out his heart to Allah, begging Allah to help him, to make the temptation go away, to make all the madness stop. If Allah didn't help him, who would?

Salim finished his own prayers and returned to the bedroom, took off his pajamas, and went into the bathroom to clean up and prepare for work. Bilal got to his feet, took his pajamas off as well, and pushed the bathroom door open slowly. He found Salim standing at the sink, brushing his teeth.

"I'm sorry, Salim," he said quietly, standing close to him and keeping his eyes down. "I'm sorry about everything. I want to help you, if you need my help. I don't want to be selfish. I don't know what's wrong with me. I'm not thinking very clearly these days."

Salim continued to brush his teeth.

"I know you like to…do things…in the mornings…sometimes," Bilal said softly. "Let me help you."

Salim put his toothbrush back in the holder and turned to stare at Bilal for a long minute.

"Please?" Bilal said, raising his eyes to look at him. "You have to tell me how to make it right with you. I can't stand it. I messed up—I'm sorry. Tell me how to fix it."

"You need to grow up, Bilal," Salim said angrily. "Stop acting like a child."

Bilal nodded and waited for him to continue.

Salim said nothing further.

Bilal knelt in front of him, put his hands on Salim's hips, and took the flesh—it had become hard while they were standing there—into his mouth. He sucked it slowly, the way he knew Salim liked. Salim did not stop him. Bilal sucked on it as if his life depended on it, as if he could make everything better just as long as that piece of flesh was pleasured and satisfied. Salim came without warning Bilal, and Bilal choked down his ejaculation. He remained kneeling in front of his brother when he was finished, waiting for his brother to tell him what to do.

Salim went to sit on the toilet and gestured for Bilal to come stand in front of him.

Bilal did.

Salim put his hands on Bilal's hips and pulled him closer, looking up into Bilal's eyes. Then his eyes drifted down Bilal's body to his right hip, and the six burn marks he'd made there the night before.

"I told you to stop doing this," he said angrily.

"I'm sorry," Bilal said. "I won't do it anymore."

For a long time, Salim said nothing. He rubbed Bilal's belly. He let one hand drift up Bilal's stomach to his chest. Then his other hand cupped Bilal's buttocks.

"You've got to promise me that you won't do anything else to shame this family," Salim said, looking up to him. "You keep yourself away from this American perversion. You keep away from that Internet crap. You go to school, you get good grades, and you keep your mouth about our business. You think about this family first, not yourself. Act like this family matters to you. Stop being so selfish and childish about everything. You hear me?"

Bilal nodded.

"I want things to be right between us too," Salim said, pulling Bilal into an embrace. "I want it to be like it used to be—in the old days. I want to know that I can trust you again."

"You can trust me," Bilal said.

"You're the only one in this family who understands me," Salim said. "You're the only one who knows how to help me. Sometimes I think Allah has been far too cruel to me, expects too much of me—I'm only human. I need someone to love me, to touch me, to make me feel good. If I didn't have you, I don't know what I'd do. I love you, and I'd kill anyone who laid a hand on you. But I need to know that you love me just as much, that you're not making a fool out of me."

"I love you," Bilal said. "You know I do. I always will."

Salim seemed encouraged by these words, and he kissed

Bilal passionately. Then he bent his head down and took Bilal's penis into his mouth. Bilal knew he was forgiven, that it was going to be all right. This made him feel happy. It was as if a dark cloud had lifted and the sun was permitted to shine once more.

"We have to stop," Bilal said, keeping his eyes fixed on the textbook in front of him. He didn't dare look at Muhammad.

Trig class had yet to start, and few of the other students had arrived.

"We have to what?" Muhammad asked, bending close to him.

"We have to stop," Bilal whispered.

"Stop what?"

"You know what I mean."

Muhammad frowned and Bilal risked a glance.

"I can't do this," he said quietly. "It's wrong. It's a sin, what we're doing. You know it and I know it, and I promised my brother I would stop it, that I wouldn't bring shame on my family. I'm sorry, but that's how it has to be."

Muhammad made a sour face. "Your brother again. The same one who beat the shit out of you, who put welts up and down your back? That piece of shit is more important to you than I am, when all I've done is try to love you and take care of you? You're fucked up, Bilal. You are seriously fucked up."

"Well, whatever I am, it has to stop," Bilal said. "You have to stay away from me."

"You're full of shit," Muhammad replied, glowering at him.

Bilal turned away and stared blankly at the front of the classroom.

"Oh, no," Muhammad said, shaking his head. "It doesn't work that way. You don't just turn your feelings on and off like a goddamned faucet."

"Watch your mouth," Bilal said, giving him an angry glance.

"Don't tell me what to do," Muhammad snapped. "We're not doing anything wrong. Don't tell me that now you're going to start taking that fundamentalist crap seriously?"

"What we're doing is a crime," Bilal said, glancing around to make sure none of the students filing into the room was listening. "The people of Sodom were destroyed for it. How much simpler can it be? The Prophet said those kind of people should be killed wherever you find them. You can't just rationalize all of that away."

"The next time your brother beats you, maybe he could beat some sense into your stupid head."

"He wouldn't have beat me at all if I hadn't been messing around with this crap. You're making a mess out of my life!"

"I am?" Muhammad said, incredulous. "You really are fucked up, aren't you?"

"You don't understand," Bilal said.

"That's for sure."

"I have to do what my brother wants."

Muhammad stared at Bilal angrily. "What about what I want?"

Bilal didn't answer—Nu Haidar had spotted them and was now headed their way.

"What are you queers up to?" Nu said as he put his books on the table and took off his jacket.

"I'd appreciate it if you'd stop calling me a queer," Muhammad said through clenched teeth. He opened his trig book and let it slap against the table.

"Pardon me," Nu said, rolling his eyes and sitting down.

"You're always hanging around us, so what does that say about you?" Muhammad pressed. "We three queers of Orient are?"

"You're in a good mood," Nu said.

"Maybe you ought to think before you open your trap,"

Muhammad suggested. He threw a bitter glance at Bilal to say the message was meant for him as well.

Bilal frowned miserably.

Mr. Washington strolled in, and class got underway. As Washington wrote problem sets on the blackboard, Muhammad scribbled a note to Bilal.

You can't do this to me.

Bilal looked at the note, glanced at Muhammad, and turned away.

Muhammad scribbled another note.

Please tell me what's wrong.

Bilal said nothing.

As Mr. Washington was finishing his work at the blackboard, Muhammad wrote a third note.

Fuck you.

The words struck Bilal like physical blows. He suddenly felt nauseated. Clutching his belly, he got quickly to his feet and excused himself to go to use the restroom.

When he got to the restroom, he locked himself inside one of the stalls and burst into tears. He felt more wretched than he could ever remember. He just wanted Salim to be happy so that there would be peace in the house. That morning, kneeling in front of Salim and performing oral sex, he had been so sure of himself. But how was he going to push Muhammad away? How was he going to stop what they had started? How was he going to turn his feelings off and pretend that he didn't love Muhammad as much—if not more than—he loved Salim?

He heard the bathroom door open, then footsteps. He tried to quiet himself. There was a knock on the stall door. It was Muhammad.

"Bilal? Let me in," he said.

Bilal stared at the lock on the door and didn't move.

"Come on, man, hurry up. Someone's going to come."

"Go away," Bilal said weakly.

"Just open the door, Bilal. I'm sorry. I didn't mean to say that. Just open the door. Come on."

Bilal put his face in his hands and sobbed.

"I'm not leaving till you open this door," Muhammad said loudly.

Bilal reached out and undid the lock. Muhammad let himself in, shut the door, locked it again, and turned to look down at Bilal. He sat on the toilet seat, his face in his hands.

"I'm sorry," Muhammad said.

Bilal wouldn't look at him.

"What's the matter?" he said gently.

Bilal looked up at him, red-eyed and helpless.

Muhammad crouched down, put his hands on Bilal's knees, and gazed softly into Bilal's face. "Come on, man, whatever it is, we can work it out. That's what couples do, you know."

"We're not a couple," Bilal said.

"Yes, we are," Muhammad replied. "I need you, man. Don't do this to me."

"You don't need me," Bilal said bitterly.

"Yes, I do. You make me crazy. Just looking at you makes me horny. What am I supposed to do with myself now?"

"If you're so horny, you can just have sex with your little brothers. You don't need me for that crap."

Muhammad frowned. "What the hell do you mean by that, Bilal?"

"They're your little brothers," Bilal said, exasperated. "You can do what you want. There's no shame in looking on the nakedness of your brother, you know."

"Is this some Kurdish thing that the rest of us don't know about?"

"Oh, so now you're going to make fun of me? You're going to tell me that joke again—what do you get when you cross a Turk with a Kurd? Oh, you get a Turd! Ha ha ha! That's so funny I forgot to laugh."

"No one's making fun of you, man."

"Why don't you leave me alone?"

"Why don't you tell me what's going on?"

Bilal looked at him wearily. "What do you care?"

"You have to ask?" Muhammad replied.

Bilal fell silent again. Part of him wished Muhammad would go away; another part of him hoped he wouldn't. He was comforted by the boy's presence and his concern.

"Why don't you tell me what's really going on here?" Muhammad said.

"Why? So you can use the *f* word on me again?"

"I said I was sorry, man. You were making me mad. I can tell by the way you're acting that something's wrong, and I want to know what it is. What is this crap about doing what your brother wants? Did he find out about us?"

Bilal looked at Muhammad for a long time. "Didn't you ever make the twins give you a blow job…or something?"

Muhammad looked aghast. "No, I never made the twins give me a blow job! The thought never crossed my mind. Why should it? They're morons. Why would I want to have sex with them?"

Bilal shook his head. The words were now on the tip of his tongue, but he couldn't say them.

"What?" Muhammad asked. "Spit it out. It's not like we have any secrets, is it?"

Bilal raised his eyebrows. "Don't be too sure about that."

"And what's that supposed to mean?"

Bilal let out a long sigh. *Here I go again,* he thought.

"I've been having sex with my brother since I was nine years old," he said. "That's what that means."

Muhammad looked at him carefully. "Oh, Bilal," he said.

"I thought everybody did it," Bilal said. "I mean, I thought all brothers had sex with each other. Don't they?"

Muhammad's face filled with disbelief. "No, Bilal, not in this country."

"Don't lie to me!" Bilal said

"I'm not lying! That's just not the way it is!"

"I'm serious. Zubair—he never made you give him a blow job or something? I mean, he's your older brother. It's no big deal."

Muhammad's disbelief gave way to pity. "It's a crime in this country, Bilal."

"It's not a crime!" Bilal said, offended.

"Then what do you call it?"

"He needs me to help him," Bilal said. "Is that so wrong?"

Muhammad shook his head. "It's wrong to make kids have sex with you. If Salim's doing it to you, then you've got to make him stop. You don't have to put up with that."

Bilal wanted to defend Salim, defend himself—but how?

"It sounds like you could use a friend," Muhammad said. "Why are you trying to push me away?"

"My brother won't let me be a faggot," Bilal replied. "If he catches us, there'll be trouble. Who knows what he'll do to you, or what he'll do to me? It has to stop. It's not that I want it to stop, but I don't have a choice."

"You always have a choice."

Bilal laughed a small, bitter laugh.

"Why don't you just talk to me?" Muhammad suggested. "Just tell me what's going on, instead of pushing me away. Wouldn't that be easier?"

Bilal gave him a despairing look and shook his head. He'd

been a fool to believe that anything could get better.

"Does anybody else know about this?" Muhammad asked.

"I told your dad—the other day."

"And what did he say?"

"He said he was going to think about it and see if there was something we could do."

"See, my dad will help you," Muhammad said confidently.

Bilal turned his hands over and stared at his palms.

"Sometimes I feel like I'm being ripped in half," he said quietly. "When I'm with you, I feel happy. I feel like everything is normal. And yet Salim says it's wrong, that it's a crime to be a homosexual—but what else can I be? I didn't ask to be this way!"

"Your brother's one to talk about what's right and what's wrong," Muhammad said.

"What he's doing isn't considered wrong," Bilal said, looking up to him. "Don't you know that? In Arab countries, Muslim countries, guys don't have access to girls, so they go after their little brothers. It's common. If not their little brothers, then some guy in the neighborhood, some little kid—everybody turns a blind eye to it. Nobody thinks anything about it. It's better than these guys getting some girl pregnant, or making some girl lose her virginity."

Muhammad rolled his eyes. "Straight out of the Days of Ignorance," he said, referring to pre-Islamic times.

"Well, that's how it is," Bilal said defensively.

"So it's all right for your brother to be doing this to you?"

His gut told him it wasn't right, but tradition argued otherwise.

"What a mess," Muhammad said, shaking his head.

"It's not my fault!" Bilal snapped.

"I didn't say it was your fault. I said it was a mess, and it is. Tell me: Do you like it?"

Bilal shook his head.

"What does he do?" Muhammad asked. "Do you have to give him blow jobs? What, exactly?"

Bilal gave Muhammad an anguished look.

"I mean, is he hurting you? Is he raping you? Does he do it all the time or just once in a while?"

"He does everything," Bilal said.

"He rapes you?"

Bilal nodded.

"And do you like it?"

"No," Bilal said, offended. "It hurts!"

"Then he should stop it. We should talk to my dad and find a way to make him stop it."

Bilal regarded Muhammad carefully. He expected Muhammad to be sickened, repulsed—but he wasn't. "You're not disgusted by me?" he asked.

"Why should I be?" Muhammad asked, genuinely puzzled. "You haven't done anything wrong, Bilal. I'm disgusted by your brother, but not by you. Never by you."

Muhammad and Bilal spent their lunch break in the computer lab—Muhammad said he wanted to print out some information from a couple of Web sites for Bilal. Nu had gone elsewhere, mad at them for ignoring him.

Bilal looked at the printouts. "Signs of domestic violence?" he said, reading from the first sheet and raising his eyebrows.

"Just read," Muhammad said quietly.

Bilal scanned the first sheet, which contained a list of abusive behaviors to watch for. The list was designed to help a victim determine whether he or she was being abused or living with an abuser. Typical patterns of abusive behavior were "name-calling, mocking, accusing, blaming, yelling" or "always claiming to be right (insisting statements are 'the truth')" or "making light of behavior and not taking your concerns about it seriously" or "shifting responsibility for abuse, claiming that you caused it" or "using physical size to intimidate, control, frighten" or "making threats to hurt you or others" or "degrading treatment based on sex or sexual orientation," along with "using force to obtain sex or perform sexual acts" and "slapping, kicking, punching, pushing, grabbing."

Bilal put the paper down and looked at Muhammad in stunned silence. Almost every one of those statements applied to Salim. They described the sort of relationship Bilal had with his brother. Their accuracy was frightening.

"Keep reading," Muhammad said.

The next page was a test to help victims determine whether a particular person or relationship was possibly abusive.

> Do you control your behavior to avoid that person's anger?
> Does this person make you nervous?
> Does this person make you feel wrong, stupid, crazy?
> Do you feel helpless, trapped, unable to get out
> of the situation?
> Are you afraid to disagree with this person?
> Has this person ever forced sexual contact?
> Does this person make excuses for abusive behavior?

If pressed to answer these questions, what could Bilal say? Just about every question on the page deserved a "yes." At the bottom, he saw—with no small amount of horror—the following sentence, in bold type:

> **If you answered yes to even one of these questions,**
> **please get help!**

"Does any of it ring a bell?" Muhammad asked very quietly.

Bilal didn't reply.

"I'm just trying to help," Muhammad said, gathering up the sheets of paper. "Then again, I might be overreacting, or sticking my nose where it doesn't belong. Maybe it's all some sort of cultural thing that I just don't get. I just want you to know that I care about you, and if you need help, all you've got to do is ask."

Bilal's mind raced. Each time he thought he had things under control, the world turned upside down again.

"This is all about Salim, isn't it?" Muhammad asked.

Bilal nodded.

"What about Hakim?"

Bilal considered the question. He took the sheets of paper from Muhammad and looked through them again. Astonished, he realized that not even one of the statements or questions applied to Hakim. He was not afraid of Hakim, did not modify his behavior to please Hakim, did not worry about being hit or slapped or punched or walked in on while he was in the bathroom. Hakim never ridiculed him or made him feel stupid. Hakim never asked for sexual favors, never showed the slightest interest in Bilal's body or sexuality, never used his physical size to threaten and intimidate.

He put the papers down, feeling very strange.

"So, what about Hakim?" Muhammad asked again.

Bilal shook his head. "He's never done anything to me. I mean, none of this applies to him."

"But it does apply to Salim, doesn't it?"

Bilal nodded.

"And what does that tell you?"

Bilal was not at all sure.

That evening, while Bilal was sitting with Fatima at the kitchen table and doing his homework, the picture Muhammad had given him slipped out of his history book, where he had been keeping it. Bilal saw the flash of dark skin and the yellow bathing suit just as Fatima grabbed it.

"What's this?" she asked, giving him a knowing, naughty smile.

"Give it back!" he said.

"I just want to see," she said primly, looking at it. "Oh, it's a picture of your boyfriend. He's cute, isn't he?"

"Give it to me!" he pleaded.

"What's it worth to you?" she asked.

"How'd you like to die?" he countered.

"One might think you were in love."

"Fatima, goddamn it!"

"The little baby wants his little boyfriend's picture—oh, how sad."

Neither of them noticed Salim hovering just outside the kitchen in the hall that led to the bedrooms.

"Is he a good kisser?" Fatima asked.

"That's none of your business."

"You are in love, aren't you? Bilal's got a boyfriend!"

Bilal turned around, saw Salim lurking in the hall, and froze.

"What is this about?" Salim asked very quietly as he stepped into the kitchen.

Fatima, startled, glanced around at Salim and went pale.

"Give me that picture," Salim said.

Fatima handed it to him, afraid he might strike her.

Salim looked at the picture for a long time before he turned his gaze on Bilal. "You want to explain to me what this is?"

"He's my friend," Bilal said weakly.

"Fatima seems to think he's more than your friend. Is that right? Is this nigger your boyfriend?"

"Don't use that word," Bilal said.

"I'll use any fucking word that I want," Salim replied slowly. "Now I asked you a question. Is this fucking nigger your boyfriend?"

"He's my friend," Bilal repeated. His hands began to tremble, and he lay them in his lap.

"Don't lie to me, Bilal," Salim said in a low, dangerous-sounding voice.

"He's my friend!"

"Is that all he is?"

Bilal didn't answer for fear of giving away too much.

Salim ripped the picture in half, then shredded and threw the pieces into the trash.

Bilal watched Salim's performance in silence. He was so weary of these confrontations, so weary of feeling afraid.

Salim strode to where Bilal sat and loomed over him. "You're going to mock me, is that it, Bilal?"

Bilal looked up at him fearfully. "I forgot about that picture. It's nothing."

Salim rapped him on the back of the head with his knuckles. Bilal winced.

"What are *you* looking at?" Salim demanded, turning his attention to Fatima.

"What am I looking at?" she repeated. "It appears to be a king-size prick, if I'm not mistaken."

He charged around the table, grabbed her by the hair and dragged her from her chair.

"Oh, you're such a big man!" she shouted angrily. "Picking on girls! Why don't you pick on someone your own size?"

Salim did not merely slap her; he slugged her. She went down in a heap on the floor, but quickly scrambled back to her feet, in a furious rage.

"Go to hell, you monster!" she screamed. Her lips were blood-ied. "You don't scare me!"

He advanced on her again. She darted to the kitchen counter, grabbed a frying pan, and turned around, brandishing it at him.

"You put that down," he said.

"You make me, you fucking pig," she replied. Blood dripped from her chin.

"Don't you talk to me like that!"

"I'll talk any goddamned way I want to," she growled as she blazed with rage.

Salim did not advance any further, but neither did he retreat.

Mrs. Abu appeared, roused by the shouting. She stood at the door to the kitchen. "What are you doing?" she demanded.

Salim turned to glare at her. "This is not your business, Ma."

"What are you doing?" she asked again, her voice high-pitched, bewildered.

"Oh, get a clue, Ma," Fatima said. "What does it look like?"

Salim turned back to Fatima. "You put that frying pan down," he said very quietly.

"You—make—me," Fatima replied, enunciating each word very sharply. "You—fucking—make—me—you—fucking—piece—of—shit."

Salim clenched his fists, and the veins bulged on the sides of his neck.

"Come on," Fatima said, trying to entice him. "Just give me a reason to beat your fucking head in, and don't you think for a minute I won't do it."

Salim continued to glare at her.

Bilal got up from the table, clutching his chest—he could not breathe. Everything was rushing around inside his mind—it was all madness and chaos. His body felt strange, as if he didn't belong to it. He gasped, trying to draw in air, but his chest tightened, and he could do no more than wheeze helplessly.

"Now look what you've done!" Mrs. Abu said accusingly as she hurried over to take Bilal in her arms. Bilal shrieked when a sharp pain in his chest wracked his body. He collapsed into his mother's arm, unconscious.

When Bilal came to, he was lying on the kitchen floor on his back. His mother was kneeling beside him, rubbing his chest ,and telling him to breathe. "It's all right, Bilal," she said. "Everything's all right."

He could not remember, at first, what had happened. Then he looked around for Salim and was relieved to discover that he was not in the room. Fatima was standing at the kitchen sink, running water and dabbing her split lip with a washcloth.

Bilal sat and looked at his mother.

"Come on, get up," she said, encouraging him to stand.

"Thanks for your help," Fatima said angrily. She turned back to the sink and spat.

"Leave him alone," Mrs. Abu said. "What he gets from his brother is plenty enough already."

As Bilal took a bath that evening, he used both hands to give himself "horse-bites"—he grabbed the flesh on the insides of his thighs and squeezed until he could no longer stand the pain of it. This produced horrible-looking red marks that eventually became bruises.

After the first horse-bite, he settled back in the warm water, enjoying the absence of pain and relative stillness of his mind. But soon he began to feel upset again, so he gave himself another horse-bite. This time, with his right hand, he squeezed the flesh on his left calf as hard as he could until he began to feel faint. The pain screamed up his leg and into his belly.

Again he leaned back in the tub and enjoyed a reprieve from his agony, but now tears stung his eyes. He grabbed the flesh just below his left breast and gave it an intense horse-bite. Pain shot through his body and surged up into his head. All of his muscles tensed. The breath got caught in his throat. He held on till he couldn't stand it anymore, then he began to cry.

He thought about the razor beneath the tub. He considered slicing his wrist just a little bit just to see how painful it might be if he ever got serious about putting an end to things. But he remained in the tub, knowing that if things got any worse, the pain of the razor would not deter him.

He felt like he was dying anyway—what difference would it make if he actually killed himself? At least the pain would go away. He was so sick of that dark cloud that always hung over his head, threatening to unleash its fury.

As he always did toward the end of these sessions, he began to masturbate. It relieved his tension and upset, and for a few minutes he could forget himself. But afterward a horrible guilt always swept over him—he knew it was sinful to masturbate, sinful to seek such pleasures outside of marriage to a woman. This time, after he came, he felt such shame and anger with himself that he inflicted two more horse-bites on his inner thighs to punish himself for his uncontrollable lust.

Salim walked in on him in the middle of this ritual.

The boys' bathroom door had no lock—Salim had removed it ages ago. Last summer Bilal had tried to install a new lock, but Salim had removed it as soon as he saw it. For that act of defiance he had beaten Bilal savagely with the switch.

Hakim and Bilal tacitly understood that if the door was closed, then the bathroom was being used. It was only polite to wait one's turn. Salim, on the other hand, paid no heed to social graces. Bilal could be sitting on the toilet taking a shit, and Salim would barge in, look around, and leave. Bilal had absolutely no privacy.

Salim had a towel around his waist. After he closed the door, he removed his towel, sat down on the edge of the tub, and put his feet into the bath water. His penis was fully erect.

Bilal looked at the hard flesh and felt his stomach knot up in pain. He knew he was expected to sit in front of it, pleasure it. Hadn't they just had sex this morning? He feared Salim was going into one of his horny phases—there were times when he badgered Bilal for sex every day, sometimes twice a day.

Bilal moved in the tub so that he was sitting in front of Salim. He bent forward and took the hardness into his mouth. He did everything that Salim liked—using both a hand and his mouth, rubbing Salim's perineum, which made his brother crazy, keeping the thing in his mouth until Salim grew soft after he came.

When Bilal was finished, he got out of the tub. Salim would want to have his own bath.

Salim grabbed him by the hips and inspected his chest and legs.

"What are all these marks?" he demanded.

Bilal shrugged helplessly.

"Didn't you just tell me this morning you were going to do stop doing this?"

"I forgot," Bilal said.

"You forgot?" Salim repeated. He stood, and the muscles on his chest and belly rippled as he moved. "Maybe I need to remind you."

Without warning, his right hand flew out, striking Bilal on the cheek.

Bilal put a hand to his stinging face and kept his eyes lowered.

"Are you going to forget again?" Salim asked, his voice dangerously quiet.

Bilal shook his head. "No," he said. "I won't forget."

CHAPTER NINE

The next day, Muhammad told Bilal his father wanted to talk to him after school, so Bilal and Fatima followed the Jackson kids to the rectory.

"What is this about?" Fatima asked as they walked across the parking lot.

"I can't tell you," Bilal said.

"You can't, or you won't?"

"I can't, not right this minute."

"Your inability to tell it like it is wearies me, Bilal," Fatima said. "I've got homework to do."

"Well, go do it then," Bilal spat.

"I just feel like I have a right to know what's going on," Fatima replied.

"Fine," Bilal answered. "I'm trying to figure out what we can do about Salim. So why don't you run home and tell him I've been talking to the Imam about him so you can get me in trouble, and maybe he'll deck you again as a way of saying thank you."

"You know I wouldn't tell him anything," she said. She stopped, grabbed his arm, and forced him to stop too. "Bilal, look, this is serious. We're in trouble. Salim's out of his mind now. We have to call the police. We have to do something. When you fainted last night, you probably saved my life. Oh, I can talk big, but what can I do? What, really? If he had come after me, that would have been the end of it. He's gotten to the point where he doesn't care anymore—any little thing sets him off now."

"Well, telling him he's a king-size prick probably isn't helpful," Bilal replied.

She smirked. "Bilal, are you aware that brothers and sisters routinely insult each other? And if the man is making an ass of himself, I have the right to tell him that and not get my head beaten in for it."

Bilal raised his eyebrows and nodded. She had a point.

"So what is this about?" she demanded.

Bilal gave her a very abbreviated account of his conversations with Muhammad and the Imam.

"He fucks you!" Fatima exclaimed when he was done, making Bilal wince. "I can't believe this. And just when were you planning on telling someone?"

"I'm telling you now," he said.

"And he's been doing this since you were nine?" she asked.

He nodded. He felt a flush of embarrassment spread across his face.

"Oh, Bilal," she said. "No wonder he never lets Ma and me go into your room. Look. If anybody's going to do anything, it has to be me and you. Hakim's oblivious. Ma's stuck in the old days. We're the ones who are going to have to do something. I want to know what the Imam says. I want to be with you when you talk to him."

"Fine," Bilal said.

When they got to the Jackson's house, Fatima stood with Bilal and Muhammad at the door to the Imam's office.

"Why don't you come with me too?" Bilal asked, glancing at Muhammad.

"It's not my place," Muhammad said.

"Please?"

Muhammad considered Bilal's request for a moment. "We'll ask my dad," he said.

The three of them went into the Imam's office, and he offered them a smile from behind his desk, where he was talking on the telephone. When he finished the call, Muhammad said, "Bilal asked me to come with him, Dad."

Malik looked from Muhammad to Fatima and then to Bilal. "Well," he said to Bilal.

"I told them everything already," Bilal said softly.

The Imam smiled. "Sit down then, all of you."

They sat.

"Bilal, I've been thinking about our options, and I guess there's a few things I have to say to you before we get to that. Are you sure you want Muhammad and Fatima here to listen to all of this?"

Bilal nodded.

The Imam folded his hands across his belly and regarded Bilal for a long moment. "Thing is, Bilal, your brother has a long history of abuse—going back to when you were nine—and I've got to admit that I'm bothered by that. Folks in law enforcement will tell you that pedophiles and sex offenders are, almost without exception, impossible to rehabilitate, mostly because they refuse to admit that what they're doing is wrong. If we're going to do something, we're going to have to really do something. Threats and confrontations, like we did the other day, are probably not going to be helpful. In fact, if I knew then what I know now—

if you had told me everything that was going on that night your brother kicked you out—I would never have confronted him like that. He's a lot more dangerous than you let on that night, isn't he?"

Bilal sighed and nodded.

"Sexual abuse is very damaging, Bilal," the Imam said. He sat forward, put his hands together on his desk, and stared intently at Bilal. "Nothing's going to mess a kid up faster than sexual abuse. It's very confusing for a child to comprehend what's going on, and the worst thing about it is that your boundaries—physical, but also emotional and psychological—are being violated. Your body belongs to you, Bilal, and no one else. Parents and adults are godlike figures to a child, and when they take advantage of their power and of a child's trust—and that's what sexual abuse is all about—well, the results are not good."

Fatima took one of Bilal's hands into one of her own and squeezed it.

"Now, I'm saying all of this, Bilal, because my concern is for you, not your brother. Salim is an adult, and he can take care of himself. As an adult, he's responsible for what he does, and no one else. He has no right to blame you for anything, or to try to pretend that you're somehow responsible for what he's been doing. He rationalizes and justifies his behavior while ignoring the pain he's causing you, Bilal, and that's just sick. I want you to keep these things in mind while we're talking."

Bilal was quiet, taking it all in.

"What do you suggest we do, Dad?" Muhammad asked.

"I'm getting to that," Malik said, nodding his head. "My first impulse is to call the police and let them handle it, because this is a criminal matter. But there are other options. Bilal could leave home and live elsewhere, get away from the situation. We could confront Salim and demand that he leave and live elsewhere, instead of Bilal. The riskiest is for Bilal to study up on sexual abuse and start insisting that Salim stop. You can educate yourself, figure out what's inappropriate behavior, and insist that your brother refrain from it. Sometimes that's all that's needed—you stick up for yourself, stop being silent about the abuse, let the person know that you're not going to be a victim anymore."

Bilal considered all of these options in silence.

"Now, Bilal," the Imam said, "I don't like any of them aside from the first—calling the police. From what you've told me about Salim, I have questions about his mental state. He seems to be a violent, angry man. If he's arrested for child abuse, Salim will be inventoried—they'll do psychological tests, see if there's something wrong with him, see if there's anything that can be done to help him. That may be exactly what he needs."

"But what about my family?" Bilal asked. "If he goes to jail, what are we going to do? How are we going to pay the bills?"

The Imam turned his palms up and smiled kindly at Bilal. "Those are secondary worries. We can all sit down together and figure out how to tackle the situation and get the bills paid. It might mean that you and Fatima will have to go get part-time jobs. We may have to check into some government assistance programs, or something like that. We'll find a way."

"He'll be so humiliated if he's arrested," Bilal said quietly, eliciting a snort from Fatima.

"Yes, he would be," the Imam agreed. "And whose fault is that? Is that your fault, Bilal? Are you expected to suffer in silence so that he can be spared the embarrassment of being found out?"

Bilal shook his head. "I think I've been embarrassed enough because of him," he said.

"Now, it's asking a lot of you, Bilal, but I suggest is that you file a report about your brother and have him arrested. Tell the police what you've told me and let them deal with it."

"And what happens after we do that?" Fatima asked. Bilal was glad to hear the word "we."

"It's up to the courts after that," the Imam said. "He'll be arrested, probably denied bail, given the nature of the charges. A hearing will be held to determine if a trial is warranted, and it will be. The trial will be held—that could be a year or more in the future. He'll be sentenced. He'll serve his time. By the time he gets out, he'll no longer be in a position to abuse Bilal anymore."

Bilal thought about his brother being sent away, and felt a rare surge of hope. If Salim was sent away, all the madness would stop—the fights, the arguments, the screaming, the whippings. But there was price: turning Salim in. Betraying his brother.

"There's no other way?" he asked, gazing pleadingly at Imam Malik.

"There's no other safe way—not that I can think of," Malik said gently. "You must be ready for this to stop by now, Bilal. You must be sick of it. You deserve to be safe when you're at home and to know that no one's going to hurt you there."

Bilal looked at the Imam with wide eyes. He was deeply grateful for the man's help, but it all weighed so heavily on him.

"There's one more thing," the Imam said. "We need evidence, Bilal. Now, we've got those pictures, and that's a good start. Your family can testify to what he did, to how he threw you out of the house. But we're going to need more than that; otherwise, it's your word against his. We have to consider the possibility that he may deny everything to the police—claim that you're making it all up and that he didn't do anything wrong. And if he does, we'll have a problem, unless we've got evidence that will convince a judge that your brother is lying."

"What kind of evidence?" Bilal asked.

The Imam sighed and knit his brow. "That night you came to my house, when Salim kicked you out—if we had taken you to the hospital, the hospital would have been forced to investigate. It's called mandatory reporting. If a child—or even an adult, for that matter—shows up with suspicious injuries like welts or unexplained bruises or broken bones, then the hospital is required to notify the police to find out what's going on. If there's been a sexual assault, they can perform what's known as a PERK—a physical evidence recovery kit—to document the assault. The evidence from the PERK is used to begin an immediate investigation.

"Now, I hope you don't get another beating at your brother's hands, but if you do, you have options. You can go to the hospital, and mandatory reporting will kick in. If he assaults you again sexually, you should go to the police immediately, and they will take you to the hospital for the PERK and handle everything that needs to be done. At the very least, you should just get on the phone and call me, and I'll be over right away, no matter what time it is."

Bilal walked home with Fatima. His head spun with all the things that the Imam had said.

"We should just call the police," Fatima said, breaking into his thoughts when they were a block away from their apartment.

Bilal shook his head. "We need evidence. What if we turn him in and he denies everything and there's not enough evidence to charge him—what then? Then we're screwed."

"That's one way of putting it," Fatima replied. "I wish you had told me all of this a long time ago. I would never have let him do all that stuff to you."

Bilal said nothing.

"Bilal?" she said. "Why didn't you tell me?"

What could Bilal say? When the abuse started, he had enjoyed it. He had willingly participated, had not considered that what he and Salim were doing was wrong. How could he explain this to Fatima? How could he tell her that there was a time when he had enjoyed having sex with Salim?

He said nothing, and they walked in silence. .

After dinner, Hakim put on his jacket and said he was going to clean up the leaves in front of their half of the duplex. A few minutes into the chore, Bilal joined him. Hakim, surprised by this unexpected help, sensed something was on his brother's mind. As Bilal held open a trash bag to receive an armload of leaves, Hakim asked, "What is it?"

"I have to tell you something," Bilal said quietly. He glanced nervously at the windows of the apartment, afraid Salim would see them talking.

"About him?" Hakim said, smiling.

Bilal nodded.

"Don't worry about him," Hakim said. "He's probably praying or something."

They moved further toward the sidewalk, just to be certain they wouldn't be overheard.

"You remember how you walked in on me and Salim?" Bilal asked.

Hakim frowned.

"You told me about that one night, when you came home drunk," Bilal said.

"I did?"

Bilal nodded.

"What else did I say?"

"You were telling me about Mary-what's-her-name and her big hoochies."

Hakim grinned.

"Do you remember that?" Bilal asked earnestly.

Hakim shrugged. "I don't remember telling you that, but yeah, I remember walking in on you. I didn't stick around for a good look or anything."

Bilal fell silent, letting the garbage bag go slack and looking at all the leaves. It was awkward—he didn't know what to say. He was embarrassed, ashamed. He didn't want Hakim to know about what Salim and he had been doing. But now there was no choice but to tell him.

"I told Imam Malik about all of this," Bilal said after he had explained the situation to Hakim. "He thinks I should turn Salim in to the police. I don't want to get him in trouble, but you just don't know what he does to me, how much it hurts, how it makes me feel…you just don't know."

Hakim frowned, raked more leaves, and didn't answer right away. "You know you can't turn him in, not to the police," he said, after a long silence.

Bilal told him about the last whipping—about the underwear being stuffed in his mouth, about the rape afterward.

For a long time, Hakim leaned against his rake and stared at the wintry clouds overhead. "Look, Bilal, in the old days, buggering your little brother was not exactly a crime."

Bilal gave Hakim an exasperated look.

"You don't go to the police about stuff like that," Hakim said. "If you don't like it, you just tell him to stop."

"Like he's going to listen to me."

"Bilal, you're not going to the police," Hakim said firmly, giving Bilal a hard look. "That isn't how we do things in this family."

"Well, then, how *do* we do things?" Bilal asked angrily.

"In Iraq, if you went to the police, they would laugh at you. You can't embarrass the family by running off to the police and having him arrested."

Bilal could believe he was hearing this from Hakim. "But it hurts!"

"Well, if you didn't like it, why didn't you ask me for help?"

"I was afraid—he told me I would be sent to a foster home if anyone found out about us. I didn't even know that what he was doing was wrong until the Imam started telling me about sexual abuse. I didn't even know there were words to describe what he was doing."

"It doesn't hurt that much," Hakim said dismissively.

"You try it!" Bilal said. "Let somebody stick their dick up your ass and see how you like it."

Hakim sighed and shook his head. "Make him stop, Bilal. You know, all you ever do is accept things in silence. You never fight for yourself. Just once, I'd love to see you stand up to that prick and tell him to fuck off. If you don't fight for yourself, everybody's just going to walk all over you all your life. If you don't like what he's doing, tell him to take his dick and stick it up his own ass for a change. If you don't like people hurting you, Bilal, you need to learn to tell them not to."

Bilal realized that he was not going to get any help from Hakim. "Well, thanks for nothing," he said angrily. He dropped the bag of leaves and stalked off.

He found Salim in the bedroom sitting on the bed and looking at the handful of photographs they had brought with them from Iraq. The look on Salim's face was total bewilderment.

Bilal felt such hatred for Salim that he wanted to get the razor from beneath the bathtub and use it to slit Salim's throat. But for once Salim looked vulnerable. Before Bilal knew what was happening, his anger had given way to tenderness.

"This is you and Papa," Salim said softly, holding out one of the photographs.

Bilal took it and looked at it. In the picture, he was standing behind his father and peering around one of his father's legs with an impish grin on his face. His father, wearing traditional Kurdish clothes and a dark prayer hat on his head, smiled at the camera. They were standing in front of the mosque where his father had once preached.

Bilal closed his eyes and felt something tighten in his chest. He was in no mood for a trip down memory lane.

"I messed everything up," Salim said, gazing at the pictures spread before him on the bed.

"No, you didn't," Bilal said. He was surprised to notice his hand on Salim's shoulder.

"Yes, I did. I'm still doing it. I put you in that school to keep you away from these American perversions, but they found you anyway. I wanted you to get a good education and meet a nice Muslim girl and have your own family, and now you're telling me…I wish I had never been put in charge of this family. I can't do anything right. I've lost Hakim. I'm losing you. Fatima will abandon her religion the first chance she gets. What did we come here for? To lose our religion and be like these godless Americans?"

Salim's words had never sounded so preposterous to Bilal. "It's not your fault," he said gently.

"It *is* all my fault," Salim said, looking up at Bilal now. "I'm not just saying that. I think someone should know, in case something happens to me."

"Nothing's going to happen to you." Bilal kept his voice even, but he was annoyed. Salim had used the I'm-going-to-kill-myself ploy before.

"I'm not going to make it much longer," Salim said. "I want to be with Papa."

Bilal sat on the bed next to Salim and resigned himself to the drama.

"Really, Bilal, someone needs to know what I did. It's about what happened that day when they took Papa and me away. You know Papa used to write things—those pamphlets. They talked about being Kurdish—about being proud of ourselves and reminding us of our history. He also talked about Islam—about how we had the right to be Sunni Muslims and that there was nothing wrong with us, no matter what the Iraqis might say about us or do to us. All of those pamphlets, Bilal—he was trying to tell us not to be ashamed of who we were, to put aside our bickering and ally ourselves with other Kurdish tribes and work together to reestablish Kurdistan."

Bilal had heard it all before. It used to make him proud to hear Salim tell stories about their father. Now it just made him weary.

"You don't know what it was like in those days," Salim said. "All the men coming and going, talking to Papa, trying to print those pamphlets to send them out into the villages—it was so dangerous, always looking over your shoulder and wondering if you were going to get caught. All the times we moved, from house to house, village to village..."

Salim sighed and shook his head. "Eventually, the secret police caught him. They came and took Papa and me away. When we got to their headquarters, the first thing they did was beat both of us. They beat me first and made Papa watch. Then they beat Papa and made me watch. And then they took us to this room, and they put Papa in a chair, and tied him to it so he couldn't move. And then..."

His voice trailed off. Bilal saw that Salim's eyes were closed and he touched Salim's hair and gently stroked it. "What did they do?" he asked.

Salim's face grew clouded and bitter. "Bilal, you know that, for an Arab, raping a man is the same as taking his manhood from him. It's the same as treating him like he was a woman.

There's nothing worse you could do to a man than that. If you kill him, at least he has some glory—he's a martyr. But if you rape him, he will live the rest of his life in shame. There is no glory in it. Only shame and silence."

Salim's voice became a soft rasp.

"Did they do that to you?" Bilal asked, frowning. Wasn't that what Salim was doing to *him*?

Salim nodded slowly. "They made Papa watch. They wanted Papa to see his firstborn son forever shamed. They wanted him to know that, after they killed him, his family would be led by someone who had lost his manhood. And Bilal...there were a lot of men there in that room, and five or six of them did it. There was a table in the room, about ten feet away from Papa. They made me lean on that table while they did it. They stripped me, tied my hands behind my back, and they were laughing while they did it."

Salim hung his head. Bilal felt a confusing mixture of pity, tempered rage, and love for Salim. The secret police had poisoned Salim's spirit, and Salim had passed that poison to Bilal.

"When they were done with me, they turned their attention to Papa. I started begging them not to kill my Papa. I was naked, crying, half out of my mind. I begged them and begged them, and the more I begged, the more they laughed. They said I was yapping like a Kurdish dog looking for a treat.

"Then they untied Papa and made him stand against the wall. Well, he could hardly walk—he was in such pain from the beating they'd given him. They kicked him and told him to crawl like the animal he was. Then they dragged me over there and made me kneel down right beside him."

Salim gasped, and fat tears rolled down his cheeks. He turned to look at Bilal with wide-eyed horror.

"Then they shot him in the head, three or four times. After that, they gave me back my clothes and told me to go home and tell everybody what they had done, that they knew there were others and they would be next if we didn't stop what we were doing."

Salim wept quietly, and Bilal continued to stroke his hair.

"But that's not your fault," Bilal said. "You didn't mess anything up."

Salim shook his head. "You don't understand. I had a friend: Jafar. He was a faggot. We all knew that. But he was fun. I was with him one night. Jafar saw someone…a man. We were in an alley…Jafar wanted to follow him, so we did…the man turned around…parted his robes…wanted Jafar to touch him…so Jafar did…and then they started doing things…"

Salim closed his eyes. Pain tightened his face.

"What then?" Bilal asked.

"The man was one of the secret police."

Bilal was confused. What did this have to do with Papa?

"They took us in. Arrested us," Salim said. He put his face in his hands.

Bilal regarded Salim uneasily. Why was Salim hanging around with a gay man? What were they doing walking around the streets together? "What happened?" Bilal asked.

Salim looked up and gave his brother a bitter smile. "Well, Bilal, they realized who I was—who my father was." He turned his face away.

Suddenly, the pieces fell into place in Bilal's mind. Their father had been caught because Salim had been arrested. After all their constant moving around and trying to evade the authorities, in the end their father was caught because Salim had been hanging out with Jafar.

"I told them I wasn't going to tell them where I lived. I wasn't going to give my father away. They could do whatever they wanted, but I wasn't going to betray him. But they did things…they did so many things to me…what could I do? So you see, it is my fault. It's all my fault. Papa would still be alive. We would never have had to suffer all of this. We'd be back home, where we belong, if it hadn't been for me."

Bilal didn't know what to say to any of this.

Salim sighed heavily. "If anything ever happens to me, you just remember what I said."

"Don't talk like that," Bilal said.

"You don't know what it's like for me," Salim replied. "You don't know what I go through, how much I hate myself for what I did. Those Iraqis took my manhood, and if they could see me now and the mess I've made of this family, they would laugh themselves silly."

Salim began to weep again.

Bilal thought about his father. The grief was so fresh and sharp in his mind, it was as if his father had just died that very day.

There was a hole in Bilal's heart—sometimes he thought of it as the black hole in his soul. It had been created by his father's death. Nothing had ever been able to heal that wound. Whenever he got near it, he could feel it sucking him in, dragging him down, pulling him into its painful embrace so he ran from it, tried not to think about it, pushed the thought out of his mind.

He had loved his father very much—he still did and always would. No one would ever replace him. And Bilal feared nothing would ever take away the pain of his absence.

Salim pulled away from Bilal's touch and disappeared into his own dark place. Bilal got up and went into the bathroom to feel his own grief and cry his own tears.

CHAPTER TEN

Ramadan, the Muslim month of fasting, arrived at the end of the week. Bilal guessed that was partly the reason for Salim's slide into depression.

During the month of Ramadan, Muslims refrained from food, water, sex, cigarettes—the intake of any substance at all—during the day. The fasts ended each evening with an *iftaar* feast. Muslims were encouraged to do extra good deeds during the month—to work on perfecting their Islam, their submission to Allah. It was a time of both penance and celebration. It was also a month of short tempers and foul moods. The mornings were okay, but as the day progressed, good cheer was harder and harder to find. Since they didn't live in a Muslim country and couldn't just shut down for a month as they had in Iraq, they had to go to work and school, all the while fasting, which made it even harder.

For a poor family like Bilal's, it was bittersweet time. No doubt Salim felt their poverty even more keenly—they did not have the means to throw lavish *iftaar* feasts of their own. And since Muslims were encouraged to do charitable works during the month, families like Bilal's wound up being the recipients of that charity—another reminder, as if any was needed, of their difficult circumstances. The gifts of food and money were welcome, of course, but it was embarrassing for all of them to be so needy.

Despite all that, Ramadan was Bilal's favorite time of the year. The fasting did not bother him. Their poverty did not bother him. He enjoyed the feelings of friendliness and closeness, not just with his own family but within the whole community. Before the month was out, he and his family would be invited to *iftaar* feasts at all of his and Fatima's schoolmates' homes. They would get to stay up late every night and have shorter days and less homework at school.

The real treat for Bilal: Salim would try to remain celibate the entire month. Happily, he usually succeeded.

Imam Malik and Mrs. Jackson invited the Abu family and the Haidar family for one of the first *iftaar* feasts, on a Saturday evening, as they did every year.

Bilal and his family walked the six blocks to the rectory in the early evening darkness. The girls and women congregated together in the kitchen, and a fuss was made over Mrs. Abu's chicken dish—it was always popular because of the exotic Kurdish spices she used. The boys and men remained in the living room, plates soon on their laps. Salim kept to himself—he was still angry about his confrontation with the Imam.

Bilal sat in a quiet corner with Muhammad and Nu. The three boys ate and talked about their schoolwork and their friends. Ahmed Haidar joined them, sitting next to Bilal and making small talk. Muhammad's older brother Zubair arrived too. The twins sat nearby, bored because there was no one their age to play with, until Hakim and Zubair began roughhousing with them. Nu and Ahmed joined them for a game of Monopoly, leaving Bilal and Muhammad to sit by themselves—which was exactly what they wanted.

"Have you been thinking about what my dad said?" Muhammad asked.

Bilal sighed and recounted his conversation with Hakim, which had effectively ruled out the idea of going to the police.

"So where does that leave you?" Muhammad asked.

Bilal had no answer. It left him, of course, right where he had started.

"Have you been abstaining from sex all day?" Muhammad asked in whisper. He shot Bilal a playful look.

"Of course," Bilal said, frowning.

"It's nighttime now," Muhammad pointed out. "We could sneak off to the bathroom and…you know, freshen up."

Bilal grinned in spite of himself. When he got up to follow Muhammad to the bathroom, he did not notice Salim's eyes on him.

Inside the bathroom, with the door locked, they quickly peeled off their clothes. They were so horny for each other, they could hardly stand it. They stood kissing, embracing, and caressing each other. They tried very hard to be quiet.

For the next twenty minutes, Bilal forgot all about Salim and Hakim and his family and all the problems that were dogging him. Instead, he gave himself over to making love with Muhammad. He lay on the carpet on his back—now that the welts were healing—and taught Muhammad how to use lotion to make love to him the right way. Feeling his friend inside him—a boy he loved and delighted in—was like a revelation. He did not care about the initial pain. He wanted Muhammad to enjoy their lovemaking, take his pleasures from Bilal's body, and empty himself inside Bilal.

They were more intimately connected than they had ever been, and Bilal, as he lay beneath Muhammad, thought about what the Imam had said about boundaries—he didn't want any boundaries between him and Muhammad.

"This is crazy," Muhammad whispered. Bilal was dazzled by the sight of Muhammad's bare skin and thrusting hips. "You make me feel so good."

"I want you to feel good," Bilal said, touching Muhammad's chest. After the boys had reached their climaxes, they lay together, panting softly. Muhammad caressed Bilal's face with gentle kisses.

When they rejoined the others, they didn't notice Salim staring at them with a strange sort of fire in his eyes.

When the Abus got home, Bilal changed into his pajamas and waited for Salim and Hakim to finish their bathroom routines, then went into the bathroom to do his own. While he was washing his face, he thought about a Billie Holiday song called "Sunny Side of the Street," and sang a few words from it to his reflection in the mirror as he patted himself dry: "I used to walk in the shade with my blues on parade."

He was high from sex and eager to get back to Muhammad, to make love again. Everything felt right in his world at that moment. Everything felt light, airy, hopeful, and positive.

He was putting his toothbrush away when the door quietly opened and Salim stepped in.

"I'm not interrupting anything, am I?" Salim asked, closing the door behind him.

Coming from Salim, it was an odd sort of question. Bilal frowned at him.

Salim stood behind him and addressed Bilal's reflection in the mirror. "I need you to help me, Bilal. I'm not feeling so good."

He rubbed his hardness against Bilal's buttocks, closed his eyes, and pulled Bilal into an embrace.

Bilal stared in the mirror. He watched the joy drain from his face.

Salim reached around the front of Bilal's pajama top, undid the buttons, pulled the fabric away, and tossed it on the floor. Then he went for the pajama bottoms, pushing them down.

Bilal closed his eyes. His belly wrenched into a knot, and he was finding it hard to breathe. Why couldn't he just tell his brother to stop? Tell his brother he didn't want to do this anymore? Why did he have to accept this torment in silence?

Salim rubbed against Bilal and pushed down his own pajama bottoms. He got lotion from the medicine cabinet, slicked himself up, and thrust himself inside Bilal's body, pinning him to the sink.

"Do you have to?" Bilal asked quietly. "Hakim's going to walk in and see us."

"He's sleeping," Salim said, moving his hips quickly back and forth.

Bilal gripped the sink and fought to catch his breath.

"It hurts," he said, glancing at Salim in the mirror. "I don't want you to do this."

Salim stopped and looked at him in the mirror. "Is that what you told Muhammad?"

Bilal grew wide-eyed with terror.

"I saw you and Muhammad go off to the bathroom," Salim said in a low voice.

Bilal felt his gut twist inside him.

Salim stared at him coldly. "I'm not exactly sure what I heard at the bathroom door, but it sounded like two people were doing something in there. Do you know what that might be about?"

Bilal wanted to die. Did Salim know what they had done?

"Do you know what that might be about, Bilal?" Salim asked more aggressively.

Bilal lowered his eyes. His face said everything there was to say, told Salim everything he needed to know.

Salim continued to fuck him, giving Bilal a hateful look now. He became rough, slamming his hips against Bilal as if he meant to hurt him.

"I can tell that nigger's been fucking you, hasn't he?"

Bilal refused to look at him.

"I thought you promised me you were going to stay away from that business. Isn't that what you promised me?"

Bilal grimaced as his brother punctuated his question with a quick, painful thrust. Strange pain, sharp and stabbing, spread through Bilal's lower back.

"Stop it," Bilal said. He reached behind him to push futilely at Salim's hip. "You're hurting me!"

"Were you and Muhammad having sex in that bathroom, Bilal?" Salim asked.

Bilal didn't answer.

"Did you let him fuck you? Is that what you did, Bilal?"

"Who gives a shit?" Bilal demanded.

"I do," Salim said.

"It's not your business what I do!"

"Oh, but it is, and don't you forget it."

Salim banged his hips against Bilal's buttocks, and the pain Bilal was experiencing increased dramatically—he felt like something had ripped inside his body. With every thrust of Salim's hips, he felt sharp, agonizing pain. He gripped the sink with both hands, feeling like he was going to throw up. Salim finally came, groaning and gasping, his fingers digging into the flesh of Bilal's hips.

Salim removed himself, pulled up his pajama bottoms, and stared at Bilal in the mirror.

Bilal put his hand to his backside, feeling that something was terribly wrong. His fingers came away with blood on them.

Salim made him turn around. "You're like a cheap whore who throws her legs up for every goddamned hard-on that walks by, aren't you, Bilal? Now, I told you not to betray me, didn't I?"

"I'm bleeding," Bilal said, not looking at him.

"I told you not to shame this family, didn't I?"

Bilal began to sob.

"I told you this was not acceptable, didn't I? I guess you didn't hear what I said. I guess I'm going to have to work harder to make myself understood."

Salim smacked Bilal full across the face, causing his head to spin to one side.

"Ow!" Bilal exclaimed, both startled and hurt.

"Are you understanding now?" Salim asked. "Or is there still something that's not clear to you?"

"Stop it!" Bilal cried.

Salim struck him again. "You think I'm going to sit by and let other people fuck my little brother? You think you can go into some nigger's bathroom and let him touch you like that?"

Bilal screamed, hoping to wake Hakim.

Now Salim gave Bilal the back of his hand, sending Bilal's face hurtling in the other direction. Several more blows followed in quick succession—Salim was in a complete rage now.

"Are you listening to me?" Salim bellowed. "Do I have to teach you the hard way about what is and what is not acceptable in this family?"

Salim slapped him again.

"Would you stop it?" Bilal yelled, his face ablaze with pain. The taste of blood was on his lips.

"Well, what am I supposed to do, Bilal? Obviously, talking to you doesn't work. Obviously, you're not getting the point here. You think you can mock the words of Allah? Didn't you promise me that you were going to keep away from this perversion? And now you're going to mock me by going off with that boy into the bathroom and letting him fuck you?"

"Why don't you leave me alone?" Bilal cried, daring now to raise his eyes. "It's not your business what I do. You have no right to punish me. I'm not your fucking property. All I have to do is tell the police what you're doing, and you'll go to jail."

The unexpected act of defiance surprised Salim, who gaped at Bilal as if he might not have heard properly. Then a hard coldness stole over his features. "Tell the police?" he repeated. "You're going to tell the police? You think that's what you're going to do, you four-eyed piece of shit?"

Salim's voice grew dangerously quiet. He walked out of the bathroom. Before Bilal could gather his thoughts, Salim returned with the switch. "You're going to tell the fucking police on me?" he asked very quietly.

Bilal stared at him, at the switch, and glanced at the door. If only he could get past Salim and escape to the Imam's house.

Salim gave him a dirty look, as if the sight of Bilal disgusted him. He raised the switch and brought it down sharply, catching Bilal across the shoulder.

Bilal screamed, jerked away, and made a dash for the door. Salim grabbed Bilal with one hand and, with the other, loosed a hail of blows on Bilal's back, shoulders, and buttocks.

The bathroom door banged open and Hakim charged in. Salim continued to strike Bilal, screaming at the top of his lungs about Allah's wrath and retribution.

Hakim snatched the switch away, only to have Salim turn on him.

Bilal gasped and tried to catch his breath, only vaguely aware of his brothers punching and screaming at each other. Salim grabbed Hakim's head and smashed it against the wall. Hakim fell backward in a daze. Salim whirled around immediately—Bilal saw him coming and could nothing more than scream. Salim gripped Bilal's left hand and began to twist it, staring into Bilal's eyes with undisguised fury.

"You're going to turn me into the police? Is that what you think you're going to do, you four-eyed faggot?"

The pain in Bilal's wrist quickly became excruciating.

"Stop it!" Bilal pleaded, trying to twist out of Salim's grip.

"You're going to defy me, you fucking piece of shit?" Salim bellowed.

"You're hurting me!"

"Is this what Papa died for, so you could go to America and be a stupid faggot?" Salim demanded.

"Stop it!"

"You're not the one who had to watch Papa die, are you?" Salim asked, glaring at Bilal. "You're not the one who listened to him scream, are you? You're not the one who was there when they blew his fucking brains out, were you, you little four-eyed faggot? What do you know about pain? Crying all the time about every goddamned thing—well, I'll give you something to cry about, won't I?"

Salim twisted Bilal's wrist even further, and Bilal saw white-hot flashes of light streak across his field of vision.

"Is this what I get?" Salim demanded. "I can't take a wife because of you and your fucking tuition and fucking school uniforms, and you're going to turn me into the police! Well, you can go to hell, you ungrateful son of a bitch! You can fucking rot in Gehenna with the Iraqi pigs that killed Papa!"

Salim wrenched Bilal's wrist violently, and something snapped.

Salim balled his free hand into a fist and punched Bilal, sending him sprawling to the bathroom floor. Bilal's mind spun into blackness.

When Bilal regained consciousness, he was lying on his side by the bathtub. His left arm lay at an odd angle on the floor, and one of the bones in his wrist was protruding from the skin. Blood pooled on the carpet. He was aware of Hakim hovering somewhere nearby, screaming for Salim to get a towel.

"Bi?" Hakim said in a quaking voice. "We've got to wrap this in a towel to stop the bleeding. You listening to me? Do you hear me? It's going to hurt a little, but we've got to do it. Do you hear me?"

Bilal found Hakim's face and brought his eyes into focus. He didn't want to move his wrist—it was throbbing with a terrible sort of pain—but Hakim had to lift it so he could get the towel around it.

"Come on," Hakim. "We've got to do this."

Bilal let out a small scream as his wrist was lifted. An angry bolt of pain shot up his arm. Hakim worked quickly, wrapping the towel around the wrist to try to staunch the flow of blood. When he was finished, he helped Bilal sit up and lean against the tub.

The door to the bathroom opened, and Bilal saw his mother standing there, looking at the three of them in horror.

"Ma!" Bilal said, crying out to her.

"What's wrong with Bi?" she asked.

"He's all right," Salim said angrily.

"No, he's not all right," Hakim said. "You broke his hand, you fucking moron."

"Broke his hand?" Mrs. Abu repeated. She ignored Salim's angry gaze and knelt down to look at Bilal. There was a lot of blood on the floor. Hakim's hands were bloody from trying to help. And Bilal himself was ashen—he was clearly in shock. She held her head in her hands, refusing to let her eyes believe what they were seeing.

"He raped me, Ma," Bilal said feebly.

"What is this about?" Mrs. Abu asked, looking up at Salim.

"It's none of your goddamned business," Salim said coldly, glaring at her.

"He raped me," Bilal said again.

"Like Muhammad raped you?" Salim snarled. "Is that the story, you piece of shit? When you were bending over and letting that nigger fuck you, was he raping you too? Who else has been raping you these days?"

Bilal felt despair suffuse his body like poison.

"What is this about?" Mrs. Abu asked again.

"He was having sex with that nigger in his bathroom while the rest of us were eating," Salim said.

"But what is he talking about?" she said, looking from Hakim to Salim. "What is this about rape?"

"Oh, it doesn't hurt," Salim said dismissively. "He's always whining about every goddamned thing."

"So you did? You violated your little brother?"

"What difference does it make?" Salim asked. "Everybody is fucking him—why shouldn't I do it too? The little faggot likes it."

Bilal began to tremble. Hakim gripped his wrist tightly and clenched his teeth together—he was now very angry.

"What happened to his hand?" Mrs. Abu asked.

"Why don't you ask Salim?" Hakim spat.

She turned to look at him, but Salim wouldn't look at her.

"Tell me you didn't do this," she said quietly. "Please, Allah, how could I raise a son like you?"

"Ma, don't start," Salim said.

"I want to know what happened!"

Hakim cursed under his breath. "Your wonderful son Salim twisted Bilal's arm until it made a popping noise and blood started spurting out."

A stricken look came over her face, and she put her hand to her throat.

"He has to go to the hospital," Hakim said, looking over his shoulder again at Salim. "Do you hear me?"

"We don't have any money," Salim said.

"Well, this is an emergency. We should call an ambulance."

"They charge for that," Salim said.

"Well, then we'll get a cab."

"We don't have any money," Salim said again.

"Well, what then—do you want him to walk?" Hakim was exasperated.

"Oh, it's not that bad," Salim said dismissively. "He's a sissy, fucking crying all the time about every goddamned little thing. I'm sick of him."

"He's got to go to the hospital!" Hakim exclaimed.

"And I suppose you're going to pay the bill," Salim said, giving him a dirty look.

"He has to go! We have to get him dressed. Where are his sweats?"

"Get out," Salim said to Mrs. Abu.

"Why?" Mrs. Abu demanded, angry. "He needs my help! What's wrong with you?"

"I'm not going to have you looking at him while he's naked," Salim snapped.

"He's my son!" she snapped back at him. "He's bleeding! Look what you did to his back!"

Bilal could not see it, but his back and shoulders were covered with welts, some of which had begun to bleed. He was also bleeding from the rectum.

"You're such an idiot!" Hakim exclaimed, glaring up angrily at Salim. "Has anyone told you that lately? You're worried about Ma looking at his little dick—are you totally out your mind? I'm sick to death of this fucking Muslim madness, your fucking rules, your fucking regulations, your fucking mad mullahs!"

"That's spoken like the fucking *kafir* pig you are!" Salim shouted back angrily.

"Remind me someday to get a gun so I can put it in your mouth and pull the trigger," Hakim said.

"You shut your fucking mouth!" Salim shouted.

"You make me!"

A shouting match rose like a squall, and Bilal could stand it no more. He'd had all he could take. He began to cry. Then, suddenly, he began to scream. It was a wounded, desperate sound that welled up from deep within him and could not be silenced. He was so frightened, so overwhelmed, in so much pain, that all he could do was howl and shriek until he suddenly settled back against the tub and fell utterly still.

The doorbell rang. The sound of it startled Salim, Hakim, and Mrs. Abu, who were gaping at Bilal.

Bilal opened his eyes and looked around the bathroom. He was losing track of time; he was beginning to feel as if he was outside his own body.

"Who the hell is that?" Salim bellowed.

"I called the Imam," Fatima shouted from the living room.

Within moments, Imam Malik strode into the bathroom. His large presence seemed to occupy even more space in the crowded bathroom.

"What in the name of Allah is going on here?" the Imam demanded. He crouched down to look at Bilal, who glanced at him briefly, then closed his eyes.

"Why the hell did you call him?" Salim asked in Kurdish when Fatima peered into the room.

"Because someone needs to take him to the hospital, you idiot," Fatima replied.

"I didn't give you permission to call anyone!"

"Well, it's too late now, isn't it?" she said.

The Imam stood up. "Fatima, get a blanket."

In seconds, she fetched one and handed it to him.

He used it to cover Bilal. "Bilal, can you hear me?"

Bilal opened his eyes and looked up at him.

"I'm calling the police," Malik said.

"Fatima, tell him it was an accident," Salim said.

She hesitated. Everything was about to come undone.

"Tell him, goddamn it!" Salim snapped.

"Why should I lie for you?" she demanded.

"Because I'll fucking kill you if you don't."

"He raped me," Bilal said softly, opening his eyes again.

"What did you say?" the Imam asked.

"He raped me," Bilal repeated, louder now, some of the wind coming back to him.

"You shut the fuck up!" Salim shouted.

The Imam got swiftly to his feet, whirled around and strode right up to Salim until their noses were almost touching.

"Get away from me," Salim said in English. There was a bit of fear and uncertainty in his voice.

"Or what?" the Imam demanded. "You think you're going to do to me what you did to this boy here? Is that what you think?"

Salim began to smile.

"Fatima, call the police," Malik said, not taking his eyes away from Salim.

Salim laughed. "Yes, call police," he said in English. "You like that—you want call police?"

Malik stared at him.

"Tell him," Salim said in English, looking at Bilal. "Tell him what you do—the bathroom, your friend. Tell him. Yes, tell him, Bilal. Tell him what you do, you faggot."

"What's he talking about?" Imam Malik asked.

"Your son fucking my brother. Raping my brother."

Malik frowned.

Salim nodded. "Yes. The bathroom. Fucking. You know, fucking? Your bathroom. Fucking. We eat, we talk, your son fucking my brother."

Salim made an obscene gesture with his hands, as if to make sure the point was absolutely clear.

Imam Malik looked at Bilal, who closed his eyes. He was so ashamed of himself that he wished he could die.

"Bilal, what is this?" the Imam asked.

"Yes," Salim said, seeing an opening. "You make trouble? You want call police? Okay! Everybody know your son fucking my son—I mean, fucking my brother. Yes, everybody know. You want?"

"Are you threatening me?" Imam Malik demanded angrily, turning to glare at Salim.

Salim grinned, nodding his head. "You tell police, I tell mosque. Trouble for me, trouble for you, no? You want? You want like that? Your son—Muhammad—the pig. The pig fucking my brother. I tell all people. You tell about me. I tell about you. Muhammad, faggot. Bilal, faggot. Fucking, fucking, fucking, like the animal."

Imam Malik's jowls quivered with rage.

In Kurdish, Salim said, "Fatima, tell him I don't want my family shamed, just as he doesn't want his family shamed. But if he wants to make trouble for me, I'll make trouble for him. Tell him if those men at the mosque knew what his son was doing with another boy during an *iftaar* feast, they would ask for his resignation. If he can't rule his own home, how can he rule anything else?"

She translated.

Imam Malik backed away from Salim, shook his head, and knelt by Bilal. He took a cell phone out of his pants pocket and dialed 911.

Salim watched him, a little less certain of himself now. He said nothing while Imam Malik spoke to the emergency operator—giving details of the situation, providing the Abu family's address, explaining who he was.

When he was finished, he put the phone back in his pocket, stood, and turned to Fatima. "Fatima, tell your brother that Bilal needs to go to the hospital. He needs treatment. I'm not going to say a word about what went on here—that's not my place. It's up to you and your family to decide whether you want to notify the police and file charges, not me. But this boy needs to go to the hospital, and I'm going to make sure that he does."

After Fatima conveyed the Imam's words, Salim said, "He's afraid I'm going to tell people his son is a faggot. He's afraid he's going to lose his job. Well, he should be."

When Fatima had translated for him, the Imam was silent. Salim continued to smirk, enjoying himself. Imam Malik did not look at him, but crouched next to Bilal and offered him a sly, conspiratorial smile.

"Did you rape him?" Hakim asked quietly in Kurdish, looking at Salim.

"He's a fucking liar," Salim said.

"I am not," Bilal said, turning his attention from the Imam to his brother.

"And anyway, it doesn't hurt—you're just exaggerating," Salim said dismissively.

"Just like it didn't hurt when those Iraqi pigs raped you?" Bilal sneered.

Salim put a hand to his face, and something odd passed over his features.

"When you were bent over that table and they were fucking you like a dog, do you mean to tell me that it didn't hurt?" Bilal hissed. "Are you just exaggerating? Is that it? Do you think it feels any different to me when you're doing the same damned thing? You think it doesn't hurt? You think I like it?"

"You let that nigger fuck you!" Salim cried, losing his smugness.

"So what!" Bilal shot back. "That's not the same thing and you know it, and it's not your business anyway."

"Everything is my business!" Salim said.

"Good—you can explain yourself to the police, then, because I'm turning you in and I don't care what happens to you. You can sit down and tell them all your 'business.'"

"No one's going to the police," Hakim said, turning to look at Bilal. "That isn't how we do things."

"To hell with how we do things!" Bilal said.

"We'll take care of this, but we're not going to the police," Hakim said. "This is not just about you, Bilal. It's about this whole family. If you go to the police, you could get us all put out on the street. You'll bring shame on all of us."

Bilal glared hatefully at Hakim. "So he can do what he wants and to hell with me?"

"Salim is going to keep his hands to himself from now on," Hakim said, "and you're going to keep your mouth shut, and that's the way it's going to be."

"You're not in charge of this family," Salim said.

"And you won't be either, if you go to jail for child abuse," Hakim observed.

There was an uncomfortable silence.

Finally, Hakim looked at Bilal and said, "If they ask you what happened, you're going to tell them it was an accident. You're going to keep your mouth shut. You are not going to put this family at risk and get the police involved in our lives. I want your promise."

Bilal glowered at Hakim. He did not want to make a promise he knew he was not going to keep.

"I want your promise," Hakim said again.

"Fine. I'll tell them it was an accident," Bilal said.

A few hours later, at the hospital, a doctor walked into the small private room that Bilal had been assigned. The doctor shut the door behind him and gave Bilal a long once-over with his eyes. Then he sat on a stool next to the bed, looking carefully at Bilal's face, touching his cheeks and lips and gently turning his face back and forth.

"I'm Doctor Damian," the man said. "How are you feeling now, son?"

Bilal shrugged. His hand had been put into a cast—a nurse with frizzy hair had told him he probably wasn't going to be able to play a violin for a long time. The rectal bleeding presented a more difficult problem. The emergency room doctor had given him something for the pain and said that surgery was probably going to be in order.

Bilal lay on his side. Dr. Damian pulled back the blanket, moved the hospital johnny out of the way, and looked at Bilal's back and buttocks.

"What happened to you, son?" he asked quietly.

Bilal looked over his shoulder and past the doctor. Through the small pane of glass, he saw Salim's shoulder. He had told the paramedics that he'd been fighting with his brother and had fallen down, breaking his hand and hurting his stomach. He told them it was an accident—just like he had promised Hakim.

When Bilal didn't answer, the doctor closed Bilal's gown and pulled up the blanket. He was an older man, graying at the temples, with bright, clear eyes. But there was a look of unmistakable sadness on his face. "Look, son, I've seen a lot of injuries in my day, and I can tell when a person falls down, and I can tell when someone's been beaten, and I know the difference. Heck, the nurses walking around here would know the difference. Now, son, do you want to tell me what's going on?"

Bilal lay still and turned his head away.

"Are you afraid to tell me?" the doctor asked. "You're not going to be punished. You're not going to be kicked out of the country. You didn't do anything wrong. If you're afraid, just tell me and I'll make some arrangements."

Bilal didn't answer.

"Son, let me tell you this. From your face, I can tell you've been slapped around or punched. From your back, I can tell you've been beaten with what appears to be a stick or a long piece of metal. You also have other marks on your body that are suspicious—burn marks, it looks like, and cuts from something like a razor or a knife. There are also other welts, fading now, maybe from a previous beating. Now with your wrist, I can tell that you didn't fall down and break it. Somebody twisted it, and they twisted it until it broke. From the rectal bleeding, well, I have my suspicions. One doesn't get a tear in that area by falling down, son. It suggests to me that maybe you were molested, that maybe somebody did something to you. Now, if you want to tell me what's going on, it'll be confidential. If you need help, I can get you police protection. It's my duty as a physician, when I see these sorts of injuries, to intervene, to say something, to try to help. Can't you look at me, son, while I'm talking to you?"

Bilal turned his head and looked at the doctor.

"Do you want my help?"

Bilal shrugged.

The doctor was not happy with this response. "You do understand me? You speak English, yes?"

Bilal nodded.

The doctor frowned, then shook his head. "Is this some sort of family thing? You want to protect your family? Are you afraid they might take you away from your family?"

Bilal nodded, just slightly.

Again the man frowned. "Okay, son. I'm going to call these gentlemen in, and we're going to have a talk. I suppose I ought to tell you up front that I'm required by Missouri law to intervene, to notify the police, who will conduct an investigation to determine what's going on here. This will be done for your own safety. I can't release you from this hospital unless I know that you'll be safe when you go home."

"It was an accident!" Bilal said. Panic seized him, and he sat up in the bed.

"You're lying to me. You know it, and I know it."

"But I don't want to be sent away from my family," Bilal said.

"And I doubt that will happen," the man replied. "If someone in your immediate family is physically or sexually abusing you, then that person will probably be removed from your home environment. That's how it works. It's not likely a judge will want to take you away from your family, son. That only happens in extreme cases."

Bilal clutched the blanket to his chest and said, "Don't tell them I told you anything—I don't want to get in trouble. I promised them I wouldn't say anything. Now they're all going to be angry at me!"

"Never you mind about that," the doctor said. "I'm going

to tell them what I'm required by law to do—and then we're going to do it. We're going to take good care of you, and I don't want you to be worrying. Okay? Now, the fact of the matter is, I've already notified the police, and they're waiting outside. So we're all going to have a talk now. Okay? Let me handle this, son. You don't need to say a word."

The doctor went to the door and asked Salim, Hakim, and the Imam to come into the room. They were followed by two police officers. Salim glanced at the officers nervously.

They all gathered at the foot of Bilal's bed.

"Now again, who are you?" the doctor asked Imam Malik.

"My name is Imam Malik Jackson. I'm the boy's pastor, though we don't use that word. The family doesn't have a car, so they asked me to bring Bilal to the hospital. I'm a resident psychiatrist at the Missouri Medical Center."

"So you're familiar with mandatory reporting?" the doctor then asked.

The Imam nodded. The same sly smile he had given Bilal earlier played across his lips again.

"And do you know what's going on here?"

"I'm not in a position to say," Malik said.

The doctor turned to Salim. "Tell me again, Mr. Abu, what happened?"

Salim cleared his throat nervously. "He fell."

"He fell," the doctor said, nodding his head. "He fell. Now, Mr. Abu, that's very interesting, because I've treated all sorts of patients with all sorts of injuries, and if I didn't know better, I'd say he *did not* fall. I'd say something else happened. In fact, I might bet my professional career on it."

The unfamiliar setting, the language barrier, and the presence of the police dampened Salim's usual arrogance. He made no reply to the doctor's statement and lowered his gaze.

The doctor continued. "Mr. Abu, it's very interesting. If I didn't know better, I'd say your brother was beaten. With a stick, maybe—something sharp, maybe a long piece of metal. Beaten with such force that the skin was broken in several places. Do you know anything about that?"

"I don't understand," Salim said quietly.

"The marks on his back," the doctor said. "He's got seventeen welts on his back. Going from his back down to his buttocks and the backs of his legs. A lot of other wounds on his body too that are highly suspicious—burn marks, cuts. I don't think he got all of them by falling down. Do you know anything about that?"

Salim looked confused, and Bilal had to translate.

"He like cut," Salim said in English, making cutting gestures. "He like do. By himself."

"By himself?" the doctor repeated.

Salim nodded.

"So he made all those marks himself, did he? He's a cutter. Is that it? Likes to hurt himself, cut his body, things like that?"

Salim nodded. Bilal shifted nervously in the bed where he sat.

"Tell me again about the wrist, then. You say he fell, struck his hand on the edge of the bed?"

Salim nodded.

"And somehow, while he fell, he also wound up with anal tearing?"

Salim looked lost, and Bilal translated again.

"Is that what you say happened?" the doctor pressed.

Salim nodded, licking his lips and looking uncomfortable.

"Well, that's interesting, Mr. Abu. You want to know why that's so interesting?"

Salim bit his lip.

"It's interesting because when you break a bone, well, each break is different. I can look at an X-ray of a broken bone and tell you right away how it probably happened. If you fall down and strike the bone directly, you get a certain sort of break. You follow me? Now, what's so interesting is that I don't see that sort of break here. What I see is the sort of break that comes from twisting. Let's suppose for the sake of argument that someone twisted his arm a bit too far. That's what I'm seeing here. Now of course, I'm sure none of you twisted his arm until it broke. I mean, that would be illegal—reckless endangerment of a child, bodily assault, assault and battery, domestic violence, child abuse. Of course, nothing like that is going on here, is it?"

Hakim and Salim were mute as statues.

"What is he saying?" Salim finally asked, looking at Bilal, who tried to translate as best he could.

Salim's face went ashen. Hakim began to smirk.

"Now it's a damned shame," the doctor said quietly, "that the patient won't tell me what really happened. He's trying to protect you. Or someone. And I think he's doing that because he's afraid of you, afraid of what you might do to him if he tells the truth. But the plain fact of the matter is that his injuries are so suspicious that he doesn't need to say a word to me or anyone else in this hospital—they speak for themselves. Someone beat this boy, and if I'm not mistaken, someone raped him and someone broke his wrist. Now, I'm required by Missouri law, Mr. Abu, to investigate this matter. I'm going to keep Bilal here at the hospital. I'm going to ask you gentlemen to please leave—you'll not be permitted to see Bilal again until we've figured out what's going on here. These police officers are here to ask you some questions so that we can get to the bottom of things. I do hope you'll cooperate."

Salim looked at Bilal, confusion in his eyes. Imam Malik interposed himself between Bilal and Salim.

"What is he talking about?" Salim demanded.

Bilal translated what the man had said.

"What do you mean, these pigs are going to ask me some questions?"

"It's called mandatory reporting," Bilal replied. "It means that if a child shows up at a hospital with suspicious injuries, they're required by law to investigate."

Salim's face went slack, as the gravity of the situation began to dawn on him. "You knew that, didn't you? You tricked us!"

Bilal nodded his head and smiled.

Hakim gave Bilal a resentful look. "You promised me!"

"I promised you I would tell them that it was an accident. That's what I did."

"But you knew!" Hakim exclaimed.

"So what!" Bilal snapped. "Yes, I knew. So did the Imam. And what were you going to do to help me? Nothing! You were going to let him keep right on hurting me. Well, I'm sick of it, and that closet case isn't going to hurt me anymore."

Salim glanced nervously at the police officers, who sensed trouble was about to erupt. "How could you do this to me?" he asked, giving Bilal a despairing look. "How could you betray your family like this? What the hell's wrong with you?"

"What's wrong with me?" Bilal said, raising his voice angrily. He held up his hand, showing Salim the cast: "This is what's wrong with me—this and a little bit of anal tearing and another set of welts on my back. No, the real question is: What's wrong with you? What's wrong with this family?"

He turned to Hakim. "How can you let him do this stuff to me and not help me? Are you really that worried about what people are going to think? What about what I think? What about someone in this family being loyal to me for a change? Or do I need to start raping people too?"

Hakim looked vexedly between Salim and Bilal. "You're both a fucking disgrace," he said.

Competing emotions played across Salim's face, but mostly he seemed scared. "You tell these people I've done nothing wrong!" he screamed at Bilal. "Don't you shame this family!"

"Mr. Abu, would you come with us please?" one of the officers said, taking Salim by the arm and steering him away from the bed.

"You tell them!" Salim shouted over his shoulder. "You tell them I've done nothing wrong! Don't you betray this family, you fucking faggot! I'll fucking make you pay! I'll fucking kill you!"

"Now, Bilal, we've got several things to do at this point," Dr. Damian said after Salim, Hakim, and the police officers had left, along with Imam Malik. "I know you're not feeling well, and we'll try to be quick about it, okay? We need to get these things done, then you can sleep a bit before you go off to surgery in the morning."

A nurse and two more police officers entered the room. Dr. Damian explained they were there to witness the examination and question him afterward. Bilal stared at all of them, overwhelmed.

"We're going to keep you here for a few days," Dr. Damian said, "and if we haven't figured things out by then, you'll be put in state custody. You probably don't want that to happen, so it might be better for you to just answer our questions and let us help you. Now, are you afraid someone's going to retaliate if you tell on them?"

Bilal hugged his knees to his chest and nodded.

"And does that someone live in your home?"

Bilal nodded again.

"Well, I can see why you're afraid. The most likely thing that's going to happen is that this person will be removed from your home and jailed, if necessary, or ordered by the court to stay away. And if you're so afraid of this person that you don't want to tell us anything, well, son, that tells me that this person is probably one bad apple and somebody needs to do something about him."

Bilal took his eyes away from the doctor. He felt sick to his stomach.

"Now, if you tell us who this person is, we won't waste time chasing our tails," the doctor said. "We'll zero in on the right person, and we'll get to the bottom of it. You might be worried about what's going to happen to that person, but it's really out of your hands now, son. If that person has been breaking the law by physically abusing you, we're going to find that out and deal with him accordingly.

"What we'd like to do now is hear your side of the story and then hear his and then talk to the other people in your family. That way we figure out who's telling the truth—see whose story holds up and whose doesn't. I can make it a little easier for you by telling you that your brother Salim has already raised my suspicions by the way he behaved. I'm not sure what he was saying to you, but he seemed very agitated and upset when the police wanted to talk to him, and that's always a pretty good clue as to who has something to hide. Am I right? Is he the one we ought to be looking at?"

Bilal looked at the four faces staring at him. There was only kindness in all of them. "Yes," he said.

"Do you want to tell what went on this evening, how your hand got broken?"

One of the police officers flipped open a pad of paper and began to take notes.

In a quiet voice, Bilal explained what had happened that evening—from the party at Imam Malik's house and his encounter with Muhammad in the bathroom to Salim's raping him, beating him, and twisting his hand until it broke.

"That tells me that we might have some confused evidence

when we examine it," the doctor said, "but at least we know to watch out for it. Now this other person—what was his name?"

"Muhammad," Bilal said.

"When the two of you were…he wasn't trying to hurt you?"

"Of course not," Bilal said.

"The two of you are very close?"

Bilal nodded.

"And how old is he?"

"The same age as me. Sixteen."

The doctor nodded. "Okay, son. Don't worry about that. The police will need to verify your story with your friend, but it will be nothing more than that. You won't get in any trouble for that, just so you know. You're pretty sure, though, that your friend didn't cause this problem?"

Bilal said he was sure.

"And how long has your brother been doing these sorts of things to you?" the doctor asked.

"Since I was about nine," Bilal answered. He was embarrassed to look at the doctor.

"So this is not an isolated incident?"

Bilal shook his head.

The doctor asked many more questions about Salim's behavior. All the while, the second, Italian-looking police officer watched him while his partner made copious notes.

"We're going to do a PERK on you, now, Bilal—that stands for physical evidence recovery kit," the doctor said. "It's what we do when we suspect there might have been a sexual assault. These police officers are to witness the collection of the evidence and then immediately take that evidence into custody so that it becomes police property. After that, we should be finished for the time being. Okay?"

Bilal nodded.

The nurse opened the evidence kit, which contained many small plastic envelopes and swabs, each labeled. The doctor worked quickly, taking clippings from Bilal's pubic hair, checking under his fingernails, swabbing and bagging evidence gathered from his genitals and anus. The doctor then examined him, pointing out the welts on his back to the police officers and noting the many cuts on various parts of Bilal's body.

"Did you make these cuts, son?" the dark-haired officer asked. He introduced himself as Lieutenant Tarantino. Bilal felt sure he had seen him in the neighborhood around their apartment.

Bilal bit his lip and nodded.

"Your brother had nothing to do with them?" the officer asked.

Bilal shook his head.

"And the burn marks? Your brother didn't do any of those?"

Bilal shook his head again.

Lieutenant Tarantino gave Bilal an encouraging smile. "It's not uncommon," he said. "It's known as cutting, or self-mutilation. It's a way of crying out for help, a way of saying something's wrong in your life and you need someone to notice and pay attention. I think it also suggests a lot of anger, and maybe since you can't take your anger out on your brother, who deserves it, maybe you take it out on yourself."

Bilal frowned. That sounded just about right.

"Now, there's just one thing I'd like to clarify, before we leave," Lieutenant Tarantino said. "I know you must be tired now, so I won't take up your time. When we're talking about sexual abuse, Bilal, we're including all sexual activity that might have occurred between you and your brother, since this is activity happening between an adult and a minor. I guess I want to put your mind at ease on the matter, since the child involved often feels responsible for what happened, or feels like he was a willing participant—especially since the activities are not always painful. Sometimes they're even quite pleasurable, and this can cause a lot of confusion.

"As far as the law is concerned, your brother is an adult, and involving you in any sort of sexual activity, regardless of what it was or whether it hurt or not, is sexual abuse.

"What I'm trying to say is that even if your brother didn't force you to do anything, he's still in the wrong, Bilal, and you have nothing to be ashamed of. I've seen too many kids like you who think they're responsible for what happened, or that it's somehow their fault. But Bilal, it's not about sex at all. It's about an adult abusing his position of authority or trust to use a child for his own gratification, regardless of the harm it might cause. When you get in front of a judge, he doesn't care one way or the other about whether some of it was pleasurable—that's not the point. It's about your brother, who's an adult, taking advantage of you because you're a child."

Bilal listened to the officer's words intently. He did blame himself, didn't he? And he didn't consider all of Salim's behavior to be abusive—it hadn't occurred to him to think of receiving a blow job as sexual abuse. But that's what the man was saying. What had Salim done to him? What was he doing to Salim?

CHAPTER ELEVEN

Bilal fell asleep, only to be roused shortly afterward and prepared for surgery. He was afraid while the nurses prepped him, but they assured him there was nothing to worry about. They offered to explain what the surgery would involve, but he did not want to know. Soon he was gazing up into the masked face of the anesthesiologist and counting backward from ten.

When he woke again, he thought he had just nodded off for a minute, but he was back in his hospital bed, and it was broad daylight. He moved around to try to ease the cramps in his back and saw his mother sitting by the bed. She had obviously been crying.

"Bilal?" she said. "You all right?"

He managed a small smile. "Aren't they going to do the surgery?" For some reason, he thought they had decided not to, and had sent him off to let him rest.

She frowned. "They already did the surgery. This morning. It's almost noon now. The doctor said you should try to lie as still as possible."

Bilal became aware of a pain in his stomach or back—he couldn't quite tell where—and stopped moving. His mouth was dry, and Mrs. Abu got a glass of water for him. The way she looked at him made him feel guilty.

"Was he arrested?" he asked quietly.

His mother nodded.

He settled back on the bed and watched her for a long time. He could see the anger just beneath the surface. "I'm sorry, Ma. I had to tell them the truth."

"I know," she said quietly.

"What happened?"

She shrugged. "I don't really know, Bilal. They questioned your brothers, kept Salim, and told Hakim he was free to go."

"Where's Hakim now?"

She pursed her lips. "He's in the cafeteria with Fatima. Muhammad too, I think—he came this morning to see you."

She lapsed into silence. Bilal searched her face, which was filled with unspoken reproach.

"I said I was sorry, Ma. What did you want me to do?"

She shook her head and put a hand to her throat. "They're not going to kill him, are they?"

"Kill him?" Bilal said, incredulous.

"You know, like when they took your father away."

Bilal shook his head. "No, Ma, they're not going to kill him."

"You never know," she said, not looking at him.

Bilal looked at her carefully. She had an exhausted, haunted look. Bilal tried not to be angry with her. She still didn't know much about American ways. In her experience, when someone was taken away by the police, nothing good would come of it.

"It'll be all right," he said, trying to comfort her. "They do things differently here."

She shrugged and tried to put on a brave face. "The doctor said you could have died without the surgery—you were bleeding internally. A few days, it could have become infected—I forget what he said exactly. He used some big word. You know how they are. So you had to come. And of course, they had to ask questions—I mean, just look at your face. They're smart people, aren't they? It had to happen sooner or later, didn't it?"

Bilal considered this in silence. She was trying to justify things, make sense of them.

"The Imam told me not to worry about the bills," she said. "We'll get by, somehow, he said. I guess we will."

"We will," Bilal replied.

"The Imam's such a nice man, isn't he?"

Bilal nodded.

"Muhammad too. What a nice boy. He was so worried about you, anxious to see you. It's good to have nice friends like that."

It is indeed, Bilal thought.

"Don't listen to me," she said, trying to compose herself. "I'm just a bit worried about things."

She sighed and pulled a tissue from her purse. Her face was pained, uncertain. "Your father would never have treated you this way. Your father always used to call you Honey Bird. You remember that? 'How's my Honey Bird today?' He was so sweet on you."

She fell silent, then put her face into her hands and began to cry.

He let her cry. Eventually, she went to sit by the window. She stared out of it, not speaking, the way she always did when she was upset.

After a while, the door to Bilal's room opened, and Hakim, Fatima, and Muhammad appeared.

"Hey," Muhammad said, smiling.

"Hey," Bilal said.

Hakim glanced at Bilal but did not speak to him and went to sit with his mother.

"How you feeling?" Fatima asked.

"Not so good," Bilal said.

"You don't look so good either. And look at that cast."

Bilal did. It felt strange, heavy, and annoying.

"You've been missing all the fun," Fatima said.

"What fun?"

"Oh, I don't know—police interrogations, evidence collecting, search of the premises, social workers visiting, all of that. Even Muhammad got taken aside and interrogated. Caused quite a stir, you did."

Bilal frowned.

"I'm not complaining," Fatima added, seeing the frown. "It's about time somebody did something."

"What's going on now?"

"He's been arrested. Waiting for his hearing. Denies everything. It's been so quiet at home, we decided to come here so we could get a bit of excitement. Don't know what we're going to do with all that peace and quiet."

"We're going to find out," Bilal said a bit darkly.

"Yeah, and it might be wonderful," Fatima replied. "You did the right thing. It's about time somebody told the truth about something in this family, isn't it?"

She gave Muhammad a knowing look. "Well, I'll just leave you two to get reacquainted." She bounced away, positively beside herself with happy feelings. Bilal felt annoyed.

Muhammad reached out and took Bilal's good hand, being careful with the IV. "I'm glad you're all right, Bilal. I've been worrying myself sick about you. I'm sorry I got you into trouble."

"You got me into trouble?" Bilal asked.

"You know," Muhammad said. "We should have been more careful."

"Why?" Bilal asked. "We weren't hurting anyone. It's nobody's business what we do."

"Well, you know."

Bilal sighed and shook his head. "I'm so tired of having to feel ashamed of myself. We didn't do anything wrong. We didn't hurt anybody."

"I know," Muhammad said again.

Hakim left his mother by the window and stood at the foot of Bilal's bed. Muhammad, without needing to be told, excused himself, leaving Bilal alone to stare up at Hakim.

Bilal swallowed dryly. His brother didn't look happy. Not one bit.

"I'm sorry," Bilal said.

Hakim said nothing. His eyes were full of confusion, hurt, and uncertainty.

"I didn't mean for any of this to happen," Bilal said. "I know you're mad at me, but what could I do?"

"I'm not mad at you," Hakim said quietly.

"Well, why are you looking at me like that?"

"I guess I didn't really understand, until the police started questioning me, how serious all of this is, how much he was hurting you. I keep asking myself why I didn't help you. You asked me to help you, and I didn't. I told you to stick up for yourself, like that was going to solve the problem. Now Salim's in jail, and I'm the oldest male in the household, and I'm supposed to take care of things. What a lot of crap that is."

"Better you than him," Bilal said.

Hakim looked haggard. "Well, I've been asking myself what it means to take care of you, to take care of this family. Salim was always in charge, you know. My opinion was never asked for, never wanted. So I never gave it much thought. But anyway, if I'm going to be in charge of this family, there's going to be no more arguing, no more hitting, no more people getting hurt. I guess I have to ask myself why I've been sitting back and doing nothing about it all this time. What kind of person does that make me?"

Bilal went home on a Saturday morning. The house seemed much larger—in a not entirely comfortable way—without Salim's presence.

Hakim and Fatima went to the market. Mrs. Abu drew a bath and made Bilal sit while she used a sponge to wash his back and gently wipe his shoulders. He could not sit properly—he had to lean to one side—but his pain was lessening.

He looked up at her. He studied the lines on her face, the gray hair she kept swept back from her forehead and tied with a string. She had prominent, proud cheekbones and clear, gray eyes. But she seemed withdrawn and less certain of herself in the aftermath of all the drama. Bilal thought she seemed to be shrinking.

"Does it hurt?" she asked, patting his cast, which lay on the rim of the tub.

He nodded. "A little, but it's not too bad."

She had him raise his arms so she could wash beneath them.

"Your father would never do this. Your father never laid a hand on you kids, not like this."

Bilal said nothing.

His mother gently wrung water from the sponge to rinse the suds from Bilal's shoulders and back, the way she had once done years ago, when he was much younger.

"Ma, what am I going to do?" he asked.

"About what?"

"About what I am."

She hesitated for a moment. Water dripped from the faucet. "And what are you?" she asked, resuming her task.

"You know what I am. Everybody knows."

She was silent and regarded him intently. Then she started rinsing his back again. "Well, of course, you're different," she said quietly. "We all know that. But someday you'll find a girl. You'll see."

"No, I won't," Bilal said. "You're not listening to me, Ma. I'm not interested in girls, and I never will be."

She had nothing to say to this.

"I don't want you to be ashamed of me, Ma," he said. "You know I don't want to shame the family. But I have to tell the truth. I can't keep lying all the time."

"You can always tell me everything," she said gently. "Whatever it is, Bi. It's your father, isn't it?"

Bilal looked at her, uncomprehending.

"Your father," she repeated. "You miss your father. So do I, Bi. Not a day goes by…"

"What's that got to do with anything?" he asked.

"You miss him. I've often heard folks say that if a boy grows up without his father, he'll be unnatural. He'll want to go… look for his father…in other men—something like that."

Bilal gave her an exasperated look.

"That's what they say," she said primly. She washed his hair, using a plastic bowl to scoop up water and pour it over his head. Then she used the sponge to wash his left arm, all the way down to the cast, being careful not to get the cast wet.

"Are you ashamed of me?" he asked.

"Why should I be?"

"Because I'm a faggot," he said. He expected her to wince, but she did not.

"You don't know that," she said, pausing to look at him directly.

"Yes, I do."

"You're too young to be worried about that."

"Ma."

"You are," she said.

"Ma, the boys at school have been talking about girls for years now, and I'm the only one who isn't interested. I'm sixteen. Girls don't excite me."

"Well, what does?" she asked, perplexed.

"Muhammad Jackson," Bilal said. "Every time I see him I know what Nu is talking about when he says he wants to get his hands on Britney Spears's tits."

"You shouldn't talk like that," she said. Now she winced.

"I'm just telling you, Ma. It's not like every guy makes me horny. Just some of them. Like Muhammad."

"Well, he is good-looking, isn't he?" she said.

"He certainly is," Bilal said. "He makes me want to take my clothes off and jump into bed with him."

"Bilal!" she exclaimed.

"Well, he does, Ma. That's what I mean. Girls don't interest me. Guys make me crazy. And I don't want to be this way, but I can't stop it, and I don't know what to do about it. I hate myself. I hate being this way. But what can I do?"

She offered a long, weary sigh. "Bilal, it just isn't done. A man takes a wife, makes his own family. He becomes a husband, a father. But two men together? It just isn't done, Bilal. It's unnatural. It's wrong. You're just going to get yourself into a lot of trouble if you try to do it that way. You need to think about getting married, taking a wife."

"How can I take a wife when girls don't interest me?"

"Well, we all have to make sacrifices," she said quietly.

Bilal rolled his eyes, and for a moment they sat in silence.

"Would you still love me, Ma, if I really was gay?" he asked, looking up into her eyes.

She looked astonished. "Really! How can you ask me a question like that?"

"I need to know, Ma."

"Bilal! What's wrong with you?"

"Ma, I want to know. Would you?"

She pursed her lips. Instead of answering his question, she changed the subject. "Do you remember how your father used to call you Honey Bird? All the time, Honey Bird this, Honey Bird that. He said you were like dipping a finger in the honey jar—so sweet. At the mosque you were so well-behaved. Everyone thought you were a little angel—your teachers, all the parents in the neighborhood. Everyone liked you. Your father didn't have any nicknames for the others, but for you, it was always Honey Bird. 'How's my Honey Bird today?' 'Honey Bird's gone to school.' 'Where's that Honey Bird of mine?' Do you remember that?"

Bilal felt his lower lip tremble. He could hear his father's voice in the back of his mind. *You been good today, Honey Bird?*

He remembered that his father had a desk where he sat to write his Friday sermon. Bilal remembered how—he must have been five or six—he used to stand in front of the desk and then duck his head. His father would say, 'Oh, Honey Bird's gone away! Where did that Honey Bird go?' Bilal would dart up, catch his father's gaze, then dart back down. His father never tired of the game.

The memory of it made Bilal's heart ache. In the chaos of his father's death and their escape from Iraq, they had never had time to mourn him properly. They were too busy surviving.

His mother smiled. "He was so fond of you. He never played favorites, but he was fond of you, and he thought the world of you. Salim and Hakim were always fighting, you know. Like two bear cubs, two little wolves, always fighting over every little thing. Drove me to distraction. But you, when you came along, you were just a sweetheart.

"Salim loved you too, you know. He was crazy about you—crazy about his baby brother. He liked to help feed you, and he was always dragging you around, trying to get you to play with him. He was so proud—he'd tell everybody. 'This is my baby brother. Lay a hand on him, and I'll kill you!' That's the way he was."

She fell silent, and Bilal looked carefully at her face. When she started talking about the old days, it meant she was tired—tired of the struggle in America. Tired of not being able to speak English, of not being able to get along properly. Tired of the daily battle just to survive.

A long silence passed as they finished Bilal's bath.

His mother helped him dress, then he lay down on the sofa in the living room to take a nap. She sat with him, holding his hand.

"Ma, you didn't answer my question. Would you still love me if I was gay?"

He expected her to tell him not to be so silly, that of course she would love him. But she said nothing, and turned away with a fretful look on her face.

"I need to check on supper," she said abruptly. She rose and went into the kitchen to check a pot of rice she had put on the stove a few moments earlier.

CHAPTER TWELVE

On the evening before Salim's hearing, the rest of the Abu family sat at the kitchen table eating dinner, keenly aware of Salim's empty chair. Tomorrow he would either be released or jailed pending his trial—unless someone posted bond on his behalf. After word had gone around the community about the reason for his imprisonment, that was not likely.

"What is this hearing business about anyway?" Mrs. Abu asked, not for the first time.

Fatima rolled her eyes. "Ma, I've told you a million times. You have a hearing. The judge decides if the case warrants a trial or not."

"Yes, but what does that mean?" Mrs. Abu asked impatiently. "I'm not a lawyer, you know."

"It's designed to be fair to the accused," Fatima said. "If the police concoct some story about some guy and want to try him, they have to convince a judge first that the case deserves a trial. They have to present evidence. If the judge sees it's all a setup, he releases the accused and that's that. If he thinks a crime really has been committed, then he sets up a date for the trial."

Mrs. Abu pursed her lips. "Well, that's not how they did it in my day."

"And thank Allah for that," Fatima replied. "Anyway, we'll find out tomorrow what's going to happen."

"If he's released, he's not coming back here, Ma," Hakim said.

Mrs. Abu gaped at him. "Where's he supposed to go?" she asked.

"If he comes here, then the government will start investigating, and Bilal and Fatima will probably be taken away," he said. "It's already bad enough as it is, and I don't want it to get any worse. He'll just have to make it somehow on his own. They've got halfway houses and other things. He'll probably be just fine."

"You can't just leave him to fend for himself," Mrs. Abu said.

"Don't be too sure of that," Hakim replied. The way he said it reminded Bilal of Salim.

"But he's your brother!" she exclaimed.

"And so is Bilal," Hakim replied, looking at her very carefully.

"And what does that mean?" she demanded.

Hakim pushed his plate away from him, interlaced his fingers, and lay his hands on the table. "It means we should have done something a long time ago before it got out of hand," he replied quietly. "It means, Ma, that we should have never let him slap Bilal and Fatima around the way he did. We should have taken responsibility for their safety. We have to stop pretending that this is not a problem. And, *In'shallah,* we will."

"Well, where's he going to stay?" Mrs. Abu pressed.

"Ma, don't!" Hakim snapped angrily. "Just don't start with that crap. He's not staying here. We have my salary. We've got money from the bread. We're going to be fine. If I have to, I'll take another job, maybe part-time, just for some extra money. But we'll get by."

"But he's my son!" she cried, putting her hand to her throat.

"Even so," Hakim said. "If they release him, he's going to have to take care of himself."

There was silence. Bilal and Fatima exchanged wide-eyed looks and waited for either Hakim or their mother to speak again.

"Look," Hakim said, "It's not going to happen—he's not going to get out. There's too much evidence against him, and he's not going to be able to talk his way out of all of it. They have the results of the lab tests they did, and Salim is going to be nailed, and he knows it. He can say what he likes to the judge, but the fact is, his semen was found right where Bilal said it would be found, and they have the medical reports of what Salim did to Bilal that night, and that's the end of the story. So just stop it with this nonsense. There's no point in worrying about it."

"Do you know what they do to guys who go to jail for molesting kids?" Bilal asked, gazing at Hakim.

Hakim regarded him coolly. "It won't be any worse than what he did to you, will it?"

Bilal had nothing to say to that.

"It's all your fault," Mrs. Abu said quietly, turning to look at Bilal. She no longer tried to hide her disgust. "It's all your fault!" she repeated loudly. "Are you happy now? You had to run and tell the police everything, didn't you? And to hell with the consequences! To hell with what happens to the rest of us! Poor little Bilal had to shoot his mouth off because he never thinks about anybody other than himself, just like his miserable little sister. Both of you are Americans—you're not Kurds! Both of you think only of yourselves, always talking about your rights and your feelings and what you want and what you need and the way you think things ought to be. What about this family? What about loyalty to your family? If you had just kept your mouth shut, none of this would be happening. Oh, no, you had to tell the whole world! You had to shame this family, didn't you? Well, I hope you're happy now. And when we can't put food on this table, don't you say a word to me about it. Don't you dare complain to me about an empty stomach."

Bilal gaped at her in disbelief.

"Ma, what in the hell's wrong with you?" Hakim asked.

Fatima, across the table from Bilal, sat back in her chair and regarded her family as if they'd all just sprouted antennae from their heads.

"First my husband, now my son!" Mrs. Abu snapped. "What's next? Are they going to drag me away for being an unfit mother?"

"Ma, I told you to keep your mouth shut," Hakim said angrily. "It's not Bilal's fault. What part of this are you not getting? Salim has been raping him since he was nine years old. Salim told him he would kill him if he said a word to anyone about it. Salim said he was going to rape Fatima—is that what you want? Are you going to defend Salim now? You want him to come back, and we'll just pick up where we left off?"

She would not look at any of them. Her eyes darted about the room and blazed with fury.

"What about me?" Bilal asked, feeling suddenly outraged by his mother. "Don't I count for shit in this family? How would you like it if someone was sticking their dick up your ass all the time?"

"Don't you talk to me like that, you dirty homosexual!" she shouted.

Bilal recoiled as if she had slapped him.

"You think your father would have wanted a homosexual for a son? Is that what you think? At least your brother Salim had enough respect for himself to keep his mouth shut when he took up with men. But you—oh, no, you have to shoot your mouth off and tell the whole world about your perversion. You disgust me! And now, thanks to you, I'm losing my oldest son, and what do I get for it? An effeminate little homosexual who's having sex with other boys and will probably get himself expelled from school. I'm supposed to be happy about that? You're a disgrace to the family. What's next—are you going to go have sex with the neighbor's dog? You've been having sex with everything else from what I hear."

Bilal stared at his mother in astonishment. He wanted, at once, to slap her and to burst into tears.

"Ma, how can you talk like this?" Hakim asked.

"If he didn't like what Salim was doing," she said, "he could have told Salim to stop it. He didn't. Obviously, he liked it. Who's fooling who? Is he going to play the victim now and blame his brother for everything and get him sent away to prison? Well, for what? So they had sex! So what! It's not the end of the world. And look at him! He's in the bathroom having sex with that Muhammad—what a hypocrite!"

Hakim put his face in his hands.

"Ma, you are so full of shit that I'm going to have to put some boots on to wade through it," Fatima said. "I mean, who knew? I thought Salim was the only wacko in this family, but apparently not. Apparently, he learned it from you."

"You watch your smart mouth!" Mrs. Abu yelled.

"Better a smart mouth than a stupid one," Fatima replied.

"You shut up!"

"Ma, get a clue," Fatima said. "Have you, perhaps, spent even so much as one minute pondering the thought that maybe, just maybe, Bilal might be gay because Salim sexually abused him when he was a child? Do you think Bilal woke up one day and said to Salim, 'Hey, Salim, let's have sex? Let's mess up my whole life? Let's see if we can't inflict massive amounts of damage on my emotional and psychological well-being? Yes, go ahead, stick that big penis in my tiny nine-year-old rectum?' Is that how you think it was, Ma? Are you going to blame Bilal because Salim has a thing for little boys? Ma, will you, like, just get a clue? Are you out to lunch here, or what?"

"You and your smart mouth!" Mrs. Abu snapped. "How dare you talk to me like that!"

"Well, wake up, Ma! Stop blaming Bilal for something that's not his fault. What the hell's wrong with standing up and telling the truth once in a while? All we do in this family is lie ourselves to death. Why shouldn't we be sick of it? Bilal's trying to tell you the truth about who he is—would you rather he sit there and lie to you? Why do you have to sit there and ridicule him for telling you the truth?"

"The truth killed your father," Mrs. Abu said, grimacing. "Who the hell cares about the truth? What does it get you?"

Fatima shook her head and waved at her mother dismissively.

"You lost your father because he was more interested in the truth than he was in his family," Mrs. Abu said angrily. "We wouldn't be sitting here today if he hadn't been running his mouth all the time. Now Bilal is going to be running his mouth all the time too, telling the whole world his 'truth.' You want your brother to be a homosexual? Is that what you want, Fatima? You want people to make fun of him? You want this community to shun him? You want people to whisper about him behind his back? You want him to get expelled from school? What is it that you want, Fatima?"

Hakim held up his hands to try to put the brakes on their runaway situation. "Ma, we don't live in Iraq anymore. We don't have to do things like they did in the old days. You don't go around hating and ridiculing people because they're different. People don't do it to you—or at least they shouldn't—and you shouldn't do it to other people. That's what Papa was fighting for. He was fighting those Iraqis who ridiculed us and who decided that we couldn't be what we were. I'm proud of Papa, and I'm proud that Papa stood up to those pigs. And look, your son Bilal is just like him, isn't he? Bilal's going to stand up and tell the truth and to hell with the consequences. You should be proud of him, instead of sitting there and defending Salim."

She glowered at Hakim, but offered no reply.

"You know what I think?" Hakim asked. "I think Salim is no better than those Iraqis pigs who killed Papa. That's what I think. He's a self-righteous prick, and he doesn't care about the people he hurts. He ridicules people. He demands that everybody see the world the way he does, and if you don't, then you're nothing but a fucking *kafir* pig—how many times did he call me that, Ma? What makes him any better than the Iraqis?"

There were a few moments of heavy silence. Then Hakim spoke again. "I'll tell you something else, Ma," he said. "Bilal's not the only one in this family who's a homosexual."

"What are you talking about?" Mrs. Abu asked.

"You don't know, Ma?"

Mrs. Abu stared at Hakim. The frown on her face deepened the lines around her eyes and mouth.

Fatima leaned forward and looked at Hakim intently.

"Don't you remember Salim's friend, Jafar?" Hakim asked.

Mrs. Abu nodded warily.

"Jafar was gay, Ma. And they were friends—they hung out together all the time. And I caught them having sex once. They were just going at it out in the courtyard in the middle of the day. The rest of us were inside because it was hot, and they were out there fucking like dogs."

Mrs. Abu's fury gave way to blank detachment.

"And did you, Ma, perhaps conveniently forget what happened when Papa was arrested? Wasn't he arrested because Salim and Jafar were caught by a member of the secret police who'd seen them raping a little boy in an alley? Did you forget that, Ma?"

She turned her face away from the table.

Fatima, who had never heard this bit of history, looked flabbergasted. Bilal was surprised—that was not the version of the story Salim had told him.

"What about all those other things you're conveniently forgetting, Ma?" Hakim was implacable. "Do you remember Rami? That little kid who lived next door to us? Do you remember his father coming over to our house and talking to Papa about how Salim was forcing that little boy to have sex with him? Do you remember how ashamed we all were? Did you forget that too, Ma?"

Mrs. Abu was completely withdrawn and gazed out the window over the kitchen sink.

Hakim went on. "So, on the one hand you have a hypocrite who's been molesting little kids because he can't be honest about who he is and he's too terrified to go out and have sex with a real man. On the other hand, you have Bilal, who's trying to make Salim stop hurting him—and you're defending *Salim*, Ma? At least Bilal and Muhammad aren't hurting anyone, and at least they have the balls to be honest about what they're doing. That's a lot more than I can say for your son Salim.

"And because of your son Salim, we lost Papa, and now we're all sitting here at this fucking kitchen table in this fucking country. You're going to defend that piece of shit after all he's done to this family? After he led them to Papa? After he hurt those little boys? After what he's done to Bilal? You're just going to sweep all of that under the carpet and forget about it, Ma, and sit here and call Bilal a 'dirty homosexual'? Well, I haven't forgotten, and I never will, and if that pig lays another hand on anyone else, I'll kill him, Ma—I swear to God I'll kill him myself."

There was more silence. No one touched the food, which had long ago grown cold.

"It's not too late," Mrs. Abu said quietly, turning her gaze from the window and back to her children. "Bilal can drop these charges at the hearing tomorrow. Tell them we don't want to proceed. I just want my son to come home. I want my children to be together. We can work these problems out. We can make him get help for himself. We can make sure he doesn't hurt Bilal anymore. I just want our family to be together. Is that so wrong?"

Bilal, Fatima, and Hakim exchanged glances filled with weary disbelief. Was there no end to this?

"Do you know what he said to me today when I visited him at the jail?" she asked. "Do you want to know?"

The three of them looked at her.

"He said he was going to kill himself," she said. "He was going to take his own life—unless these charges were dropped. Is that what you want?"

"What a loser," Fatima said under her breath.

"Ma, he's always talking about killing himself," Hakim said. "What else is new?"

"Yes, but this time he meant it. I could tell, by his eyes. We're all he has—are you going to take that away from him? Are you going to sit back and do nothing and let him go to prison for who knows how many years? And why? Because he was having sex with his brother? He's not exactly the first person to do that."

Bilal stared at the food on his plate. This was typical of Salim, wasn't it? Manipulative. Self-centered. Not a word of apology for his misdeeds. Not a shred of concern for the people he hurt. Only a constant preoccupation with himself.

"Ma, are you listening to what I'm saying?" Hakim asked. "If Salim comes back here, the government people will start investigating, and we'll lose Fatima and Bilal. Is that what you want? Because that's what will happen. We can't change things now. What's done is done. Salim brought all of this on himself, and he has no right to blame anyone else, or to try to make us feel guilty by threatening to kill himself. He has to live with the consequences of his own actions. And it's not like he wasn't warned."

Mrs. Abu put her face in her hands and began to cry. They watched her in silence, for a few moments, then Fatima stood and began to clear the table.

After the table was cleared and the dishes washed, Bilal went to the boys' room, lay down on the bed, and cried some tears of his own. He felt nothing but a deep, bruising shame. It was not his fault that Salim was in jail, yet he blamed himself for getting his brother in trouble. It would not be his fault if Salim took his own life, yet he would blame himself for that too.

He tried unsuccessfully not to think about the fact that his mother and Hakim knew—all those years, they knew—what Salim had done to other boys, and what Salim was doing to him. And they had done nothing to stop it. All the fear he had felt, all the pain, the confusion—and all along, they knew. At any point, they could have stopped it.

His hand in the cast was itching. He banged it against the wall angrily, wishing he could take the damned thing off.

Allah was punishing him for having sex with Muhammad. Allah was swift in His wrath, swift and terrible in His retribution. Bilal had mocked the words of the Quran, mocked the teachings of Islam, had engaged in shameful, perverted acts, and now he was paying the price.

He heard the door open and felt someone sit on the bed. He did not turn to see who it was.

"I'm sorry," his mother said in a weak, hoarse voice.

He did not reply. He suddenly hated her, hated the fact that she was ashamed of him, that she had let him suffer all these years and had done nothing about it.

"I didn't mean those things I said," she said.

He did not answer.

"Bilal, I didn't know what to do!" she exclaimed. "I tried to make him stop. You don't know how many times I pleaded with him to stop it. Can't you forgive me?"

At that moment, he had no forgiveness for her in his heart.

"Bilal, I don't have anything left. I've lost everything. I was trying to hold on to my kids. What else do I have? What did you want me to do? I was afraid to tell anyone. I thought the government people would come and take all of you away. It would have killed me if they did that. What did you expect me to do?"

Her words only made Bilal feel worse. He felt she believed he had no right to be angry, that he was being a silly little boy who should have just keep his mouth shut. After a few moments had passed, she rose from the bed and silently retreated from the room.

It was well past midnight when the doorbell rang.

Bilal woke immediately and roused Hakim.

The doorbell rang again.

"What the hell?" Hakim said.

Bilal followed him to the living room. His mother and Fatima stood at their bedroom door, looking frightened.

Two police officers were waiting on the front steps.

"Is this the Abu family?" one of them asked.

Hakim motioned for Bilal.

"Yes, it is," Bilal said, wiping sleep from his eyes.

"Are your parents home?"

"My mother doesn't speak English well," Bilal said.

The officer gave Bilal a grim look. "Son, I'm sorry to have to tell you this…I have some bad news. Salim Abu—is that your brother?"

Bilal nodded.

"What is it?" Mrs. Abu asked.

Bilal turned to see her hovering in the doorway between the hall and the living room and clutching the seams of her housecoat.

The officer took a deep breath. "Son, I'm sorry to have to tell you this. Your brother took his own life this evening, just about an hour ago. I'm very sorry."

Bilal felt like someone had slugged him in the stomach. Tears sprang to his eyes, and he turned to Hakim to explain what had been said. Hakim shook his head in disbelief.

"Son," the police officer said, "I'm sorry. We have something we need you to look at. It's a note. We don't know what it says. It was found with your brother's body. Can we bother you to look at it? We need to know what it says—for our investigation. I'm sorry to have to bother you with it."

Bilal managed to nod. The officer handed him a piece of paper with Salim's handwriting on it. There were three words, written in Kurdish. Bilal looked at those words and felt a wave of nausea rise from the pit of his stomach.

The note said, *Fuck you, faggot.*

He put his hand to his mouth and handed the note to Hakim.

"Son, can you tell me what it says?" the police officer asked.

Hakim turned to the officer. "It says 'fuck you'—that's what it says."

"I'm so sorry," the police officer said. "I needed to know. I'm sorry."

Bilal turned from the door and fled to the bedroom.

"Bilal, come on," Mrs. Abu said, trying to coax him from the corner by the bed in the boys' room. He'd been there for almost two hours, hugging his knees to his chest, his face in his hands.

She pulled his uninjured arm, trying to get him to stand up.

"Don't you touch me!" he shouted.

"Bilal, please," she said. "Come on, honey."

"Get away from me!" he screamed at her.

"Bilal, please."

His tears alternated with wailing and sometimes shrieking. Every so often, he banged his cast loudly against the wall.

"It's not your fault," she said gently.

"Don't lie to me," he replied in a manic voice that frightened her. Snot ran from his nose, and he tried to wipe it away with his cast. "I got what I wanted, Ma. And you'll get what you want too, you just wait and see! I'll take Papa's razor and cut my fucking throat. Then you can be happy too, Ma—just as fucking happy as I am!"

"Don't talk like that!" she pleaded.

"Don't tell me what to do!"

Fatima entered the room and put her hands on her mother's shoulders. "Ma, just leave him alone," Fatima said.

"Can't someone just tell me why?" Mrs. Abu said, raising her voice.

"Ma, Salim was sick," Fatima said. "He was sick, Ma. Are you listening? He was not well."

"He looked fine to me!" Mrs. Abu cried.

Fatima sighed and stroked her mother's hair. They'd already had this conversation three times.

"I just don't understand any of this," Mrs. Abu said. "I just don't understand what's going on here."

Hakim rose from the sleeping mat where he'd been sitting and gently pulled his mother and Fatima away from Bilal. Then he crouched in front of Bilal and took hold of his arms.

"Let go of me!" Bilal screamed.

Hakim would not. He pulled Bilal into his arms.

"You think it's my fault!" Bilal shouted. "You all think it's my fault. I know you do. And I'm sorry. I made a mistake. I should have kept my mouth shut. But you'll see. I'm going to fix it. You'll see."

"Bilal, be quiet," Hakim said gently. "Enough is enough. It's not your fault, and no one thinks it is, so just be quiet now."

Bilal began to run out of steam now. "Allah is punishing me," he said. "I never wanted to be like this. Why is He punishing me?"

"No one's punishing you," Hakim said. "Just be quiet now."

"Don't touch me!" Bilal shouted, pulling away from him.

"Bilal, please," Hakim said.

"Keep your fucking hands off me! All those years, and you knew what he was doing—I hate you! I hate all of you! Don't you fucking touch me!"

Hakim held his brother firmly, and Bilal fought him.

"Oh, God!" Bilal exclaimed. He started gasping and the color drained from his face.

Hakim picked him up, lay him on the bed, and rubbed his chest. "Easy, easy," he said soothingly.

Bilal gripped Hakim's shirt in his fists and focused on Hakim's gentle voice. When he began to breathe more easily, Hakim cradled him and promised him everything was going to be all right.

CHAPTER THIRTEEN

The next day, Bilal stood between Hakim and Muhammad as they prepared to bury Salim with his head facing in the direction of Mecca. Salim had been washed, then his mother had applied scent to his body before it was wrapped in white funeral sheets. Imam Malik led the funeral prayer service.

Bilal thought of what the Prophet Muhammad had once said: "He is not of us who slaps the cheeks and tears the garments and mourns like the mourning of the days of ignorance." Excessive grief at a Muslim funeral was frowned upon. Yet the Prophet had also said: "Whoever strangles himself strangles himself into fire." Salim had done just that. He had tied one leg of his pants to a bar in his jail cell and tied the other leg around his neck. Then he had leaned into his makeshift noose, giving it his full weight until he lost consciousness.

O Allah, grant protection to our living and to our dead and to those of us who are present and those who are absent, and to our young and our old folks and to our males and our females.

O Allah, whomsoever Thou grantest to live from among us, cause him to live in Islam, and whomsoever of us Thou causest to die, make him die in faith.

O Allah, do not deprive him of his reward and do not make us fall into a trial after him.

O Allah, grant him protection, and have mercy on him, and keep him in good condition, and pardon him, and make his entertainment honorable, and expand his place of entering, and wash him with water and snow and hail and clean him of faults as the white cloth is cleaned of dross.

Bilal listened to these prayers and then the *talqin*, the brief sermon to exhort the living to remember that to Allah they must all eventually return. When the service was over, he walked behind as the men of the community—women were not allowed to attend this part of the ritual—carried Salim's body to the graveyard.

He felt very empty and very cold. Muhammad wrapped an arm around his shoulders, which provided some comfort. Bilal did his best not to cry. He would cry later.

For several days afterward Bilal lay in bed. He didn't speak or eat.

After the first day, his mother gave up trying to make him eat or communicate. She stayed in her room with the door closed.

On the following Friday after Prayers, Fatima asked Imam Malik to go see Bilal. In the afternoon the Imam and Muhammad showed up on their doorstep.

"Bilal, the Imam's here to see you," Fatima said, shaking his hip.

He said nothing.

The bedroom door opened, closed, and someone large and heavy sat down on the bed beside him.

Imam Malik did not speak. Feeling embarrassed by his behavior, Bilal rolled over and looked at him.

"What's going on, Bilal?" he asked quietly.

Bilal looked at him dejectedly.

"Fatima's worried about you. I am too."

Bilal said nothing.

"I suppose you're punishing yourself," Malik said. "That's what good victims do, isn't it?"

Bilal didn't like the sound of that statement and frowned.

"You broke the conspiracy of silence—what a bad boy you are! Now look what's happened. Your brother couldn't take the heat and opted for the easy way out. You must be responsible, Bilal. I can't see how, but even so, it must be your fault. You should have just suffered in silence and kept your mouth shut. Now look what you've done! It's all your fault! Never mind what he was doing to you. Never mind how much he hurt you. Never mind all that. You're a victim, so you should have kept your mouth shut. That way, he would never have been embarrassed, and none of this would have happened. After all, Salim and his needs were far more important than you and your needs. Who cares about you, Bilal? If someone wants to get their kicks by forcing you to do degrading things, you should just let them. After all, you're just a victim."

Bilal didn't reply, but he sat up in bed. He suddenly felt foolish hugging his pillow while the Imam spoke to him.

"Now, I suppose you ought to just lie here till you die, because that's all you deserve. Maybe you're thinking about taking your own life—maybe that'll even the score. Maybe things will be better if you do that. Anyway, at least you'll be properly punished for forgetting your place and wanting to be treated with a little respect and kindness."

"You've made your point," Bilal said. He felt anger stirring beneath his misery.

"Have I?" the Imam asked. "Have I, really?"

Bilal looked away from him.

"Bilal, for a long time, I've thought of you as being frozen like a block of ice—frozen, frightened, hiding your secrets. Not fluid and loose and free-flowing like most kids, but brittle, always looking around and wondering what other bad thing is going to happen. Well, you know what you did that night when you went to the hospital and turned your brother in? You started melting. You started softening up. You broke the conspiracy of silence, and suddenly everything was different. Salim was on the defensive and locked away where couldn't manipulate you. Now, I'm willing to bet you've been having some problems at home, because this silence thing is usually a response to family trouble—and you broke the rules. You decided that things had to change, and now you're being punished for it. Am I right, Bilal?"

Bilal did feel himself thawing. He *was* being punished, in a way, by his mother. He turned to the Imam and nodded.

"And you probably feel like Salim's death was your fault, don't you?"

"It was," Bilal said.

"Well, that's probably what you wanted, wasn't it? You were hoping he'd kill himself, weren't you? That's why you turned him in."

Bilal gave the Imam a look of horror.

"That's ridiculous, Bilal. You turned him in to the police because you wanted him to stop hurting you. You have a right not to be hurt. You have a right not to get your hand broken because your brother can't control his temper. We warned him, didn't we? Didn't we sit him down and tell him what the consequences would be if the police got involved? Didn't he know that what he was doing was illegal? Of course he did. And he chose to keep doing it anyway. So whose fault is that, Bilal? Is that your fault? Are you to blame because he couldn't control himself?"

Bilal didn't need to be told these things—he already knew the truth of them. Why couldn't he bring himself to *believe* them? Why did he choose to keep blaming himself anyway?

"What does the Quran say?" the Imam asked. "Isn't each man, according to the Quran, responsible for his own deeds, and no one else's? Won't each man and woman stand before Allah and render an account for his own or her own deeds, but not those of anyone else?"

"I know," Bilal said.

"I know you do," Malik replied. "I'm just reminding you. I'm just telling you that it's normal to feel guilty, but you have to accept the fact that it really isn't your fault and there was nothing you could have done. You had no choice but to do what you did. In fact, you had a right to do what you did, and I'm proud of you for doing it. You've decided to start using your power, and the people around you are going to be upset by that for a while. But they'll get over it. And so will you. You'll get used to using your power. And people will start treating you differently. I hope you never let anyone else frighten you into silence again, not for any reason."

Bilal looked at the Imam and felt more awake and alive than he had in weeks.

"Bilal, I know you loved your brother, and you're probably going to miss him. But don't make it harder on yourself than it has to be, eh? Don't forget there are people who love you and care about you. If you need to talk, all you have to do is open your mouth and start speaking. Don't keep it all inside. Let people help you if you need help. Will you promise me that?"

Bilal nodded. He could do that.

Muhammad followed Bilal to the bathroom. As Bilal washed his face and hands, Muhammad watched him in the mirror.

"Why don't you leave your glasses off?" Muhammad suggested. Muhammad stood just behind him and gazed at their reflections. "How did you get to be so good-looking?" Muhammad asked, running his fingers through Bilal's hair.

Bilal stared at himself in the mirror. The person staring back at him was not, in his opinion, good-looking. His hair was messed up with sleep. He had dark circles under his eyes. His face looked pale, strained.

"You look like that Mexican boy that used to go to the YMCA—what was his name?" Muhammad asked.

"Rico?"

"Yeah. Rico. When was that? Four, five years ago? That kid was so good-looking—that brown skin, those soulful eyes, that black hair—not just black hair, but I mean, *black*, black hair, just like yours. Oh, I had the hots for that kid."

"You did not!" Bilal exclaimed.

"Of course I never told you," Muhammad said, smiling. "I didn't even know I had the hots for him. I just wanted to see him, watch him, see what he looked like when he got undressed and went to the shower. Made me so horny, that kid. And that's just what you do."

"I'm ugly," Bilal said, frowning.

"So you're saying I have bad taste?" Muhammad asked. "Or maybe you just don't know how beautiful you are. I told you all the girls in school are crazy about you. 'Oh, he's so cuuuute!' You should hear Jamilla going on about you. She's just waiting for the day when she can become Mrs. Bilal Abu. Going to break her heart when she finds out that all she can do is be your sister-in-law because you're already taken."

Bilal looked at Muhammad's reflection in the mirror. Now *there* was a beautiful boy.

"Why don't I give you a bath?" Muhammad suggested. "Fatima says you've been sleeping for twelve years."

Muhammad's playfulness helped Bilal relax. Muhammad started the water in the bathtub while Bilal brushed his teeth, turned his head the other way while Bilal peed, then helped him undress. Again he made Bilal stand in front of the mirror and look at himself. Muhammad stood behind him, gazing at Bilal's reflection and running his hands run lightly across Bilal's skin.

Muhammad made him feel desirable, as if he was someone worth loving and caring for, someone worth touching and caressing. Yet he did not want to have sex.

He lowered his eyes.

"What's wrong?" Muhammad asked, sensing his change in mood.

"I'm not ready for anything right now," Bilal said quietly. "Maybe not for a while."

Muhammad turned him around and gazed directly into his eyes. "That's perfectly fine, Bilal. We have all the time in the world. I just wanted you to see how beautiful you are—at least to me, even if you don't see it yourself."

With Salim, Bilal's conscience had told him that something was amiss, that they were doing things that ought not to be done. His conscience had nothing to say about Muhammad—only that he should love him and treat him with respect and kindness. All he wanted was to love this young man and be loved in return.

"If it's a sin for me to love you," Bilal said quietly, "then I'm going to burn in Gehenna."

"So am I," Muhammad answered.

CHAPTER FOURTEEN

On Monday of the following week, Bilal went back to school. He was surprised by the number of people who came up to him to say they were sorry about his brother. He was even more surprised when Mr. Washington took him aside and said the meeting of the board had been canceled "considering the circumstances." He admitted there were was "more going on" than he had originally thought.

The Poetry Hoedown was coming up the following week, and Muhammad encouraged Bilal to stay in the competition. Only four other students had signed up, all of them girls. Bilal went to the office and put his name down on the paper, ignoring the butterflies in his stomach. What did he have to lose?

He already knew the poem that he was going to recite. He also knew it would probably get him expelled, but he did not care.

The next day, he was surprised when Hakim woke up early to say Morning Prayers with him. Since Salim's funeral, Hakim had changed too. He no longer talked about American girls and their big hoochies. He spent a lot of time reading the Quran and often went for long walks in the evening by himself. Muhammad told Bilal that Hakim had been to see the Imam about finding a better job.

On Wednesday, Mr. Washington told Bilal that the school was aware of his medical bills and that his family would need help paying them. Washington said the students would sell chocolate bars and raffle a microwave oven—donated by Mr. Junayn, who owned an appliance store—as a way to help out.

On Friday, Bilal was well enough to make the deliveries of his mother's bread again. The shopkeepers were surprised to see him and asked him where he'd been. Everyone said they were sorry about his brother.

When he was finished with his route, he rode his bike past the spot where Dreadlocks and his cronies had stopped him. That day seemed so long ago. He planned to tell them to fuck off and pick on someone their own size—or die for his insolence. Luckily, the Mercedes and Dreadlocks were nowhere in sight. That particular confrontation would have to wait for another day.

He went down to Darby's, locked his bike in front, and steeled himself.

Mrs. Darby, sitting at the cash register, looked surprised to see him. "Mrs. Darby, how are you?" he asked as he walked up to the counter.

"Well, I'm all right," she said quietly. "And you?"

"I'm fine, Mrs. Darby."

"I heard about your brother. I'm so sorry, Bilal."

He nodded to acknowledge her sympathy. "I wanted to talk to you about my mother's bread, Mrs. Darby."

A frown creased her brow.

"Mrs. Darby, my family and I didn't fly planes into those buildings. We have nothing to do with car bombs or suicide missions. We aren't terrorists. We're refugees from Iraq. My father was murdered by Saddam Hussein's government. We're not a danger to you, Mrs. Darby. I should have told you that, the last time I saw you, but I was ashamed. It's not right for people to blame us for things we didn't do—things we would never do in a million years."

"Well, you know—" Mrs. Darby began, looking a bit sheepish.

"Mrs. Darby, we don't have a lot of money, and it really helps us if we can sell our bread at stores like yours. Won't you please give it some thought?"

"Well, Bilal—"

"I want to help my mother. I want to go home and tell her we've got more orders, that maybe things will be all right. We're in a bad way right now. It would mean a lot to her."

"Oh, Bilal," Mrs. Darby said, sighing. "I was wrong, wasn't I?"

"A lot of people are angry and afraid these days," Bilal said.

"Well, all right then. Did you bring some today?"

Bilal nodded. "I brought ten loaves, not six. Can I leave all of them with you?"

Mrs. Darby gave Bilal a wry look. "You're going to be a little businessman, aren't you, Bilal? All right, then. Ten loaves. Had so many people in this store asking for Bilal's bread, I should have called your mother a long time ago. I'm so sorry, Bilal. I know you're not to blame for all the mess in the world. And Lord knows you've got enough troubles of your own. Why don't you go get that bread?"

"Thanks, Mrs. Darby," Bilal said. As he strode back to his bike, he noticed that his vision seemed wider and he felt an inch or two taller.

The school auditorium was filled with students and their friends, parents, teachers—almost three hundred people altogether. They were there for the poetry contest and to hear a special address by Imam Malik on the community's response to the ongoing war in Iraq. And there was the raffle for the microwave oven as well as a bake sale out front and a spaghetti dinner afterward.

At the foot of the stage, Bilal sat with the other four contestants—all of them girls wearing veils and long dresses—and felt terrified out of his mind. There wasn't a soul in the auditorium who didn't know about his brother—his suicide, what he had done to Bilal, their medical bills. He was convinced he would do nothing but make a fool of himself by getting up and reciting his poetry.

Yet he was doggedly determined not to get up and run away. He was going to stand up, open his mouth, and speak. To hell with the consequences. To hell with what people thought. If he did nothing else in his life, that would be fine, but he was going to get up there when his turn came and read some of his poetry.

Imam Malik gave his talk first, acknowledging the unfairness of Muslims' being treated with suspicion by angry Americans and encouraging the community to respond with patience and facts. Yet he spoke briefly, and all too quickly the Poetry Hoedown was underway.

An official from the Kansas City School District explained how the Poetry Hoedown worked and what they were aiming to accomplish that evening—to pick a winner to represent the Harun Mosque and School at the citywide finals.

The first contestant—from the look of her, she was just as nervous as Bilal—was called onto the stage. She was a seventeen-year-old girl named Hara Johnson. Bilal saw the paper in her hands tremble as she stood in front of the microphone and read a poem about motherhood.

There was enthusiastic applause when she finished. The content of the poem didn't really matter. What mattered was that she had had the courage to get up and read it.

She made a small, grateful bow to the audience before she returned to her seat.

Another girl was called up to the stage.

Bilal could hardly breathe. He was afraid he would have a panic attack and be unable to continue. His hands were sweaty. He hadn't brought a printout of his poem—he knew it by heart. Now he wished he had. What if he forgot the words? What if he got up there and his mind went blank?

"It helps to breathe," the girl sitting next to him said, whispering in his ear. "You know, just breathe in, breathe out, relax."

He gave her a feeble smile.

The friendly girl was called next. She strode up to the microphone confidently and read a very powerful poem about what it meant to be a Muslim in the world after 9/11. She received long, sustained applause, and Bilal felt a sinking feeling in his stomach—she was surely going to be the winner.

With horror, Bilal heard his name called. There was polite applause while the audience watched him get up and walk to the microphone. He stared out at the audience, totally unnerved. He couldn't open his mouth. Suddenly, he felt very self-conscious about the cast on his arm. A few people in the audience shifted uncomfortably.

What were the words?

Bilal searched frantically for Muhammad. He spotted him in the front row off to the left. The sight of his friend helped Bilal settle down. Muhammad smiled, gave him a thumbs-up, and nodded encouragingly.

"I'd like to read a poem called 'My First Suicide,'" Bilal said hoarsely.

There was more nervous energy in the audience—this was going to heavy-duty. The judges, sitting at a table off to his right, waited patiently for him to proceed.

This poem was not something that should be read in front
of his entire school—he knew that. But he was feeling reckless
and angry. He was tired of hiding and lying and pretending
to be something that he was not. The truth inside of him
demanded to be released, to be shared, to be spoken, to be
given life.

He began speaking quietly at first. Then his voice became
clearer and stronger as he went along:

> *My first suicide*
> *was on an evening in July*
> *and pills were the plan*
> *they were sticky in my hand*
> *as in twos and threes, I*
> *gulped them down with Lipton tea*
> *but death was not to be*
> *not yet*
> *not for me*
> *then came razor blades*
> *as further murder plans were made*
> *to end my misery*
> *to bleed my way to peace*
> *but despite my ardor for success*
> *I created only one more mess*
> *and death was not to be*
> *not yet*
> *not for me*
> *these empty places, empty spaces*
> *all these holes that must be filled*
> *how much better, how much faster*
> *if this body I had killed*
> *instead it's endless hours*

endless days and endless haze
as bit by bit and piece by piece
I make my way to my release
and I, despite my best,
long to die and take my rest
but death is not to be
not yet
no, not for me
you see:
you got the ball, I got the chain
you got the sun, I got the rain
you live in light, I live in pain
for me to die would be to gain
I know such words ought not be spoken
just as true things rarely are
and what's the use of too much hoping
when each day brings still more scars?
yet hope I do, I can't resist
I long to know much more than this
I long to know some happiness
a chance is all I'm asking
a chance to do my best
a chance to love somebody
to put my heart to rest
you tell me I'm not normal
you tell me that I'm queer
you tell me that the folks like me
aren't really wanted here
you tell me it's a crime
if I should feel the way I feel
you say my love is shameful
there's no way it could be real

but then, how would you know
if these shoes you have not worn?
but still that doesn't stop you—
oh, how easy falls the scorn
the hatred and rejection
how they wound and how I bleed
'cause love is not to be
it's not allowed for folks like me—
well, where then should I go,
back to pills and razor blades?
and what then should I do
to take this pain away?
and would it make you happy
if you put me in the ground
if you silenced me forever
with that stillness so profound?
Still I, despite despair,
offer up this fervent prayer
that death is not to be
not yet
not for me
the kind that comes from trying
to be what I can't be
you see:
my first suicide
was on an evening in July
and pills were the plan
they were sticky in my hand
and only now when I look back
do I begin to understand
why life was meant for me
why the truth can set you free.

So finally let the truth be spoken
here and now for all to hear
finally let the truth be said
I am queer
Yes, I am queer
And let this be a suicide
a death to lies and my deceit
a death to all my furtive hiding
a death to my dishonesty
'cause life is meant to be
both for you
and for me.

He fell silent, lowered his eyes, and adjusted his glasses nervously. He had no idea what they would make of such a poem. Mr. Washington would be furious. Half the school would be furious. He did not care. Let them expel him. Let them do their worst.

Muhammad stood up and began clapping. It was a solitary, forlorn sound in the auditorium.

Bilal looked at him, grateful. Was he the only one who was going to applaud?

Then everyone began to applaud all at once. Many people stood and looked at him with astonished faces. But Mr. Washington, he saw with a bit of fear, kept his seat and stared at Bilal as if he meant to bore holes right through him.

The applause went on and on. He did not see the looks of disgust and hatred that he had expected. He did not hear the boos and hisses of disapproval. Fellow students didn't laugh. Instead, he saw a room full of people who had listened to his truth and had decided it was well worth the hearing.

He returned to his seat, feeling a bit numb and disembodied.

Both relief and terror swept through him. He had done what he had set out to do, and he was glad of that. But he lost a little of his bravado and began to worry about the consequences.

The last girl was called, and she went up on the stage. She seemed flabbergasted and kept glancing back at Bilal. He had stolen the show. Still, she read her poem gamely. It was something about cats and dogs—Bilal could not concentrate on the words. She received polite applause, and the competition was over.

Almost immediately the head judge got up from the table and approached the microphone. It was the official from the Kansas City School District who had opened the competition. The first thing he did was call for another round of applause for the contestants, who had all done a wonderful job, he said.

When the audience had settled, he asked, "What should poetry do for us? Poetry ought to make you feel something. Poetry should express the deepest of truths, the truest of things. It ought to be fearless and go down into the guts of an issue. The words ought to be new words, fresh words, brought together in ways that no one has thought of. And that, ladies and gentlemen, is what we heard this evening. We had a young poet come up and grab us by the shoulders to tell us a deep, profound truth."

The man asked the five contestants to stand with him in front of the audience. Bilal stood apart from the girls, as was only proper.

"First, let me thank you all for participating and sharing your poetry with us. Didn't they do a good job?"

The audience clapped again.

"Now, all of you are winners in my book, but one of you must be selected to represent your school at the finals. Four of you are going to receive a plaque as a token of our appreciation for participating. One of you is going to receive the trophy."

Another of the judges came forward, carrying four plaques and the trophy. The head judge handed one of the plaques to the first girl in the line and urged her to take a bow. She did. The audience applauded. Before Bilal realized what was happening, all four girls had been given plaques and he was standing alone in front of the audience.

"Now, young man," the judge began. The audience interrupted him with thunderous applause.

The judge smiled at the audience and waited for the applause to subside.

"Now, young man, you have the heart of a poet if I've ever seen one. You're reckless. Maybe one day you will learn to speak more softly and carry a bigger stick."

Appreciative laughter rippled through the audience.

Bilal stared around him, dazed. Had he really won?

"It's my privilege to proclaim you the winner of this evening's contest," the judge said. "Ladies and gentlemen, would you join me in congratulating Mr. Bilal Abu of the Harun Mosque and School, who will be your representative at the finals?"

The judge handed Bilal the trophy, and there was more exuberant applause. Bilal's friends came forward from their seats—Muhammad, Nu, Ahmed, the boys in his class, and Fatima too. Hakim and Imam Jackson joined them all on the stage.

All their words were lost on him. He began to cry. He felt helpless, happy, terrified—he was overwhelmed by the emotions crowding his heart.

"I told you!" Muhammad said happily. "Didn't I tell you? They love you, man!"

Nu was at his other elbow. "Boy, are you going to be expelled or what? But it was cool! Did you see Mr. Washington's face? Are you really a queer? Bilal!"

Imam Malik congratulated Bilal and then got the lot of them

to return to their seats so that he could finish up the evening's program. He raffled off the microwave oven and invited everyone to the spaghetti dinner. He tactfully mentioned the fact that the proceeds were going to go to the Abu family to help them defray the expenses from their recent "troubles."

For the rest of the evening, Bilal could hardly keep his feet on the ground. It began to dawn on him that the world was not going to end because he had just stood up and publicly outed himself in front of the entire community. Finally, he began to smile and enjoy himself.

"I'm proud of you," Fatima said the following morning.

It was Friday, and they were both up to their elbows in bread dough, which they were kneading for their mother.

"I really am," she said, grinning at him. "Mr. Washington looked like he was going to have a heart attack. Everybody else thought you were pretty cool to get up there and do that."

"Yeah, well, when they expel me, maybe you won't be so proud," he said.

"They're not going to expel you," she said confidently.

Bilal appreciated her words, but he wasn't so sure.

Life was falling into a routine again. Salim was gone, but Bilal was surprised by how quickly he adjusted to his absence. He even felt a bit guilty about it. The simple truth of the matter was that he didn't really miss Salim. The peace in the household astonished them all. There was no more of the screaming and the tantrums and the sudden rages, no fear of violence, no threat of punishment—it was all gone. It was like a long nightmare had finally come to end.

Bilal looked at his mother, who was shaping dough and putting it into the tins. There was still anger hiding just below the surface of her face. She still blamed Bilal for Salim's death—and perhaps always would. That burden was hers to bear if she chose.

With his left hand in a cast, Bilal was not having much luck keeping up with Fatima. Hakim joined them at the table and said, "Why don't you go watch the ovens?" Bilal was grateful to comply.

Nothing much happened that day. Bilal made the deliveries, and Fatima walked with him to Friday Prayers. The Abus were invited to the Imam's house afterward for lunch, and they all went. They talked to their friends. They went home. They ate a quiet dinner. Bilal kept waiting for something to happen—for someone to get angry, someone's fists to go flying, someone's temper to explode. But nothing happened. Nothing at all.

On the following Monday he was summoned to Mr. Washington's office. He approached the meeting with a fair bit of dread.

"Bilal, sit down please," the principal said, motioning to one of the chairs across from his desk.

Mr. Washington regarded Bilal in silence for a long time. "I ought to expel you," he said quietly. "In fact, I want you to know that I tried, but the board overruled me. How dare you get up in front of this school and talk about your homosexuality!"

Bilal said nothing. He held Mr. Washington's gaze until the man looked away.

"I don't think you appreciate the consequences of what you've done," he went on. "You're making a mockery of this school, and I don't like it one bit."

Bilal looked at the man with hate that was bright and fierce and intense. Yet there was more in him than hate. There was sadness too. "I told the truth," he said quietly. "Isn't that what the Quran tells us to do—tell the truth? Are you saying that it's better for some of us to lie because the truth makes you uncomfortable?"

"If you were an alcoholic, you wouldn't get up and tell the whole school that, would you?" the principal asked.

"That's not the same, and you know it," Bilal said. "I've committed no sin. I've done nothing wrong. I got up and told you who I am—who I *really* am. I didn't ask to be this way. I didn't wake up one day and pray to Allah to make me a faggot. I'm trying to understand what's happening to me. And I'm trying to be honest. And if you can't accept that—if it's too frightening to you—well, that's your problem, not mine. Don't expect me to lie and hide and pretend and deny for your sake, because I refuse."

"The Islamic teaching on homosexuality is clear," the principal said gravely.

"No, it isn't," Bilal replied.

"It's very clear!" he snapped.

"No, it isn't!" Bilal insisted. "Do you really think the Prophet Muhammad—peace be upon him!—went around telling people that it was okay to murder homosexuals? Is that what you think? Did the Prophet Jesus do that? The Buddha? Gandhi? Did any of those people ever say such things? How can you believe such nonsense? If you're going to kill me, fine, but what about men who beat their wives or rape their daughters? Do we get to kill them too? What about men who sexually abuse little kids? What about murderers? What about people like Hitler and Stalin? Is it just homosexuals that you're going to throw off cliffs? Is it just homosexuals that you're going to kill wherever you find them? We're not living in the Days of Ignorance anymore, or are we?"

"It's unnatural!" the man exclaimed.

Bilal sighed in exasperation. He was not going to win a fight with this man. He was not even being heard, much less understood. "What do want me to do?" he asked earnestly. "What, exactly? I am what I am. I've never hurt anyone. I'm not going around raping the other students. I haven't done anything wrong. I just want to be honest and tell the truth—is that such a terrible thing?"

"Bilal, you have to understand that this is a very troubling issue for many, many people. Is it too much to ask that you don't rub our noses in it?"

Bilal's anger flared. "Does that mean you won't rub my nose in straight sexuality?" he said.

The principal realized he needed to back away from a volatile situation. "Look, son," he said, "we can talk about this issue and try to find out what the proper response to it is. But I'm not going to have you going around this school and getting everyone upset about it and flouting what Islam has to say about this matter. You have to do what your conscience tells you is right. I understand that. But so do I. Can't we compromise? You've challenged the school now, and we need to draw up a new policy that is fair to you, but also fair to this school and to the Islamic values that we're trying to teach. Something good can come of this, Bilal, but I need you to understand that sometimes a bit of discretion isn't the same as lying about yourself. Maybe we need to take some small steps and try to figure out how we can help students like yourself rather than discourage them."

"I'm tired of feeling ashamed," Bilal replied. "And that's all you've done so far—try to make me feel ashamed. Until you can do better, I don't know what there is that we have to talk about."

"Do you want to be expelled from this school?"

Bilal shrugged. "I don't care actually. Is that your answer to the problem, just expel every gay student that comes along? Is that how Islam deals with people it doesn't like?"

Washington now leaned back in his chair. "Son, I don't think you understand what you've done here. I don't think you understand at all. I've gotten so many calls from parents and board members and people in the community asking me why one of our students got up and talked about being 'queer'—as you say. Most of these people feel sorry for you and wanted to know what we were teaching in this school that made you feel so afraid of telling the truth. I've got parents calling me and wanting to know what they should do if one of their children turns out to be gay. I don't think you have any idea what kind of trouble you've created for us. Now, you made your point. Is it too much to ask you to tone it down a bit and give us a chance to figure out how to respond, how to best serve the interests of this school and its students?"

"You want me to shut my mouth, in other words," Bilal said.

"No. How about being a little more discreet, a little more careful about what you say to the other students? How about showing respect for Islamic teachings on premarital sex, which apply to you just as much as they do to anyone else? How about showing respect for the fact that there are different opinions on this matter and letting people know that you mean no disrespect to the teachings of Islam? Some matters are private, Bilal. There are also some matters on which Muslims may legitimately disagree, and this could be one of them. But let that discussion proceed in a mature, thoughtful manner."

"Let people like you decide what's best, in other words," Bilal said.

The principal narrowed his eyes and set his jaw.

Bilal stood up. "Expel me," he said. "I don't care. I'd rather go to a normal school anyway. I have the right to tell the truth, and I'm sick of people like you trying to shame me into silence. My father got himself killed for telling the truth, and maybe I'll get myself killed too, but at least I won't have to live with the shame of cowering in silence all the time because I was too afraid to speak up. So just expel me, if that makes you feel better, but don't sit there and ask me to keep my mouth shut, because I will not."

Without waiting for permission, Bilal turned on his heel and walked out of the principal's office.

Bilal was not expelled. In fact, the school very quickly adjusted to the presence of an openly gay student. Almost as soon as it had become an issue, it became a nonissue. Life went on as it had before. Classes were held, tests were taken, and the world did not come to an end.

Though he was teased by some of the older boys, Bilal also encountered newfound respect in the eyes of some of the other students.

He was surprised when Mrs. Owen pulled him aside and gave him the address of a gay teen center downtown. She suggested he might like to pay a visit, make some new friends, and find out how other teens were coping with their sexuality. Then she gave him a short lecture on safe sex.

It soon became apparent to most people that Muhammad and Bilal were more than good friends, but no misfortune befell them. They weren't hurting anyone.

Bilal had good days and bad days. At times, he felt perfectly fine. At other times, he felt angry, depressed, confused, and uncertain. For weeks and weeks he had nightmares—he was chased in his dreams by either Salim or a bloody man whose face he could never see—his father.

In the spring, Bilal had an unusual request: He wanted to have a funeral. His family stared at him strangely when he made this announcement over dinner one evening.

"What are you talking about?" Mrs. Abu asked, looking at him askance.

"I want to put Papa in the ground," Bilal said. "We never put Papa in the ground, like we did Salim. Until we do, I'm never going to feel right. I'm never going to be able to let it go."

"What sort of nonsense is this?" she demanded angrily.

"You'll see," he said. Although they pressed him for more details, he would add nothing further.

The next Saturday, Bilal invited some friends over in the afternoon for the "funeral." Imam Malik and Mrs. Jackson came with all their kids, including Muhammad. Nu Haidar and his family—including Ahmed—came. Some of Bilal's friends from school came too.

After Mrs. Abu served lunch, Bilal asked if they would follow him outside into the backyard. He carried a shoe box with him. In a corner of the yard, by the fence, he had already dug a small hole.

Everyone gathered around and watched him carefully.

The "funeral" had been Imam Malik's idea—a way for Bilal to symbolically bury the past and start thinking more about the future.

Bilal showed them the shoe box. "It's a coffin," he said quietly. "We never got our father's body back from the government, so we never buried him. We never put him in the ground. So I made this coffin out of a shoe box."

He lifted the lid to reveal a G.I. Joe action figure wrapped in a bit of white sheet, like a shroud. "I hope you don't think I'm silly," he said, wiping his eyes and feeling enormously sad.

"Nobody thinks you're silly," Muhammad said.

Bilal stared at the action figure wrapped in its make-believe shroud, and for a few moments he said nothing.

His friends and family moved closer to him. Imam Malik put his hand on Bilal's shoulder. Hakim stepped forward and held the shoe box with him.

"I know you must think it's strange," Bilal said, "but I have to put my father in the ground. It all happened kind of fast. Papa was killed, then we fled Iraq almost immediately. We eventually got to this country. We had to survive. We had to work. It's been eight years now. So I'm going to bury my father today. I'm going to put Papa in the ground. And then I'm going to give him back to Allah. I'm going to let go of him. I wanted you all to come so you could help me."

He turned around, knelt on the ground, and put the box in the small grave he had dug. He paused for a moment, then he began to cover it up with dirt.

Bilal cried, and Muhammad knelt next to him and put an arm around his shoulder.